The Trouble with Funerals

Mabel and Violet Mysteries, Volume 3

Joan Havelange

Published by Brown Wolf Publishing, 2025.

Published by Brown Wolf Publishing
Saskatchewan, Canada

Dedication

To my readers, the reason I write.

Chapter One

"She doesn't look a bit good," lamented Sophie Schoenberg.

Mabel Havelock looked down at Mini Frazer's body. "She wouldn't. She's dead; no one looks good dead."

The funeral director, who had ushered the two ladies to view the body in the casket, now looked steely-eyed at the women. "Pardon me."

Sophie turned to the man in the sombre black suit. "I don't think you people did a very good job of preparing poor Mini. She looks quite pekid," she tisked.

Harold Hauke, the funeral director, a thin rail of a man, looked down his skinny nose at her and glowered; he then rearranged his grimace into a sympathetic smile.

"Mother, stop criticizing," Mabel whispered. She gave the stone-faced man an apologetic smile. Her eighty-year-old mother's social filter was a little thin.

Harold Hauke drew his lips into a tight, thin line. "May I direct you to a pew?" he asked in a deep, solemn whisper.

Sophie stood looking sadly at Mini, lying in the cherry wood coffin in front of the church altar.

Mabel nudged her mother. "Yes, thank you."

Sophie took her daughter's arm, following the tall, thin man down the aisle; she stopped abruptly and turned. "I should be sitting up in the front pew with the family. Goodness knows I've been a lot closer to Mini than her family. I can't remember when they last came for a visit," Sophie said in a peevish tone.

Harold Hauke's eyes narrowed. Giving the women a stony look, he furtively motioned them to follow him.

The church was filling up; people were giving them curious looks. "Come on, Mom, you're not family." Mabel nudged her mother. "We can't stand arguing in the middle of the aisle."

"I was Mini's dear friend." Mabel nudged her mother again and whispered in her ear.

"You meant Mini when you moved into the condo. So you've only known Mini for a year. That hardly puts you in the front pew."

Mabel's mother had recently moved from the nearby town of Kipling to the little village of Glenhaven. She had taken up residence in the newly built Gravenhurst Manor, a senior's condo complex.

Sophie, looking sorrowful, followed Mabel and the funeral director to a pew. She nodded to a large lady with a bouffant hairdo. The woman nodded back and slid down the old wooden bench, making room for Sophie and Mabel.

Sophie straightened the skirt of her navy blue suit and clasped her hands together. Looking pious, she said, "I still think the family will want me in the front pew. I may have only known Mini for a short time, but we were the best of friends." The woman sitting next to Sophie gave her a sidelong glance, pursed her lips and opened her funeral program.

"Hush, Mom, please remember you are here to pay your respects to your friend Mini. Not to complain about who sits where at her funeral."

Sophie sniffed and opened her purse; taking out a lace hanky, she dabbed at her eyes. "Please, Mabel, you could be a little more compassionate. I'm still distraught. Something very odd happened the night dear Mini died."

Mabel tuned out her mother and looked around the church at the mourners gathered for Mini Frazer's funeral. The congregation was a gathering of the very old, like her mom and those who were middle age. She'd learned from reading the obituary that Mini had been a music teacher. She assumed many of the middle-aged people were former students.

"I remember taking music lessons when I was a kid. I can't remember the name of the teacher. But I do remember after a few lessons, she wisely told me to take up something else. I think she said ping pong," mused Mabel.

"Ah yes, your piano lessons. Mini was not your music teacher; it was old Mrs. Hoolway. I doled out a lot of money for those lessons; what a waste. Your brother was much more talented. He played the tuba." Sophie smiled fondly. "Do you remember him playing?"

"Oh, I remember, and I remember the racket he made when he tooted on that thing. I don't think Cyril was talented, just more persistent."

"He was talented," disputed Sophie.

"Whatever." Mabel felt the old familiar wave of jealousy. Cyril was better at most things. Her brother was usually picked as captain of their schoolyard sports. She remembered playing scrub baseball. She and the chubby boy were always picked last. And her brother would always pick Ralph, the chubby boy, before her.

"Hush." The woman in a bright purple dress turned around in the pew to admonish them. The bouffant hairdo woman in the seat beside them nodded in agreement.

"Sorry," whispered Mabel.

Sophie, ignoring the woman, tucked her hanky back into her purse.

"Do you think any of her husbands will be here? You told me Mini was married twice."

"No, both are long gone. I don't know when they died." Sophie sighed.

Two black-clad ushers went up and down the aisle, escorting mourners to their pews. A few of the mourners went up to the altar to view the deceased in her casket.

Mabel watched as Helen Graham went up to the casket and looked sadly down at Mini. Mabel's friend from Coffee Row attended every funeral for miles around. The thin, nervous woman had a reputation for going to every funeral in the community, whether she knew the deceased or not.

"A nice turnout for Mini," Sophie said, picking up a hymn book and flicking through the pages; she placed the funeral program in the hymnal as a bookmark.

In the choir loft, the organist played a hymn softly. Sun shining through the old stained-glass windows made colourful patterns on the battered old wooden pews. The church smelled of candle wax and incense. Above the dark mahogany altar hung a poorly rendered biblical picture painted by some long-forgotten parishioner. The painting was of the Last Supper with a blond Jesus presiding over it.

"Do you know Mini's family?" Mabel asked. "You said they didn't visit her much. Do any of her children live here?" Mabel, a retired nurse who spent most of her life in Kipling, had only moved to the little town of Glenhaven upon retirement.

"No, none of them came to visit Mini. As I told you, Mini was divorced twice. She had two sons from her first marriage, and both boys live in Toronto. And a daughter from her second. She lives in Ottawa and has a government job. Mini was so proud of all her kids. I can't remember what she said they did, but she was very proud of them. Personally, I think they are a bunch of ungrateful children. Poor Mini, I don't think her daughter ever visited. I'm sure I would remember if she did. Maybe the one son came. Yes, I remember he did come once, a short, chubby man. He had a wonderful sense of humour, like his mother. But I never clapped eyes on the other son."

"Well, that explains why they didn't visit their mother; they live on the other side of Canada. Little Glenhaven, Saskatchewan, is a long way to come to visit."

"That's the trouble with funerals. The family only shows up when you're dead."

"Mom, shush," admonished Mabel.

Sophie shrugged her shoulders and opened her purse, which matched her navy blue suit. She took out a tube of lip gloss and applied it to her lips. Mabel wondered briefly if her mother approved of her black slacks and the plain white blouse she was wearing. Her mother was a tiny woman with beautifully coiffured white hair. She looked like a delicate flower, but her mother was tougher than old boots. Mabel, who had prematurely white hair, never fussed and instead settled for a simple, no-nonsense bob cut. She had inherited her mother's blue eyes and temperament. But there, the resemblance ended. Mabel was portly and didn't particularly care how she dressed. Her mother, on the other hand, was always appropriately attired for every occasion.

Mabel shifted on the hard wooden bench, wishing the funeral would start. "If the church had softer seating, they'd get more parishioners," she mumbled.

"Don't complain. It could be me lying up there," her mother said morbidly.

"What a thing to say. I don't even want to think about that," scolded Mabel.

"It's a fact of life, well, a fact of death, I guess."

Mabel, knitting her eyebrows, gave her mother a disapproving look. The thought of losing her mom was a thought she didn't want to face. Eighty years old these days wasn't that old, she reassured herself.

The funeral director's helper, a squat man dressed in a black suit, closed the coffin lid. Mabel thought the man looked more suited to a wrestling ring, his black suit stretching over his muscled arms threatening to burst. He adjusted the funeral pall over the coffin and waddled back down the aisle.

The organist began to play in earnest, and the congregation stood. A doddery old priest in green robes slowly led the way down the aisle. Following the priest, a tall woman wearing a smart black dress, a young boy and a girl accompanied her.

"That's Mini's daughter, Judith Flanders, and the kids beside her are Mini's grandchildren. The boy is called Robbie, and the girl is Susan. I've seen pictures of them," Sophie whispered to Mabel.

The children looked to be preteens, eleven or twelve years old. Both were wearing black slacks and grey jackets. Mabel thought the clothes looked like school uniforms, as there was a monogram on the breast pocket of the jackets.

"I don't see Judith's husband. It looks like he didn't come to Mini's funeral. Isn't that shocking?" tisked Sophie.

A short man in a blue suit followed the woman and the children.

"Maybe that's her husband," Mabel whispered to her mom.

"No, that's Judith's brother Andy with his wife; I don't know her name. Andy never came to visit, but I've seen pictures of him and his wife at Mini's."

A man of equal stature dressed in a grey suit followed them.

"And that's Howard; he's the son I was telling you about, quite a nice man. And oh, look who is accompanying them. It's Gemma Charbon."

"Who is she?"

"Gemma is a lovely woman. She volunteers at the Manor and helps all of us seniors who live there. You know, with rides downtown, shopping and what have you. She's going to sit in the front pew with the family. I should be sitting there too. Mini and I were the best of friends."

"Don't start that again," Mabel cautioned her mother.

The family filled the two front pews, which left a large space between them and the rest of the mourners.

On the opposite side of the aisle sat four men attired in black suits with armbands.

"They're the pallbearers," Sophie whispered.

"Mom, I have been to a funeral before."

"I know, but those are local men hired to be pallbearers. They are not relatives or friends. I find this very shocking."

"Mom, stop criticizing," scolded Mabel.

"Quiet," the woman in the purple dress rebuked.

Sophie nudged Mabel. "Yes, dear, this is a sombre occasion."

"You're the one doing most of the talking," Mabel admonished in a hushed tone.

"Really, some people," huffed the bouffant hairdo lady.

Mabel gave her mother a warning look and opened a hymnal.

The organist, joined musically by the choir, began to belt out *The Old Rugged Cross*. Unfortunately, the organist and the choir were not on the same note.

Sophie cranked her neck to look up at the choir loft. "That has to be Nelly. She's got a tin ear, but beggars can't be choosers. Mrs. Ryhan, our regular organist, has to work, so Nelly is filling in. Why can't funerals be on Sunday? We could kill two birds with one stone; I'm sure the good Lord wouldn't mind."

Mabel grinned; her mother did have a way with words.

"I wonder who picked this hymn?" muttered Sophie. "I know for a fact that Mini was not fond of *The Old Rugged Cross.* She would be appalled."

"Shush, please stop critiquing the funeral; show some respect."

The organ music ceased, and the priest began to sprinkle the coffin with holy water.

Ah, ah, ah, ah, stayin' alive, stayin' alive, blasted out from Mabel's purse. It was her cellphone alert. Mabel dug frantically in her purse, hunting for her phone.

The old priest stopped mid-sprinkle and turned, looking at the congregation.

Heads swivelled, looking for the offending cellphone owner. Sophie gave Mabel a disapproving look and shifted away from her, down the wooden bench.

Mabel dug. Tossing Kleenex, car keys, her address book and her pocketbook out of her purse, As *ah, ah, ah, ah, stayin' alive, stayin' alive,* continued to play out from her phone. She grabbed her offending phone as it belted out the *Stayin' alive, Stayin' Alive,* one more time and shut it off. She ducked her head. Maybe no one knew it was her phone.

The bouffant hairdo lady and the purple dress woman both stared at Mabel and shook their heads.

The priest waited for silence; his gaze lingered on Mabel. He then turned back to bless the casket. Finished with his blessing, the priest shuffled to the pulpit, acknowledging the family with a kindly smile that brought a radiance to his old-lined face. In a surprisingly clear voice, he announced, "The family has asked Mrs. Gemma Charbon to give the eulogy." Nodding to Gemma, he shuffled behind the altar and sat on a high-back wooden chair.

Gemma Charbon rose from her seat and unwrapped her white and gold shawl from her shoulders. She paused to clasp the hand of the daughter. Then Gemma, the tall, attractive woman with broad shoulders, strode to the pulpit. Her erect posture made her seem even more imposing. The long dark blue skirt of her dress swirled with each confident step. Mabel's heart sank. In Gemma's bejewelled fingers was a raft of notes.

Gemma tapped on the mike with the tips of her well-manicured nails. She tilted the microphone up, paused, sighed, and then nodded to the family sitting together in the front pew. "I had the great pleasure of knowing your dear mother." Gemma flicked a strand of her long, auburn hair from her cheek. "We would sit for hours chatting about life and our love of music. It surprised Mini that I knew so much about music. I, of course, play the piano, and I am an accomplished violinist." Gemma closed her long eyelashes over her brown eyes momentarily and smiled sadly. "Unfortunately, I never got to play for her."

Mabel silently groaned as she jammed her effects back into her purse. The woman droned on and on, listing more things about herself than about Mini. When Gemma did mention the deceased, it was how the death of Mini affected her. The family looked uncomfortable, and the kids became restless.

Mabel tuned out the woman, wondering who called her on her cellphone. Maybe it was Violet. Her friend had gone to the Regina airport to pick up a man from England, Neville Hawthorne.

She and Violet had met Neville when they went on a cruise down the Nile in Egypt. He was coming to visit Violet for a month. He said he was eager to see what life was like on the Canadian Prairies. Mabel had taken a dislike to the man, although she couldn't put her finger on the reason why. But she didn't trust him, and she thought Violet was making a mistake inviting him to stay with her. Mabel looked at her watch. Gemma had been talking for 20 minutes.

MABEL AND SOPHIE SLOWLY followed a long line of funeral mourners down the crowded carpeted stairs to the church basement, where a luncheon supplied by the ladies of the church awaited.

"Good lord, that woman went on and on," grumbled Mabel. "I so wanted to get up and walk out of there. But we were trapped. You can't just walk out of a funeral, although I so wanted to."

"Who is critiquing now?" Sophie asked.

"Yeah, we were a captive audience," a croaky voice from behind agreed. "I thought Gemma would never shut up."

"Now, now," scolded Sophie. "Gemma might be a talker, but she is always there to help us. Don't you forget that, Charlie."

Mabel glanced over her shoulder at a tall, gaunt man, his bald head nearly covered in liver spots.

Sophie paused on the stairs to do the introductions. "Dear, this is Charlie Sweeny. The Sweenys are neighbours of mine; they live in the Gravenhurst Manor in an apartment on the same floor as mine. They moved into the manor right around the same time I did. Oh, and this is my daughter, Mabel."

"And this is my wife, Linda," Charlie said.

Linda was as tall and thin as her husband. "Hello, nice to meet you. Sophie said she had a daughter. It's nice you are finally able to visit your mother. Did you come for the funeral?" Linda offered her hand; blue veins showed through her translucent skin.

Mabel awkwardly turned on the steps to shake Linda's hand. It was like shaking hands with eggshells; she was afraid she would break the frail woman's hand. "No, I live here in town." Mabel gave her mother an inquiring look.

"Oh, do you? I don't think I've seen you at the condo." Charlie looked over Sophie's shoulder at Mabel.

"No, you wouldn't have meant Mabel. She doesn't visit me very often, even though we live in the same town." Sophie shuffled forward.

"Mother, you could make God feel guilty."

"Mabel! That's blasphemy."

"And kill two birds with one stone on a Sunday, isn't?"

"I wasn't the one who interrupted the service with their nasty cellphone ring," reminded Sophie.

"Was that you?" Charlie asked with a grin on his face.

"Maybe," Mabel said, blushing. The people behind them on the stairs were muttering their disapproval.

"Never mind, dear, we all make mistakes," Sophie said. She glanced apologetically at Charlie and his wife. "Mabel is not used to going to church either."

"Thanks a bunch," Mabel grumbled as they edged down the stairs one step at a time. "Now, not only am I a delinquent daughter, but I'm also an atheist."

"Of course, you're not an atheist, dear. But when was the last time you attended church?"

Feeling guilty, Mabel sighed. She had to admit it had been a while.

"Excuse me, excuse me." A young, thin blonde woman holding a Tupperware container above her head snaked her way through the crowd of people on the stairs. "I'm helping with the luncheon," the young woman said as she elbowed her way past Mabel and her mother.

Sophie and Mabel stood at the bottom of the stairs. The line of mourners had halted. Homer, a small, bent man with a walker, had slowed everyone to a standstill. The white-haired man thumped his walker toward the food tables.

Long tables covered with white plastic tablecloths, set in rows down two sides of the wood-panelled basemen. A paper cup and a folded napkin were on the tables in front of each chair. Sugar bowls, small cream jugs, and plastic stir-sticks set in the middle of the tables. Down the center of the room were the food tables, laden with trays of sandwiches, cheese, pickles, and fruit platters. Next to a big coffee urn, more trays are filled with small cakes and tarts. A friend of Mabel's, Mary Woodhouse, was presiding over the coffee urn. Mabel waved at the flushed-faced woman, but Mary was busy pouring coffee and didn't notice her.

Homer, the skinny little man with the walker, filled a paper plate with a mound of sandwiches. The plate precariously balanced on the handrail of his walker. Mabel hurried over to him. "Do you want me to help you?" she asked, reaching for his plate, brimming over with sandwiches and dainties.

Homer looked at her with rheumy eyes. "Get your own plate." He jerked his plate from her hands. Sandwiches and dainties flew, and a salmon sandwich landed on Mabel. The salmon slid down the front of her white blouse.

"You cantankerous old—"

"I'll help him," Mary interrupted. Bending, she gathered up the sandwiches and dainties off the floor. "You go and clean yourself up, dear."

"Stupid woman, she tried to steal my food," muttered Homer.

Mabel looked around the room, embarrassed. She hoped it was a long time before she attended another funeral.

Chapter Two

Mabel opened the back door of her little bungalow and shooed her orange tabby cat, Gertrude, out onto the step. Standing on her back steps, she rubbed her bare arms; the early morning air of September had a bite to it. She looked at her garden. Now that all her vegetables had been harvested, she needed her friend Henry Hawkins to bring his garden plow to work up her garden. The leaves were changing from green to brilliant orange, gold, and red. A prelude to winter, but it was warm, and the farmers had lots of good weather ahead to harvest their crops.

She closed the door, walked over to her sink, and picked up a dishcloth, wiping the crumbs off her red arborite countertop. Mabel rinsed the dishcloth, then tossed it back into her old white porcelain sink. A hiss and a yowl grabbed her attention. She pulled back the bright white and red flowered curtains on the window over her sink and looked out. Gertrude's back arched, her ears flattened, and her tail twitched. A stray grey cat had entered Gertrude's domain. Gertrude leapt off the step, hissing and yowling. Mabel grinned as the grey cat scampered out of the yard. Her cat was old, but she was feisty.

She dropped the curtains and wandered over to her wall phone. Mabel paused, debating, should she call Violet? She missed talking to her. Mabel hadn't heard from her friend since she'd picked up the Englishman Neville at the airport. She guessed Violet was too wrapped up with her new boyfriend to bother with an old friend. Mabel felt a pang of jealousy; she was being pushed to the sidelines by Neville. Maybe she should invite them for supper? She reached for the phone as it rang.

"Hi, Violet. I was just thinking about you." Mabel played out the long phone cord back to her chrome table. Pulling out a chair, she sat.

"Sorry to disappoint you; it's just your poor old mother."

"Mom, don't try playing the old lady card; it won't work on me." Mabel kicked out another grey chrome chair and put her feet upon it.

"Old lady card?"

"The oh woe is me. I'm a little old lady who needs help, card."

"Huh," snorted her mother.

"Anyway, what's up? We just saw each other yesterday at the funeral. I still have my blouse soaking. It smells like a fish."

"Oh, only once a week. Is that all you want to see me?"

"I visit you more than once a week." Mabel twisted the long cord around a finger.

"Well, now, you do. You've been away so much I almost forget I have a daughter."

"Don't exaggerate; you know that's not true."

"I won't be here forever, you know. Family is important. You'll realize that when you get old like me."

Mabel sighed. Her mother was a master of guilt. "I was busy with my daughter in Edmonton. Your granddaughter Melina wanted me with her when she gave birth to my granddaughter Rene."

"Yes, dear, of course. Did you know it's quite unsettling to be the mother of a grandmother? All the same, I'm glad everything turned out well for them both, and everyone is healthy."

"So, you see, I wasn't neglecting family. I was with another family member."

"Yes, but don't forget you were off gallivanting when I moved," Sophie accused.

Mabel flipped the long telephone cord back and forth, making little skipping rope motions with it. She'd heard her mother lament this story many times before.

"It's not easy selling up and moving at my age."

"I know, but you could have waited until I got home.

"You went to Egypt, and I was all alone."

"One trip, I go on one trip, and you decide to move. You can't blame me for that. You could have waited."

"You helped the RCMP solve a murder at the golf course."

Mabel stopped whipping her telephone cord and frowned at the sudden change in topic. Her mother was a consummate manipulator. What was she up to now?

"Yes, Violet and I did. Why?"

"And that's why I'm calling. I have a job for you."

"With the cops? What did you do? Cheat at bingo?" Mabel teased.

"Don't get snarky with me, missy, and how can you cheat a bingo?"

"It was a joke."

"Well, not a very good one. Anyway, I need your help."

"You need me to run some errands for you? No problem."

"Not an errand, dear. I need you to find out why Mini died."

"Mini? She died of old age."

"People don't die just because they reach a certain age. They die because of some illness or accident. Or maybe, even something else." Sophie's voice became softer.

"Of something else?" Mabel sat up straight in her chair and swung her legs down to the floor.

"Yes, something else. Mini was as healthy as a horse."

Mabel rolled her eyes. Mini was at least eighty. "An eighty-year-old horse."

"Eighty-year-old horse! That is very disrespectful."

"Sorry, but you said it first."

"I did not."

"Forget it; I'm sorry I phrased it that way. But Mini was at least eighty."

"Yes, but a healthy eighty. Sure, she had a little high blood pressure, but it was minor."

"A little high blood pressure?"

"Yes, a little."

"Next, you will tell me she had a slight heart attack. There is no slight about it."

"Mabel, did I say she had a slight heart attack? No, I didn't. I'm telling you, something is not quite right with Mini's sudden death."

Mabel laid her head back and closed her eyes. Only her mother would think an aged friend who died at eighty was a sudden death. "What do you want me to do?"

"Find out, for goodness' sake. Why do you think I'm telling you this?"

"And just what am I supposed to find out? I can't break into the coroner's office and look at his reports."

"Ask him."

"Why would he tell me?"

"Why wouldn't he?"

"It's called patient confidentiality."

"Mini isn't his patient. And Mini is dead, and in my opinion, her death is downright suspicious. Now, are you going to do something? Or not?"

Mabel sighed. Gathering the telephone cord in one hand, she slid the kitchen chairs back into place. Her mother was not going to let this thing with Mini go. So, she might as well get it over with, and truth be told, she was bored; she had nothing else to do. Violet was too busy with her new boyfriend to golf. "Okay, I'll come over, and you can tell me why you think Mini's death is suspicious." Mabel suspected her mother just wanted her to visit. Who would want to harm an old lady like Mini?

Chapter Three

Mabel took in a deep breath; it was the smell of autumn. Golden leaves showered down on the sidewalk, swirling in the light breeze. Soon, they would no longer be soft but brittle. Mabel smiled, remembering how, as a child, she delighted in crushing the leaves and feeling the crunch underfoot. She slung her purse over her arm, enjoying the warm sun as she walked along the sidewalk toward the Gravenhurst Manor, the senior's condo on the far side of town. The school bell from the Glenhaven Public School rang out, calling the children in from recess. And she could hear shouts and shrieks of laughter as they ran from the playground to the school. Mabel paused to admire the two new houses on her street. They had knocked two old houses down to make way for the new. A new potash mine located south of the town brought big changes to Glenhaven. The little town was experiencing a building boom. She wasn't sad to see the two dilapidated houses demolished. New homes had sprung up, and old homes were sold at astronomical prices. Mabel wondered momentarily what her little bungalow was worth. She quickly shook off the thought. She was happy in her little house.

In the once-vacant lot next to the dental office, three men dressed in coveralls and hard hats climbed up a scaffold. The building, when finished, would house a gym, a new ice-skating rink and a swimming pool. As she passed Pam & Ally's café, she wondered if the new fast-food cafes opened near the highway were taking business away from them. She hoped not.

Mabel paused at the post office to chat with her neighbour, Wanda. The walk to the seniors' condo took longer than planned, as she kept meeting friends and neighbours on the street. It was nice that not everyone was a newcomer to the town.

A large black raven perched on the Gravenhurst Manor sign cawed at her, the sign set on the green lawn in front of the new two-story building. The manor, which had twenty-five modern suites, was geared to seniors. The condo had been built to free up housing. However, many of the residents living at the manor were from out of town. Which still left a housing shortage in Glenhaven. The big two-story white building with its blue roof had a grand entrance. Two pillars supported the gabled porch entrance. Through the large glass double doors, Mabel gained access to the vestibule. On a wall inside was a brass plaque with the residence names and condo numbers. Below each name was an intercom button. This was a safety feature which guaranteed safety for the seniors living there. The lobby doors only opened if the residents buzzed their visitors in, releasing the lock on the next set of glass doors into the foyer. Mabel supposed this was a selling point; the seniors were assured of their safety. Her purse strap slipped down over her arm as she pressed the button to her mother's condo unit.

"Who is it?" Her mother's voice sounded tinny over the intercom.

"It's me, Mabel."

"Who did you say you were? I don't recognize the name."

"I'm a door-to-door salesman selling insurance. Open the darn door, Mom and quit playing games." Mabel sighed. Her mother had a way of making her feel guilty. The door buzzed and opened.

A tall, lanky man in a pair of patched old coveralls with a big brown belt cinched around his waist came out the door. A ring of keys hanging down from the belt jingled as he walked.

"Afternoon," mumbled the man. He paused; faded blue eyes gave Mabel the once-over. "Your new? I ain't seen you around here."

Mabel detected suspicion in his voice. "I'm just visiting." She edged toward the door to the lobby.

"Visiting who?"

"Sophie Schonberg, I'm her daughter Mabel. Mabel Havelock."

"Is that a fact, coming from away, are you?" The man took up a position in the open doorway with his arms crossed.

Mabel lifted her chin and stared back at the nosy man. He had to be a newcomer to town. She had never seen him before. "No, I live here in town. Sorry, I don't know your name. What is yours?"

"My what?"

"Your name."

"Farley."

"Farley? Is that your first or last name?" Mabel looked up at the gangly man over her granny glasses. Although the man had a weathered face, she thought he was in his early fifties.

"Last."

"I see. You're new in town."

"Yep."

"From where?"

"From away."

"From away, where?"

"From away."

"And where is that exactly?"

"Away."

Mabel rolled her eyes. "Do you work here?"

"Yep," he muttered, sauntering out the front door.

That man is definitely a few sandwiches short of a picnic, Mabel thought as she stepped inside the lobby. The manor still had the new, fresh paint smell. A large, sparkling chandelier hung down from the vaulted ceiling. Armchairs, set on either side of the elevator. Across the carpeted foyer, the entrance to the lounge. The lounge had the same light-blue herringbone-patterned carpet. A leather couch faced a gas fireplace, and over the fireplace hung a large plasma screen TV. Brown leather armchairs circled small tables with shiny brass lamps topped with red lampshades. In front of the two big windows, two long tables.

At one long table, Hannah Huston and Freda Jilvontee were working on a jigsaw puzzle. Mabel set her purse on a small end table and trotted over to have a peek.

"How is the puzzle coming," she asked. The puzzle looked to be half done. They had propped the puzzle box lid up against a flower vase. The picture on the cover depicted an old medieval castle with a flower garden.

Hannah, a small woman with a widow's hump, flashed Mabel a smile. Hannah's teeth were loose, and her teeth clicked as she talked. "Ah, you've finally come to visit your mom, have you?" The tiny woman picked up a puzzle piece, examined it, and then fit the piece into the castle.

Mabel pursed her lips. What was her mother telling her friends? Was she saying she didn't visit enough? She thought of her brother, Cyril. Her brother only came to visit on holidays. He lived three hours away in Winnipeg, and Mabel didn't count that as an excuse. But her mother did.

"It's about time you came to visit your mother. Your poor mom gets lonely. If Daniel and I were able to have children, I know they would be here every day," Freda Jilvontee said.

Freda was a widow; Mabel guessed her to be at least seventy. The woman had iron-grey hair curled into a bun and a long, thin nose.

"That doesn't fit." Freda's top lip curled as she removed the puzzle piece Hannah had put in.

"I'd give anything to have children," Hannah said, turning back to the pile of loose puzzle pieces, shifting them around with her index finger. "But that bugger buggered off."

"Yeah, yeah, Tom left you. We've all heard that story." Freda examined the puzzle piece she had rejected.

Hannah glanced up at Freda with a mutinous look on her face.

"I visit my mom," defended Mabel, watching Freda put Hannah's puzzle piece back in the castle.

"That's not what Sophie tells us," Homer Murphy piped up from the kitchen. The community kitchen was a smallish area with a fridge, stove, and dishwasher. A half counter separated it from the lounge. The small, bent man leaned on the grey and white marble countertop, pouring a cup of coffee.

Mabel glared at Homer as he picked up his coffee mug and hobbled over to a chair where his walker sat. There was a baseball game on the TV, but no one appeared to be watching. Charlie Sweeny stretched out on the couch in front of the TV, snoring.

Homer, balancing the cup of coffee in one hand, looked over at Mabel. "Aren't you going to help me?" he asked.

"Fat chance I'd probably end up wearing it," she growled.

Homer chuckled as Mabel did an about-face, strutting out of the lounge to the elevator. As she pushed the call button for the elevator, she heard Hannah clicking her teeth. "Poor Sophie, it's a shame when your children don't visit."

Chapter Four

Mabel stepped out of the elevator and strutted down the hallway, she was still annoyed that Hannah, Freda and old Homer thought she had neglected her mom. She rapped soundly on her mother's door.

"Who is it?" her mother called.

"It's your long-lost daughter who never visits you."

"Who?"

"Quit fooling around." Mabel opened the door and walked into her mother's condo.

They called the design of the unit her mother lived in open-plan living. The suite had a small kitchen with an L-shaped cupboard design and an island that separated the kitchen from the living room. A narrow hallway led to the bedroom on one side and a bathroom on the other. It always took Mabel a moment to adjust to all the pink and white. To her, it looked like a valentine had thrown up. A long wall behind the TV that her mother called her feature wall had pink and white stripe wallpaper. White lacy curtains hung on a brass rod across the living room window. Across from the TV was a pink couch with a matching wing-back chair. Scattered across the pink sofa, round pink and white floral cushions. A white knit afghan lay along the back of the couch. Even the padded kitchen chairs were pink. The TV, the only thing that wasn't pink, sat in a long oak cabinet with pictures of her family. Sprinkled amongst the photos, little white fairy ornaments paused in mid-flight.

"What were you doing?" Sophie asked. "I buzzed you in ages ago."

"Some guy named Farley met me at the front door. The man gave me the inquisition before he let me in."

"Ah, Farley, he is the caretaker here. I grant you he is an odd duck, but he seems to do his work. Everything is kept very clean."

"And your friends in the lounge gave me an odd reception too. Hannah, Freda, and Homer all talk as if I never visit you."

"Oh, never mind them, Freda, she is just a nosy woman. And Homer, the dear man, is just looking out for me. Come sit down, dear," Sophie invited.

Mabel doubted Homer was concerned about her mother's welfare. It was more like he was just being his usual nasty self. "Anyway, tell me what you think is suspicious about your friend Mini's death." Mabel slowly sank, feeling herself being swallowed up by the plush pink couch.

Sophie sat on the wing-back chair and pressed her hands together as if praying. "The night Mini died. We had a date to go downstairs to the lounge to play bridge with Abagail and her husband, Ned. They're the Faulks. Ned worked with your father, and they were very good to us when your dad died. Do you remember them?"

"I do, nice people."

Sophie sighed. Her eyes were sad. "I had been at Mini's place for supper, and we did the dishes. And Mini seemed fine."

"Okay, and then what?"

"I came back here to change. I like to look nice. Abagail is quite a snappy dresser."

Mabel grinned; her mother was a little vain, and no one was going to outshine her in the wardrobe department.

"Mini said she would meet me downstairs. We had decided to take some of that nice wine your brother gave me for my birthday and treat Ned and Abagail." Sophie giggled. "Well, we actually planned on getting them a little snockered. They are very good bridge players. You know, give us a little advantage."

"Go on." Mabel struggled to get off the couch. The more she struggled, the deeper she seemed to go.

Sophie leaned back in her chair and smiled. "Isn't that the most comfortable couch you've ever sat on?"

"Your couch certainly is soft." Mabel heaved herself to her feet and went to the window, tugging on Sophie's lace curtains. The sun was shining in her eyes.

The Glenhaven Senior's Condo was built on the edge of town, and from the second-floor vantage point, Mabel could see for miles. The old joke, in Saskatchewan, you can see your dog running away for days, popped into her head. But in her opinion, the golden fields and brilliant blue skies made up for any flatness. A dark red barn with a grove of trees broke up the landscape. In the distance, a big green and yellow combine. A farmer was harvesting his crop.

Mabel turned her back to the window. Closing the lace curtains had not helped; the sun was still streaming in. "So, you came home to change clothes and get the wine, then what happened?"

Sophie plucked at the tassels on a floral cushion. "I went downstairs. Abagail and Ned were already there, but not Mini. We waited and waited; I have to tell you, we all got a little impatient. So, I told Abagail and Ned I would go and see what was holding Mini up. I went to the elevator and pushed the call button. But the elevator appeared to be in use."

"Appeared to be?"

"Yes, appeared to be. Wait, I haven't finished. Anyway, I decided not to waste time and used the stairs. When I got to this floor, the second floor, I couldn't open the door."

Mabel frowned; maybe her mom was getting weak. She looked okay. But was she eating properly? "You couldn't open the door."

"Yes, that was so strange. The door isn't that heavy. Anyway, I couldn't open it so I went back downstairs and tried the elevator again. This time, the elevator was free, and I took it back up. I rapped on Mini's door, but she didn't answer. I thought maybe she was in the bathroom. Then I wondered, did she fall or something? I waited and tried the door, but it was locked, so I came back here and rang her. She didn't answer."

"Okay, and?" Mabel saw no reason for her mother to be having weird thoughts that Mini had meant with a sticky end.

"I became worried and phoned the key holder. You know, the person who has the spare key. The one we contact if there is an emergency, and we can't get into our unit."

"Yes, I know what a key holder is."

"Well, I hope you do. You're my key holder."

"Yes, Mom, I know."

"Good. Anyway, I decided this was an emergency, so I phoned Mini's key holder."

"So, who found her?"

"Gemma, she is, or was, the key holder. She had the spare key. After I phoned her, I went back. I kept knocking on Mini's door and calling out to her. But she didn't answer her door." Sophie's voice faltered. She twisted the tassels on her cushion, and the tassels became knotted. "Then I came back here to wait for Gemma."

"Did you go into Mini's suite with Gemma?" Mabel sat on the arm of Sophie's chair and put her arm around her mother, hugging her.

"Yes, and we found dear Mini. She was dead." Sophie leaned her head against Mabel.

"What happened next? Who phoned the doctor?"

"I suggested we call a doctor. But as Gemma said, Mini was dead, and even I could see that, so Gemma called the coroner."

"Why the coroner?"

"She said we needed him to sign the death certificate."

"Gemma called the coroner?"

"Yes, she did. And they made me wait with everyone downstairs in the lounge. I'm afraid we polished off the wine."

Mabel gave her mother's shoulders a gentle squeeze. "If my friend died, I'd need a drink too."

Sophie sighed and sat up, tucking the cushion behind her back. "Gemma told me the coroner declared that Mini died a natural death and signed the death certificate."

"What? A heart attack?"

"I don't know, Gemma didn't say. She just said natural causes. But I don't think Mini died from natural causes. Mini was a healthy woman. She didn't take a bunch of pills. And I know she wasn't going to the doctors."

"Mini was eighty with high blood pressure. I know it's hard to lose a friend, Mom, but you have to leave it."

"But something is not right. Something happened to Mini."

"What makes you think something happened?"

"The door would not open, and remember the elevator?"

"You said the elevator was in use."

"No, I said the elevator appeared to be in use, and it wasn't. No one came down in the elevator. I asked Abagail, and she said no one came down in the elevator."

Mabel sighed. "Okay, let's go try this door you couldn't open."

They left Sophie's suite and walked silently down the corridor to the door. "The door should open to the hallway." Mabel turned the doorknob and pulled on the door. It opened easily. "Okay, Mom, you try it."

Sophie opened the door, went out to the stairwell, and closed it. Seconds later, she reopened the door. "I can open and close a door," she muttered.

"I know you can. I'm just wondering. On the night of Mini's death, did you push or pull on the door?"

"I did both. I pushed, and then I pulled, but the door wouldn't budge."

Mabel went out to the landing of the stairwell. She pushed on the door, and it opened easily. The doors were designed for seniors. "Okay, right, the door wouldn't open, and there was an elevator issue. Was there anything else that happened that makes you think Mini didn't die of a natural cause? Like a heart attack."

Sophie brought her index finger up to her lips. "Shush, you don't know who's listening, wait."

Mabel raised her eyebrows and walked back to her mother's unit in silence. She hoped her mother wasn't becoming paranoid.

Sophie closed the door and hurried into her kitchen, turning the burner on under the kettle.

Mabel plunked herself down on the couch and promptly sunk deep into the pink-well of soft sofa cushions. Her feet came up off the floor, and she propped them up on the glass coffee table. "So, you and Gemma found Mini?"

"Take your feet down, Mabel; that is not very ladylike."

Mabel obeyed. Taking her feet off the coffee table, she struggled to the edge of the couch. "How long between the time you knocked on Mini's door until Gemma came?"

Sophie set out teacups on her counter, opening drawers and taking out teaspoons. "Well, I came back here and waited for Gemma."

"Do you want help with the tea things?"

"No, I can manage." Sophie placed the teacups on a tray. "As I told you, Gemma is Mini's representative. She had the spare key. And Mabel, this has gotten me to thinking. A fat lot of good it will do me if you have my spare key and you're off gallivanting in some foreign land. Or out on the golf course, come to that." Sophie opened a cookie jar and arranged the shortbread cookies onto a plate. She set the plate on the tray.

"Would you stop that? I went on one trip, for goodness' sake."

Sophie opened her fridge and took out a small pitcher of cream. "You won't be of any help if you're not here. I should change my representative to Gemma." She set the cream and sugar on the tray.

Mabel sighed. "Whatever, do what you want. Back to the night of Mini's demise. You phoned Gemma, and you waited here in your suite until she came. How long did that take?"

"I don't know; I sat here and waited with my door open so I could see when she came." Sophie carried the tray to the coffee table and then hustled back to the kitchen. The kettle was boiling.

"And then?" Mabel took the cups and saucers off the tray, placing them on the coffee table with a teaspoon beside each cup.

"Then, Gemma came." Sophie turned off the burner and poured the hot water into her little pink and white teapot.

"And?" Mabel felt like she was wasting time. This obsession her mother had with Mini's death might be just a worry about her own time left on earth. She should go home and phone Violet and ask her and Neville for supper. But first, cookies. Her mother did make delicious homemade shortbread cookies.

Sophie placed a pink-and-white-flowered tea cozy over her teapot and carried it to the coffee table. "Like I said, Gemma came, and I went with her into Mini's suite. And we found poor Mini dead in bed." She paused. Her hand shook, and she set the teapot on the tray.

"Okay, that doesn't sound odd to me." Mabel picked up a cookie and took a bite.

"She was in bed. Don't you see how strange that is?" Sophie threw up her hands and sat on the couch beside Mabel.

"Why is it strange? Do you want me to pour the tea?"

"No, let it steep. Mini was in bed. And it was only seven o'clock in the evening."

"No offence, but old people do go to bed early."

"Pay attention, Mabel, and don't talk with your mouth full. Remember, we were going to play bridge. It was all arranged."

Mabel wiped her mouth with a napkin. "Maybe Mini felt ill and laid down."

"She was in her nightgown, and she was in bed. And if Mini felt ill, she would have phoned me and told me she wasn't going to play bridge. Mini wasn't a rude woman; she wouldn't have wanted to snub Abigail and Ned. Or me either, come to that."

"Can I pour the tea now?"

Sophie nodded. "And don't forget the elevator that appeared to be in use when it wasn't. And the blocked door."

"Are you sure the elevator wasn't in use?"

"I told you I asked Abagail if anyone came down while I went up the stairs. Both Ned and Abagail said no."

Mabel had her doubts about the blocked door. Her mother may have gotten confused. And Abagail and Ned might not have noticed someone getting off the elevator. But to put her mother's mind at rest, she would humour her. "Okay, saying all that is true."

"It's true. Do you think I'm lying? Goodness me," huffed Sophie.

"No, I don't mean that. I mean, what about the rest of your neighbours who live on this floor? If something nefarious was going on, they might have seen whatever it was."

"No, no one would see anything. Mini died on a Thursday night."

"Oh, I see a Thursday night that explains everything," Mabel exclaimed.

"Don't be snarky. Thursday night is senior dance night at the leisure centre. Everyone goes to that. Well, except for Mini, she never went. She thought the music was dreadful. I don't think it is. But Mini was a bit of a snob where music was concerned. That's why I said she would have been appalled at the organist at her funeral. Of course, as she was dead, I suppose it didn't make any difference."

Mabel picked up her teacup. "I thought you like to dance?"

"I do, and I almost always go, but Mini wanted to play bridge with Abagail and Ned. Charlie and Linda Sweeny usually play bridge on Thursday evenings with them. Because

Charlie doesn't like dancing. But the leisure centre was hosting a new band, and Linda's brother was playing in the band."

Mabel drank her tea, wondering when her mother would get to the point.

"Linda made Charlie go to the dance. So, when Mini asked me to play bridge, I thought, why not try something different? Only we never did get to play." Sophie stirred her tea, looking remorseful.

"But, Mom, be reasonable. Why would anyone want to kill Mini? She was eighty-some-odd years old. What motive could anyone possibly have?"

Sophie looked sadly at Mabel. "When you get old, everyone thinks all you need is to be warm, fed, and propped up in front of a TV. I guess no one cares how you end your days. We're old anyway."

Mabel knew her mom was playing the old lady card. But darn it, her mother was a master of guilt. "I won't dismiss Mini's death, I promise you."

MABEL RODE DOWN IN the elevator, remembering how sad her mother looked. Was her mother, right? Did something untoward happen to Mini? The elevator and blocked stairway door were odd, but was it suspicious? Mabel sighed. She had promised her mom to look into it, but how? She stepped off the elevator and was confronted by Homer. The man had her purse draped over his arm.

"That's my purse."

"Well, it's not mine, you stupid woman. Here, take the damn thing and don't leave it lying around. Things have a way of going missing in this place."

Chapter Five

"How are you, Violet?" Mabel twisted the long cord from her phone around her finger.

"I'm fine, sorry I haven't phoned you. We've been so busy. I've been showing Neville the sights."

Mabel grinned. "That wouldn't have taken long. What was the highlight? The grain elevator?"

"Neville has never seen one of these big grain elevators, and Frank Huberdeau gave us a wonderful tour."

"Fascinating, I'm sure. Anyway, if you and Neville aren't doing anything this evening, I would like to invite you both for supper."

"Let me ask Neville."

Mabel tapped her foot and waited. Violet asking Neville if they could come for supper? Where was Violet's independence? What was her friend thinking? Good lord, was this friendship with Neville serious? Her friend had married three times and vowed she would never do it again. Violet had told her, *'If I ever tell you I'm thinking of getting married again, hit me over the head with a two-by-four.'* Maybe it was time to remind Violet of her vow.

"We would love to. What can I bring?"

"A dessert would be nice." Mabel, an impatient cook, loved good food, and her friend Violet was an excellent baker.

"WHAT DID YOU SAY WAS the name of the main dish?" Neville ran his tongue over his teeth, laying his napkin on his plate, covering his leavings.

Mabel glanced at the tall, lean man sitting at her kitchen table. Although she wasn't fond of his pencil moustache, she had to admit he was an attractive man. He had deep brown eyes and dark brown hair, with just a touch of white at his temples. "Hamburger casserole, a favourite of my husband." Mabel scraped his leftover food into the garbage can under the sink. Neville appeared to be a picky eater. Maybe she should have cooked a roast.

"Neville isn't used to prairie cooking, are you?" Violet jumped up to help.

Mabel's tall friend reached over her head, taking out Tupperware containers. She carefully put the leftover casserole evenly in each container, taking some out of one and adding it to another. Satisfied they were all even, Violet snapped the lids shut.

Violet and Mabel were exact opposites. Where Mabel was short and round, Violet was tall and lean. Mabel let her hair go grey and wore steel-rimmed glasses. Violet dyed her short hair a brilliant red and wore trendy blue-rimmed glasses. The differences didn't end with their physical looks. Violet, a thoughtful cautious woman, liked everything neat and in its proper place. Mabel, a force to be reckoned with, was a surprise to the unwary, who did not know her kindly granny look was only a facade. Despite their differences, or maybe because of it, they were best friends and had been since their nursing days. The women worked in unison, clearing the table and putting everything away.

"What do you think of Saskatchewan?" Mabel asked, placing the last plate inside the dishwasher.

"I quite like these wide-open spaces. And some chap has invited me to participate in the harvest."

"Alfred Jilvontee. I think Alfred meant for you to watch. Farm machinery, like combines, are huge and complicated to operate." Violet collected the silverware, setting the cutlery in the dishwasher, and closed the door.

"I went to visit Mom this morning, and I saw Freda Jilvontee, Alfred's aunt." Mabel poured hot water into her little red teapot, placing a bright red flowered tea cozy over the pot. "Let's go into the living room. We can enjoy our tea and dessert there." Mabel picked up the tray with a teapot and mugs and led the way. She set the tray on her coffee table and shooed her cat, Gertrude, off the couch. The cat yawned, stretched and jumped up on the big grey armchair.

Violet followed with the cream and sugar. Placing the red ceramic bowls beside the tray, she asked. "How is Freda?"

Neville gave the sofa a cautious look, brushed a hand on the couch, dislodged cat hair, and eyed the cat.

"When I saw her, she was putting together a puzzle with Hannah. You remember Hannah." Mabel went back into the kitchen, returned with two dessert plates with rhubarb pie topped with a scoop of vanilla ice cream. She gave one slice to Violet and the other to Neville.

Neville accepted the plate, wrinkling his nose at the pie.

"Violet makes amazing pies. I know this pie will be delicious. You will love it."

"Forks, dear." Violet smiled at the praise. Shifting a navy cushion, she sat next to Neville on the grey tweed couch.

"Coming up," Mabel said cheerfully as she returned from the kitchen with a slice of pie for herself and forks for all.

Mabel picked up a green ball of wool from her big armchair and tossed it to the floor. The ball of yarn rolled across the floor. Gertrude scampered after it, batting the ball. It rolled under the coffee table.

Neville took a tentative bite. "This is delicious," he agreed, gobbling up the pie.

Violet preened. "Thank you." She took the tea cozy off the pot, opened the lid, and peeked in. "I think it's steeped," she said, replacing the lid. "Shall I pour?"

"Please do," Mabel said, digging into her pie.

Violet poured the tea, adding sugar to a cup, stirring it, then passing the cup to Mabel, who accepted the mug and set it down, continuing to enjoy her pie.

"How is your mom?" Violet asked, pouring tea for Neville and herself.

Gertrude swatted at the ball of wool. It was unravelling.

Neville set his empty dessert plate on the coffee table and took a sip of his tea. He grimaced, set the mug beside his empty plate, and nudged the cat with his toe. Gertrud abandoned the wool and attacked his pant leg.

"Mom is fine. But she has this wild theory about Mini Frazer's death. Mom thinks Mini's death wasn't from natural causes because of a few odd things that happened the night Mini died. She is jumping to this unlikely conclusion."

Neville shook his leg; the cat was clinging onto his pant leg.

Violet grinned. "Hum, really, I wonder who that reminds me of?"

"Who?" Mabel asked.

Neville shook his foot to dislodge the cat. Gertrude jumped sideways back under the coffee table and crouched. Her tail flicked, then she leapt up and attached herself to his leg. Neville yelped, shaking his foot. Gertrude rolled on her back, her paws holding onto his foot.

"Two guesses?" Violet teased, taking a fork full of pie.

"I don't know what you mean. My theories are never wild. Mom keeps going on about Mini's death as if it was suspicious. But Mini was old. Who would want to kill an old lady?" Mabel set her empty plate on the coffee table and picked up her mug of tea.

Neville jumped up from the couch. "Your cat is quite aggressive." Gertrude laid flat, her ears back, her tail flipped back and forth.

"Gertrude?" Mabel set her mug of tea down. "She's just playing." She pulled Gertrude out from under the coffee table, stroking the cat, she continued. "Like I was saying, Mom has gotten a bee in her bonnet and just won't let it go."

Neville brushed off his trousers, eyeing Gertrude suspiciously. He made a wide berth around the cat and strolled over to a canvas on an easel in front of Mabel's picture window. Tilting his head one way, then the other, Neville rolled the tips of his moustache between his thumb and forefinger. "A goblin?" he asked, looking at the greyish figure with big dark circles around the eyes.

Mabel turned her head to look at the Englishman. Was he joking? "That's a self-portrait. I know I need to work a little more on the eyes. Eyes are hard to paint with glasses."

"It's coming along. Good for you keeping up with your painting." Violet piled the empty dessert plates onto the tea tray.

Mabel smiled. "Thank you. I painted Gertrude; that's the painting hanging over my TV."

Neville stood with his hands clasped behind his back, surveying the painting, centred in the middle of the picture, a large fuzzy orange ball. Green blobs with black dots represented Gertrude's eyes. A long, furry orange tail curled around the ball. Neville snorted, shook his head and grinned.

Mabel's eyes narrowed. What a snob. First, he didn't like her cooking or her tea. Now, she could tell he thought her painting lacked talent. She stuck out her chin. Good, she thought mutinously. She didn't want Neville to like anything of hers.

"Anyway, you said your mother has a bee in her bonnet. I assume that means... well, I'm not at all sure what it means." Neville turned his back to the painting, tweaked his moustache and smirked.

"Bee in a bonnet," Violet said, adding the dessert forks to the tray. "It means Mabel's mom is obsessed with an idea."

She grinned good-naturedly at Mabel. "Not that you have ever been obsessed with a suspicion."

"If you recall, my suspicions have always been right," Mabel replied indignantly.

Violet, smiling, shrugged and picked up her mug of tea.

Neville sat back beside Violet and draped his arm over the back of the couch.

"Why does your mom think someone did away with Mini?" Violet asked, looking over her mug of tea at Mabel.

Mabel related the events of the night Mini died. "Mom said everyone from that floor had gone to a dance. She thinks someone jammed the elevator. And she is sure the door from the stairwell was blocked, preventing any access to the floor. And because they found Mini in bed, my mom is positive someone had a hand in Mini's death."

Violet frowned. "Mini in bed does leave me to think she died in her sleep."

"I know. But Mom said they were supposed to play bridge."

"I assume they called the coroner." Neville picked up his mug of tea, swirled it, curled his lips and set it back down.

"Yes, but Mini is an old lady, and maybe he just assumed she died of a heart attack." Mabel took a sip of her tea. There was nothing wrong with the tea.

"But why would anyone hurt, let alone kill Mini? I guess money could be a motive. But she wasn't rich. Mini gave piano lessons. You don't get rich from teaching kids the scales." Violet set her empty mug down on the coffee table.

"Perhaps her husband had money," suggested Neville. "Sometimes, people can live quite simply and still possess a lot of money." His arm slipped down the couch, and he draped it over Violet's shoulder.

"I suppose Mini could be well off. Mom said she was married twice," Mabel said slowly. "Maybe she got good settlements from her ex's." Her eyes darted from Neville to Violet. Her friend had been married three times. Did Neville think Violet had money squirrelled away? Was he here to con her buddy out of money? She gave him a suspicious look.

"Ladies, I have to advise you these ideas of yours are pretty far-fetched." Neville lifted his eyebrows and smirked.

What an arrogant man, Mabel thought. Who said that they had any ideas about Mini's death? It was her mother's notion, and she thought her mother's theory was out in left-field. She grinned. It was time to annoy the tiresome man who stuck his nose up at everything. "Hum, I wonder if Mom could be right, a suspicious death."

"Even if Mini had money, it would be her children who would inherit. I'm sure they didn't kill their mother," Violet said.

"Well, yes, you're right. And Mini's kids don't even live here. They had to fly in for the funeral. But still, it makes me wonder?" It didn't, but it would be fun to see Neville's reaction.

"Are they still here?" Violet asked.

"I think so. They have to settle the estate and sell their mother's condo. It wouldn't hurt for us to poke around, maybe find out if she changed her will suddenly." Mabel watched with satisfaction as Neville's lips curled.

"What an extremely vulgar suggestion," huffed Neville. "How can you even think of intruding on the family in their time of grief? Most unseemly, asking questions. Questions that are none of your business." He squeezed Violet's arm. "Don't get involved." Violet's eyes widened. She shrugged off his embrace.

"It's not like I'm going to barge up to the family and ask if their mother changed her will. I have a little more finesse than that," Mabel said, suddenly upset with Neville's opinion of her.

"Well, Violet is certainly not going to be involved in this ridiculous plan. Are you?" Neville stared intently at Violet.

Violet's brow knitted in a frown. She picked up her tea mug, tapping the side of the cup with an index finger.

Mabel's eyes flickered from Neville to Violet. She should tell him she was joking. Her friend Violet would be the last person to intrude on anyone's grief.

Neville looked over at Mabel, his lips curled into a smug smile.

Mabel bristled. "We will be subtle."

"Violet, you can't possibly think this is a good idea. You will be making a huge mistake. Just because some old lady has a wild theory of how this woman Mini died. Is no reason to get tangled up in this ridiculous investigation." Neville turned to Mabel. "Sorry, but it's true. This idea your mother has is crazy."

"Hold it right there. My mom is not a crazy old lady," snapped Mabel.

"Neville doesn't mean your mom is crazy. Do you, Neville?"

"No, of course not; I'm sorry if you mistook my meaning."

Mabel folded her arms over her chest and sat back in her chair. She didn't think she mistook anything.

"What I mean is, it is foolish to upset the grief-stricken family with such a flimsy theory based on a door that wouldn't open." Neville leaned forward. "Your mom is old. Her strength would not be what yours is. And she could have just gotten confused when she pulled instead of pushed on that door."

"Mom had no problem opening the door when I was there this morning." She hadn't been sure that her mother wasn't confused either. But now, because Neville was disputing her mother. Mabel decided her mother could well be right.

"It won't hurt to ask a few questions, maybe even go and see the coroner," suggested Violet.

"Violet. You can't be serious." Neville leaned forward his hands clasped.

"Why not? You'll be busy tomorrow. You're going to combine with Alfred, remember? Mabel and I will just have a little poke around. We'll be discreet."

Mabel grinned. She doubted Mini's death was suspicious. But it was good to have Violet put Neville in his place. She didn't like the idea of him telling her friend what she could and could not do.

MABEL TAPPED ON HER iPad. She would find out about this man, Neville. Who was he? If he was a criminal, surely his name would come up. She keyed in his name, miss-spelling it. Neville Chamberland's name came up. The next thing Mabel knew, she was down the rabbit hole. She went from World War II to Africa. Then she was on YouTube, watching a giraffe in someone's backyard eating a hedge and a monkey licking an ice cream cone.

Yawning, she shut her iPad off and went to bed. Gertrude, her cat, curled up beside her. Mabel stroked the cat. She suspected she and Violet were on a wild goose chase. But it would ease her mother's mind if they did have a poke around, as Violet called it. And better yet, it would annoy that pompous man. Mabel went to sleep with a smile on her face.

Chapter Six

Violet rapped on Mabel's back door, calling, "Good morning." She entered without further ado. "You know, maybe it's not such a good idea to let people enter your house before being invited. There are a lot of new people in town. I could have been a stranger."

Mabel, sitting at her kitchen table, looked up at Violet and grinned. "I knew it was you."

Violet arched an eyebrow. "And how would you know that?"

"You called out good morning, silly. Would you like some coffee?" she asked.

"No, thanks. Neville and I had a big breakfast. I didn't want to send him off to the farm on an empty stomach."

"Alfred's wife, Ruth, will undoubtedly feed them well." Mabel cleared the table of her breakfast dishes. "Did Alfred pick him up?"

"No, I lent Neville my car. I hope he doesn't get lost. But I'm sure he won't; we were out at Alfred's farm yesterday."

"Does Neville know how to drive your car? They drive on the other side of the road in Britain. And their steering wheel is on the wrong side too." Mabel wiped off her table and tossed the dishcloth into the sink.

"There's no right or wrong side."

"You're not worried your car won't come back with a dent? Neville will be driving your car on a country road."

"Thanks a bunch; that puts my mind at ease." She'd been okay with Neville using her car. That was until Mabel pointed out the fact that Neville was used to British ways of driving. Violet compressed her lips. It was a gravel country road. "I haven't had a call from Neville that he is lost or is in an accident. So, I'm not going to worry about him or my car." She pasted an unconcerned smile on her face.

"Right, so shall we get on with our investigation?"

Violet shook off her worries. "What's the plan?"

"We go visit Mom. I bet some family members are staying at Mini's condo. There are not a lot of places to stay in Glenhaven. And the motel on the highway has seen better days."

"There is Mary's bed and breakfast."

"Let's give the condo a try," Mabel suggested.

MABEL PRESSED THE BUZZER to her mother's condo and waited for her to answer.

"Who is it?" Mabel's mother's voice echoed over the intercom.

"It's me, Mom, and Violet is with me."

"Is that my daughter? Are you sure it's Mabel?"

Violet looked at Mabel in alarm.

Mabel shook her head and shouted into the intercom. "Stop being a clown and let us in."

"There is no need to shout." The door buzzed and opened.

Violet looked with concern at Mabel as they entered the lobby. "Are you sure your mom isn't losing it? Sometimes it's hard for family members to recognize the signs of Alzheimer's in those they love."

Mabel sighed. "It's a little game she plays with me every time I visit. I have to admit it's getting a little old."

"You're sure?"

Homer Murphy hobbled out of the elevator with his walker. "Oh, it's you."

Violet smiled at Homer. "How are you, Homer?"

"Why in tarnation does everyone want to know how I am? And what business is it of yours?" Homer thumped his walker toward Mabel. He stood staring at her as if it was a game of chicken.

Mabel stared back, then sidestepped out of his way. Homer nodded smugly and stomped away with his walker.

"I see he hasn't changed his ways," Violet said, watching the old man shuffling into the lounge.

"He's a bully with that walker. And this is the thanks we get for solving that serious assault on him," Mabel snorted.

"Stumbled on the solution, you mean." Violet led the way into the elevator.

Mabel followed, and the door closed. She pressed the button for the second floor. "We didn't stumble. It was a brilliant deduction."

"If you say so." Violet hitched her purse over her shoulder and grinned. Granted, her friend Mabel was good at putting the pieces of a puzzle together. But solving the mystery was never as straightforward as Mabel liked to believe.

They exited the elevator and walked along the corridor to Sophie's suite. Mabel rang the doorbell.

"Who is it?"

Violet looked at Mabel in alarm; they had just been buzzed in the door by Mabel's mother, and she had already forgotten they were coming or who they were.

"The pot inspectors, we hear you are growing illegal marijuana," Mabel answered.

"Smartypants, come on in."

Violet grinned, relieved.

"Violet, dear, so good of you to visit me." Sophie hugged her. "Thanks for bringing Mabel. I hardly ever see her."

Violet furrowed her forehead as she looked at Mabel over Sophie's shoulder.

"Mother, stop this charade. Violet thinks you're losing your marbles."

Sophie's blue eyes twinkled. "Well, it's not too far from the truth."

Mabel chuckled. "You think you're losing your marbles?"

"Don't be silly. I mean, you went to Egypt and left me all alone."

"One trip, I took one trip," Mabel defended.

"And you never even told me you were going to Egypt."

"Mom, not that again," Mabel sighed.

"Oh, never mind, I'm pleased you have come to visit me." Sophie tucked an arm through Violet's and led her to her living room. "What do you think of my little home? I decorated my new home all by myself. Mabel was absolutely no help at all."

Violet looked around at Sophie's suite and then at Mabel, who winked. What should she say? She didn't want to hurt Sophie's feelings. But she had never seen such over the top use of pink and white in her life. "Where did you find a pink couch?"

"It's not pink, dear, it's rose. And believe it or not, I had to special order this couch in. They didn't have a rose-coloured one in stock, can you imagine?"

"I guess I can; pink, I mean, rose couches must be difficult to find. You've settled nicely in your new home. You look very comfortable," Violet said diplomatically.

"I got rid of all my old furniture from the old house when I sold it. I don't think Mabel was very pleased. But I wanted to have everything fresh and new in my brand-new home," Sophie said proudly.

Mabel shrugged. "I'm fine, Mom, and it's your furniture."

"Well, everything certainly is fresh and new." Violet didn't think Mabel looked all that fine with it.

Mabel sat on the pink wing-back chair and motioned Violet to sit with Sophie on the pink couch. Violet sunk deep into the sofa. She glanced over at Mabel, who was grinning from ear to ear.

"Are you comfy, dear? Isn't this the softest couch you ever sat on?" Sophie settled into the cushions.

"It is certainly the softest," Violet agreed, struggling to get to the edge of the couch. "Would you like to see pictures of your daughter riding a camel?" she asked.

"Yes, indeed."

Violet took a package of pictures out of her purse and began showing Sophie the sights of Egypt. She smiled as Sophie oohed over the photos.

"My, what an adventure, and you rode a camel, Mabel; I'm impressed," Sophie said as Violet put the pictures back into an envelope.

Mabel beamed.

They chatted about the events in Glenhaven, the new housing, and all the newcomers bringing business to town.

Violet decided it was time to broach the reason they were there. "Mabel and I are going to look into your concerns about your friend Mini."

"Thank goodness, I wasn't sure Mabel took me seriously yesterday."

"Well, I did. And we thought it might be a good idea to talk to Mini's kids. Are any staying here in Mini's condo?"

"Mini's daughter Judith is staying here."

"And the rest?" Violet tucked the envelope of pictures into her purse.

"I don't know where the rest are staying. I've only seen Judith in the corridor."

"Do you want to come with us? You can introduce us to Judith. It would look more natural," suggested Mabel.

"What do you hope to find out? The kids weren't here when Mini died."

Mabel stood. "I'm not sure, but we have to start somewhere. We're doing this because of you. So, are you coming?"

"Just a minute, dear, I have to freshen up."

Sophie's freshen-up took a half hour. When she emerged from her bedroom, she had rouge on her cheeks and tiny pearl earrings in her ears. She'd changed her clothes. She was now wearing a mid-calf length blue striped skirt and a pink blouse, with a white-fringed shawl over her shoulders.

"You look lovely, Sophie," complemented Violet.

"Yes, you do," added Mabel.

"Thank you. One must always look their best. You could try a little harder, Mabel."

Violet grinned; mother and daughter were very close personality-wise. But Mabel had no interest in clothes, while her mother took any opportunity to dress up.

Mabel tugged her sweatshirt with a football logo on it, sighed, then followed her mother out the door.

Sophie led the way down the corridor.

"Aren't you going to lock your door?" Mabel asked.

"There's no reason to lock my door. This is a secure building. No one can come in here to rob us. Anyone who wants to come into this building must be let in by a resident. And everyone who lives here is honest."

"Aren't you forgetting something?"

"What, dear?" Sophie stopped in the hallway.

"The fact you think someone killed Mini. If it's as safe as you say, and no one can get in. And if everyone living here is an honourable person. Who killed Mini?"

Sophie's hand fluttered to her mouth. "Oh my, you do have a point."

"I'll go back and lock your door for you," Violet volunteered.

"Would you, dear? That would be so nice. My key is on a peg just inside the door on the left-hand side."

Violet locked Sophie's door, hurried back, and gave Sophie her key.

"Was Mini in the habit of locking her door?" Mabel asked as they followed Sophie down the hallway.

"No, none of us do. Although now I think I will alert my neighbours of the danger of leaving our doors unlocked."

"Violet, did you hear that?"

"Yes, what of it?"

"A clue."

"A clue?" Sophie dropped her key into her little white purse.

"I find it strange that Mini didn't lock her door as a rule. Yet on the night she died, her door was locked."

Violet perked up. "Ah, are you thinking what I'm thinking?"

"I believe I am."

"Since I'm not a mind reader, do you mind letting me in on this little secret?" asked Sophie.

"A murder in a locked room. We've come across this before."

Sophie gave the women a hard stare. "You girls are talking in riddles; stop it this instant."

"What we mean is when we were in Egypt, there was a murder in a locked room. But we cracked the case."

"We cracked the case." Violet chuckled. "You sound like a detective from an old movie. What you mean is we bumbled around and finally solved it."

"We did not bumble. We solved it." Mabel tilted her head and stuck out her chin.

"So, what does Mini's locked door mean?" Sophie looked from Violet to Mabel.

Mabel frowned. "I don't know yet, but it's suspicious."

"Be sure to let me know when you figure it out." Sophie stopped and rapped on a door. They waited, and then Sophie rapped again.

Mabel tapped her toe on the floor. "Try the doorbell; maybe she didn't hear you."

As Sophie pressed the doorbell, the door swung open. Judith stood before them, wearing a faded pair of blue jeans and a red and black striped T-shirt. Her hair was tied back in a ponytail, and her face was drawn and void of makeup.

"Hello, Mrs. Schoenberg; I wasn't expecting company."

"Please, call me Sophie. Your mother and I were great friends."

Judith looked down at Sophie. "Yes, I know, you told me at the funeral."

Violet and Mabel shared an uncomfortable look as they stood in the open doorway. Was Judith going to invite them in?

"I found your mom the night she died. Oh, I wasn't alone when I found your mom. Gemma was with me."

"Yes, I know, Gemma told me." An awkward pause followed.

Mabel reached out a hand. "I'm Mabel, Sophie's daughter, and this is my friend Violet."

"How do you do," Judith said formally. She shook Mabel's hand first and then Violet's. "Well, I guess you might as well come in, but the place is a mess. I'm sorting through my mom's things." Judith stood back, holding open the door.

Violet followed Mabel and Sophie into the condo unit. The suite's layout was a carbon copy of Sophie's. But there was no pink here; instead, there were muted blues and greys. The cupboard doors hung open in the kitchen, and cardboard boxes lined the countertop filled with dishes. Scattered across the carpet in the living room were more packing boxes. An assortment of clothes was strewn on the couch and on the big, padded rocking chair.

"Please, just shift the stuff and sit down," invited Judith.

Sophie and Mabel sat down on the couch.

Violet picked a photo off the floor and deposited it on the coffee table. "A terrible time for visitors, we know. But we wanted to offer our condolences."

Sophie picked up her friend's sweater and placed it neatly on the arm of the couch. She sighed. "What are you going to do with all your mom's things?"

"Give it all to Goodwill or some charity. Most of this is just old stuff."

Sophie bit her lip and ran her hand over the sweater, gently pressing the wrinkles out of the garment.

Violet took a navy and white dress off a cushioned rocker and sat down. The rocker swayed gently.

"Are you doing this all on your own?" Mabel asked, shifting a black woollen coat.

"Aren't your brothers helping you? This is a big job." Violet folded the dress and placed the item in an open box.

"Just me, I'm afraid. My husband took the kids back to Ottawa," Judith said, perching on a kitchen stool. "The kids have school. And my brothers had to get back to work." She frowned. "Or so they said."

"I didn't see your husband at the service," Sophie piped up.

"Russ came later to the luncheon. He missed the funeral." Judith's voice was sharp with vexation.

"The funeral was very nice." Sophie smiled at Judith.

Violet's eyes darted from Sophie to Judith. A nice funeral? Violet avoided looking at Mabel.

"Nice? I guess so, thank you. We did want to give Mom a nice send-off."

"Nice except for the music, which was absolutely god awful," Sophie added.

Mabel, laying the black coat on the rug, looked up at her mother in alarm. Violet ducked her head and picked up another dress, folding it.

Sophie continued her critique. "Your mother, being a music teacher, would have been appalled."

Judith's eyes widened. "Appalled?"

"The organist was dreadful. Of course, that's not all your fault, dear, but if you'd picked another day for the funeral, our regular organist could have been there. She works, you see. And that hymn, *The Old Rugged Cross*, really? What were you thinking when you chose that hymn?"

Judith looked askance. "We picked what we thought mother would like."

"No, dear, your mother hated it."

"Mom," Mabel rebuked sharply.

Violet, who had folded two more garments and deposited them neatly in a box, spoke up quickly. "I'm sure it was fine, the music, I mean."

"Well, it wasn't. It was awful. Just ask Mabel if you don't believe me."

"Don't bring me into this."

The doorbell rang. Judith jumped off the stool and hurried to the door. She opened the door, and Gemma Charbon stepped into the room.

"Hello, Judith, I've come to help," she said cheerfully.

"Thanks. There is a lot to go through."

"No problem," said the tall, imposing woman as she swept into the room, dropping her big green purse on the counter.

Sophie jumped up from the couch and rushed over to Gemma.

"It's good to see you, my little Sophie." Gemma smiled and bent down to hug Sophie. "She's my little doll," she said.

Violet watched Mabel's eyes narrow, and her body stiffen. She suspected her friend felt envious. Sophie hadn't greeted Mabel with the same exuberance. Was Sophie trying to make her daughter jealous?

Gemma kept her arm around the little woman. And Sophie beamed happily up at her.

"As I said, I'm here to help, but I see you have helpers already." Gemma flashed a toothy smile at Mabel and Violet. "Who are your friends?"

"They're just visiting." Judith picked up a dinner plate off the counter, wrapping it in a newspaper. "They are just about to leave." She gave Sophie a cold stare.

"I'm Violet Fisher, and this is Mabel, Sophie's daughter. I could stay and help," offered Violet; she'd already packed one box with clothes.

"Oh, no, but thank you for your offer. But Gemma is here to help," Judith said hurriedly.

Gemma turned to Mabel. "Oh, of course, you're Mabel. I've seen your picture in your mom's cozy little home. You've done wonders with the place, Sophie." Gemma smiled at Mabel over the top of Sophie's head. "Your mom has a flair for decorating."

Mabel looked flabbergasted. Violet raised her eyebrows. A flair for decorating? Sophie? The woman had to be humouring Mabel's mother.

"Well, ladies, I don't mean to be inhospitable, but I've got a lot to do. I have to pack up all my mom's things and get this condo ready for sale. And settle Mom's affairs and her estate. So, if you'll excuse us." Judith held the door open.

Mabel tromped down the corridor. "Good lord, Mother, we were not there to critique the funeral."

"She asked how I liked the funeral?"

"No, she did not. No one asks how you like a funeral."

"Forget it, Mabel, it doesn't matter," Violet intervened.

"I guess not, but did you see how Gemma ingratiated herself?"

Unlocking her door, Sophie turned to Mabel. "Don't be unkind, dear. Gemma is well-named. She is an absolute gem. Gemma helps many of us who live in Gravenhurst. She takes us to our doctors' appointments. And is always ready to give us lifts downtown to do our errands. She even picks up our mail for us. And the dear girl never takes a thing in return. We all love her; Gemma is a gem of a person."

"I can always give you a lift; all you have to do is ask me."

"Gemma has a swanky new car, not like your old beater. I always feel like a princess when she drives me around town."

Violet grinned. "Your mom has a point. It's hard to feel like a princess riding in your old purple Pontiac."

"Mom, you always act like I never do anything for you. I'm sure Gemma thinks I never visit you. And your chums think the same thing."

"You know it's just our little joke. But maybe I've carried it a bit too far," Sophie conceded.

"A little bit too far? How about a lot too far? I'm tired of your little joke."

Sophie wrapped her arms around her daughter and kissed her on the cheek. "You need to get a sense of humour, dear."

"MY MOTHER IS ABSOLUTELY bonkers. I don't mean as out in left field. I mean bonkers. She comes out with the most outlandish things. Like critiquing the funeral." Mabel punched the button in the elevator with more force than was needed.

"The apple doesn't fall far from the tree," Violet said as she followed Mabel into the elevator.

With a mutinous expression on her face, Mabel crossed her arms. "I'm nothing like my mother."

"If you say so. But I do agree that you don't have your mom's decorating flair, as Gemma calls it."

"Decorating flair? Either Gemma has horrible taste, or she needs glasses." The door to the elevator opened, and Mabel stepped out. "That woman rubs me the wrong way."

"Are you perhaps a wee bit jealous?"

"Ha, me jealous, not a bit."

Violet gave Mabel a sidelong glance.

"And a big help you were, we didn't learn a thing."

"Hey, I packed a whole box."

"Oh, I know it's not your fault. It was my mom who got us thrown out before we could learn anything."

"Maybe there is nothing to learn."

Mabel walked with Violet out the condo door and into the vestibule. She paused and looked at the buttons on the brass wall panel. "Everyone's name is listed."

"Yes, so what?"

"We don't think anyone who is a resident killed Mini, do we?"

"No, that seems unlikely."

"So, what if someone buzzed Mini? Mini lets this person in because she knows them. And whoever she let in killed her."

"That is if someone did kill the poor woman. We have no proof of anything nefarious. It's just your mom's suspicions." Violet reminded Mabel.

"Okay, but let's suppose for a moment Mom is right, and someone killed Mini. Mini let this person in. They went to her suite because Mini is expecting them. After they kill Mini, they take her key and lock the door to convince everyone she died of natural causes. You heard what Mom said. Mini never locked her door."

"We should have asked Judith if there is a missing key?"

"A lot of time has passed. By now, the key is probably returned."

"We should go visit the coroner tomorrow and find out if there was anything at all suspicious about Mini's death." Violet opened the outside door.

Farley strolled in the door, keys jingling on his belt. "Hello, ladies."

"How are you today, Farley?" Mabel asked.

"Same as yesterday." Farley let the door slam shut behind him.

Violet grinned. "Friendly man."

"Mom says he's an odd duck. Anyway, are you coming with me tomorrow? What about Neville?"

"Oh yeah, I forgot about him."

Mabel's steps were lighter; there was hope for Violet yet.

Chapter Seven

Putting the last of the dishes in the dishwasher, Mabel looked over at her wall phone, wondering if she should phone Violet again. It had been a week since they had decided to talk to the coroner. And every time she called Violet and asked if she wanted to go with her to Kegsworthy and speak to the coroner, Neville had some excursion planned. Seriously, she fumed, this was Saskatchewan. What more did he want to see? She picked up her phone and dialled, swung the long phone cord and waited for Violet to answer.

"Hi, I was just going to call you."

Mabel's spirits rose. "Good news, I hope."

"Well, it's not bad news; I was planning on going with you to Kegsworthy, but—"

"But Neville wants to see more sights." Mabel finished for her. Leaning up against the wall, she twisted the long telephone cord in her hand.

"He wants to see the lake district."

"The lake district, where the heck is that?"

Violet chuckled fondly. "Neville wants to go to the Qu'Appelle Valley, to Katepwa Lake. The valley should be beautiful with the fall colours."

"The leaves on the trees will be stunning," Mabel conceded. "Enjoy."

"Do you want to come with us?"

Mabel sighed. The views in the valley would be spectacular, but a day with Neville, she could do without. "No, but thanks. I'll pop up and see Mom before she spreads any more rumours that I have abandoned her. Maybe I'll take her to Kegsworthy. It's not as pretty as where you're going, but it will be a change for her. And I'll talk to the coroner. I want to find out if anything was odd with Mini's death and put my mom's worries to rest."

"The drive will be nice for her. Hey, you're not taking her into the coroner's office, are you? Your mom is a little outspoken; you remember the visit with Judith."

"No, I won't. Nothing good would come of that." Mabel could hear Violet laughed.

MABEL GLANCED IN HER rear-view mirror at the long convoy of vehicles stretched out behind her. It was slow going. She was stuck behind a combine. The traffic was heavy on the two-lane highway, with cars and grain trucks, making it impossible to pass the farmer's huge farm implement that took up a full lane.

"Finally," she said as the farmer pulled onto an approach and into his field.

A blue half-ton truck zoomed from the back of the convoy, passing everyone. Seconds behind the truck, a police car with lights flashing and sirens blaring came out from an approach. Mabel and the convoy slowed down, passing the truck pulled over to the side of the road. She spotted Constable Robert Shamanski behind the wheel of the RCMP cruiser. She waved at the young constable as she drove by, hoping he would notice her. The big constable didn't notice Mabel, but the driver of the blue truck did. He gave Mabel the finger.

"How rude," exclaimed Mabel.

"You waved at him. The man thinks you're enjoying the fact he's been stopped for speeding."

"I wasn't waving at him. I was waving at my friend Robert. He's the RCMP officer writing out the speeding ticket."

"You know that young policeman?" Mabel's mother asked.

"Yes," Mabel said proudly. "Robert and I are great friends."

"Really?"

Mabel picked up speed as they passed the parked police car. "Violet and I helped him solve a murder. Well, actually, two murders."

"Oh, yes, I remember; those were very disturbing murders."

"All murders are disturbing."

"I know they are, and Mini's even more so. Killing a poor, defenceless woman. How despicable."

"Mom, we don't know if someone murdered your friend Mini. Let's just call it a suspicious death for now. After I talk to the coroner, I will know more." Mabel was secretly pleased that her mother didn't contradict her when she said that she and Violet had helped solve a murder.

She slowed her car, bringing it to a stop at a railway crossing. The crossing gate dropped, and the red signal lights flashed. A train with a long line of grain cars sped down the tracks.

"I miss Mini," lamented Sophie. "We moved in around the same time. I don't dislike the rest of the residents. But Mini and I hit it off right from the start."

Mabel shifted her car to neutral as she watched the long line of grain cars pass before her. As a child, she and her brother used to count how many cars the engine was pulling. Now, she just wished the train would hurry and pass. "Is there no one you can strike up a friendship with? What about Freda Jilvontee or Hannah What's-her-name?"

"Huston," supplied Sophie.

"Or Abagail? You play bridge with her."

Sophie sighed. "You don't have to be my social director, dear. As for Freda, I think she may be losing it. She accuses people of stealing her jewelry as if she had the crown jewels, for goodness' sake. Now she says someone stole her mail. Like anyone wants to read her mail."

Mabel looked out through the windshield at the passing train. Someone had sprayed graffiti on the side of a grain car. It looked quite artistic. She wondered what the words meant.

Sophie continued to critique her neighbours at the Gravenhurst Manor. She ended the review of her neighbours with, "Hannah and I have nothing in common."

"Do you really think someone is stealing from Freda?"

"I doubt it. Although Hannah is always sneaking around. Turning up when you least suspect it. One day, she came into my condo uninvited. It does make one wonder." Sophie's brows furrowed.

"That's not a very good reason to accuse Hannah of stealing."

"I'm not accusing her; I'm saying she is a sneaky woman, and we have nothing in common. But Abagail Faulk, now she is quite a nice girl."

Mabel grinned. Abagail was a woman in her seventies, and her mother called her a girl. The train cleared the crossing. As Mabel put her car into gear, a horn blared behind her; she glanced in her review mirror and stuck up her middle finger in the air, giving the driver the finger.

"Mabel, be a lady," admonished her mother.

"Sorry," Mabel apologized. It didn't seem to matter how old she was. Her mother still reprimanded her as if she was twelve.

As they entered the town of Kipling, Sophie tugged on Mabel's arm. "Please drive by our old house. I want to see what the new owners have done to the place."

"Okay," Mabel agreed, curious to see her old childhood home as they drove past the giant Red Paper Clip. Mabel mused aloud. "I wonder if Violet has shown Neville the red paper clip?"

"Neville? Who is Neville?"

"A friend of Violet's who is visiting from England."

"If he comes from England, where there is history at every turn. Do you really think he'd want to see a giant red paper clip?"

"I don't know. But the paper clip does have a cool history. A man bartered his way from a little red paper clip to owning a house."

"True. Turn here, dear; this was our street."

"I do know where we lived, Mom." Mabel turned the corner, and as they drove past the bungalow, she remembered sitting on the front porch. And playing 'hide and seek' in the big old elm trees with the neighbourhood kids. It was all so long ago.

"Everyone in these houses is dead," commented Sophie.

"That's silly and downright weird."

"What I mean is, everyone who lived on our street has passed on."

"That is still a very morbid thought to have." Mabel slowed her car to a crawl as they passed her old home.

"Well, they have; that's why I moved to the Gravenhurst Manor. New people have moved into the neighbourhood. Young people, people I didn't know or had anything in common with. Oh, look, how tacky! They've put up Christmas lights on the eaves, and it's only September." Sophie screwed up her mouth.

"I recognize those snowdrop lights. Those are the same lights you had me put up last year. You never took them down."

"If you had been around when I moved, they wouldn't still be hanging there."

"Don't start that again. We're having a nice day out, so let's not bicker about who was where."

"Well, I know where I was."

Mabel raised her eyebrows and shook her head. "Mother," she said.

"Yes, dear, sorry. This is a lovely drive, well, except for that train and the combine. And it's nice to see the old place once again."

Mabel decided this was as close to a compliment as she would get. She turned at the end of the street and drove to the highway. "It will be lunchtime when we get to Kegsworthy, and I'll buy you lunch."

"That would be lovely, thank you, dear." Sophie turned her head, looking out the passenger side window.

Mabel sped down the highway past golden wheat fields. Listening to Sophie expand on her knowledge about her neighbours in the condo. Mabel soon became apprised of all the gossip. Who was the snappiest dresser, the best cook, and who cheated at cards. And who had what ailment. And whose children never visited. Mabel had a sneaking suspicion she was included in this group due to her mother's warped sense of humour.

It was noon when they arrived in the bustling town of Kegsworthy. Deciding the coroner would be out for lunch, Mabel angle parked her car in front of a small restaurant with a sign that read. *Food for Rent.*

"That's disgusting. I'm not eating here." Sophie clutched her purse, looking mutinous.

"You can eat in, or have take out. It's an attempt at humour," Mabel said.

"An attempt that fails badly, I repeat, I will not eat here."

Mabel knew when she was beaten and drove to a roadside diner with a big red hip-roof. The sign swinging on a long black pole said. *Spuds Are Us.*

"How about this place?" Mabel asked as she parked her car and looked over at her mom.

"Well, it's better than the last place, but I'm not eating any greasy fries."

"I'm sure they have other items on the menu. The parking lot is almost full; that's always a good sign that the food is good." Mabel got out of the car.

Sophie folded her hands on her lap and looked at her daughter. Mabel walked around the car and opened the passenger door for her mother.

Sophie sighed and got out, straightening her dress. "My daughter takes me to all the best fast-food joints."

Exhaling deeply. Mabel's lips tightened over her teeth.

Chapter Eight

Mabel angle parked her car in front of a small grey stucco building with a big wooden door painted green.

"Would you please wait in the car for me, Mom? I shouldn't be too long."

"I most definitely will not wait in the car. What a thing to ask," snorted Sophie. She opened her car door and jumped out, her purse swinging as she hurried down the sidewalk.

Mabel slammed her car door and rushed after her mother, catching her on the doorstep. "All right, but let me do the talking, promise."

Sophie's eyes narrowed, and her lips thinned. She grabbed the doorknob and pulled the door open.

Mabel crowded beside her mother, whispering, "Remember, I'm doing the talking."

Sophie sniffed, stepping over the threshold, blocking her daughter. Mabel brushed past her and stepped into the room.

The office had seen better days. The warped, imitation wood veneer panelling that lined the walls had come away from the edges, leaving gaps at the top. A battered old wooden desk, set at the end of the long, dark, narrow room. Behind the desk sat a stern-looking woman of indeterminate age. Her dark hair pulled back from her round face into a bun. The woman looked up from her computer screen, pursing her lips.

Sophie shoved Mabel to the side, her purse striking her daughter on the shin. Mabel hopped to the desk. Sophie jumped ahead, landing on Mabel's toe.

"Geez, Mom." Lifting her foot, Mabel rubbed her toe. It hurt worse than her shin.

The woman stood up and placed her hands flat on the desk. A beaded eyeglass chain hung down from her pink-rimmed glasses. The glasses swayed across her ample bosom as she looked at them in alarm and shouted. "Ladies, ladies, what is the meaning of this?"

Mabel edged her mother out of the way. "I," she said, narrowing her eyes at her mother. She gave her a warning look. "I would like to speak to the coroner."

"You mean the medical examiner?" The woman sat back in her chair and folded her hands on the desk, glowering at the two women engaged in a shoving match.

"Whatever, I would like to speak to him; it's an urgent matter."

"Yes," agreed Sophie, clasping her handbag. She elbowed her daughter and stepped in front of her. "It's a very urgent matter. You see—"

Mabel pushed past her mother. "Mother, please let me do the talking. It's none of this woman's business. What I want to talk to the coroner about. Oh, sorry," she amended. "The medical examiner."

The woman bristled at Mabel's remark. "Mr. Flegerler is a busy man. Do you have an appointment?"

"No, but it's very important." Mabel stuck her arm out in front of her mother, who was edging her way closer to the desk.

"No one sees Mr. Flegerler without an appointment," the woman said, giving them a curt nod. She waved them back from her desk and looked back at her computer screen.

"Flegerler, Randolph Flegerler?" Sophie asked.

"Yes," the woman replied. She continued to stare at the screen, her hand moving the mouse on her desk.

"Well, for goodness' sake, Randolph, Germaine's son. My, my, little Randy Flegerler, a medical examiner. His mom must be so proud. Do you think you could tell him his mother's friend is here? I'm Sophie Schoenberg. We were neighbours when he was growing up. I'm sure he would like to see old friends." Sophie's blue eyes sparkled.

"Oh, I see. Well, you should have said." The woman heaved herself up from her desk and plodded to the closed door at the back of the room and knocked.

"Come," a voice from the other side of the door said. The secretary entered the office, closing the door behind her.

"You see how easy that was, dear?" Sophie gave Mabel a superior smile. "And you wanted me to sit in the car like a child."

Mabel grimaced. "Okay, you're right. Which Flegerler kid is he? Was he that snotty little kid who always cried when we found his hiding place? The dumb kid always hid in the same spot."

"No, that was Randy's brother, Carl. Randy was our little tattletale. We mothers loved him; that's how we always knew what you kids were up to."

"Ah, Randy, the rat, I remember him now."

The door to the office opened, and the secretary came out. "Mr. Flegerler will see you. But you'll have to wait. He's writing up an important report. Please take a seat, and he'll be with you shortly." She indicated a row of faux brown leather chairs lined up against a wall.

"Thank you," Sophie said. She remained standing by the desk, striking up a conversation with the secretary. They soon learned her name was Jennifer Lane. And Sophie knew the woman's aunt and the aunt's children.

Mabel trotted over to the row of chairs and eased off her shoe, rubbed her toe, then put her shoe back on and fidgeted on a hard chair; her feet didn't touch the floor. She listened as Sophie and Jennifer carried on a conversation about who was where and what they were doing. Impatiently waiting, she leafed through an old agriculture magazine, printed in the year 2000, extolling the use of a new herbicide, which Mabel thought now was probably banned.

Finally, the door opened, and Randolph Flegerler, a tall, thin man with long white-blond hair and washed-out blue eyes, poked his head out.

Mabel's lips twitched; she remembered Randy the rat all right. He was a sneaky little weasel. Randy never got into trouble, even if he was involved in whatever childhood escapade they had gotten up to. She walked across the floor and offered her hand. Maybe he'd changed.

Sophie scuttled past Mabel, reaching the man first. "Dear, dear Randy, how good it is to see you. You remember Mabel, don't you? You were kids together, and what fun you all had. The neighbourhood was full of children back then." Sophie rambled on. "Everyone playing outside together. Not like now, all hunched over their computer games and whatnot."

Randy smiled and shook Sophie's hand. He looked at Mabel, his faded blue eyes lingering on her. "You're Mabel? You look so different."

"We all age, Randy." Mabel smiled, shaking his hand.

"But you look so old."

Mabel tightened her lips. She didn't like the weasely little rat when they were children and she decided she didn't like him now.

"I have a few minutes free to catch up on old chums. How are you, Mrs. Schonberg? You look well," he said, escorting them into his office.

The cluttered office was a small room, and it was a mess. Cream-covered file folders covered a long table in front of a big bay window. Brown metal shelves weighed down with books, jammed up against filing cabinets, with more files stacked on top. One cabinet drawer hung open and faded vanilla files stuck out at odd angles as if he had just finished searching. Mabel thought it would be a wonder if he found anything. Violet would hate this office, except for his desk. The only thing on the desk was a laptop and a tray of papers.

"I'm just fine, thank you," replied Sophie, taking a chair near the desk.

The only other chair had another stack of files on it. Mabel wondered how efficient a coroner could be in this mess. She took the stack, plunking them on the floor next to the chair, and sat. As she watched Randy take a seat behind the desk, she decided a coroner was an excellent job for him. He always liked finding things out and reporting them. He had a lot of practice when they were kids.

Sophie placed her purse on her lap and smiled. "Your mom must be so proud of you, a medical examiner, my, my."

"Yes, she is. Mom still lives in Kipling on the same street we grew up on."

"So much for everyone being dead." Mabel arched an eyebrow and grinned at her mother.

Randy folded his hand on the deck. "What do you mean everyone is dead?"

"Mabel is just teasing me about some remark I made." Sophie scowled at her daughter. Her fingers tapped a rapid tattoo on her purse. She turned to beam a cheerful smile at the medical examiner and asked, "How is your dear mother?"

"Mother is fine." Randy settled back in his office chair. "You'll have to excuse the mess. We are changing locations. I'm transferred to Regina," he said proudly.

"So, Randy, you were the coroner who attended." Mabel searched for the right word. She couldn't very well say murder or even suspicious death. She didn't want to look a fool in front of this man.

"The term is Medical Examiner. And attended what? A dinner, a speaking engagement?" Randolph's lips curled into a mocking smile. "What are you talking about? And please use my proper name, Randolph."

Mabel plastered a smile on her face. "Randolph, you were the ahem. The medical examiner called to investigate Mini Frazer's untimely death."

"Untimely death, what a quaint term. I believe, if memory serves me, the woman was old." He leaned back in his chair. It creaked alarmingly. He clicked his mouse, and his computer screen lit up.

Mabel leaned forward to see the screen. Randy turned the laptop and scrolled down the screen. Mabel looked at her mom and waited while Randy read the screen.

"Ah, Mini Frazer, yes, I attended her, as you so quaintly put it." Randolph closed his laptop and folded his hands back on his desk.

Mabel's nostrils flared. A quaint term, she'd like to give him a quaint smack upside the head. She took a deep breath. "Okay, Randy, what did you find?"

"The name is Randolph," he growled. "Please don't use that childish name."

"Okay, Randolph." Mabel clenched her teeth. She was rewarded with a small smile. "And?"

"And what?" he asked, resting his elbows on his desk, steepling his fingers.

Mabel gave him a steely look. He was avoiding answering. "What did you determine was the cause of Mini Frazer's death?"

"You always were a snoopy kid." Randolph's lips curled into a sneer. "And childhood friend aside, you can't possibly think I can divulge information regarding Mrs. Frazer's death to you."

"So, something was wrong? I knew it." Sophie jumped into the conversation.

"I didn't say anything was wrong, Mrs. Schonberg. There was nothing wrong with her death."

"Other than she is dead," Mabel broke in. "And if there is nothing amiss, why can't you tell us?"

He stared coldly at Mabel. "That is a ridiculous question."

"I don't see why you think it's ridiculous. The Freedom of Information Act. You have heard of that, haven't you, Randy?" Mabel asked, deliberately using his childhood name.

"The Freedom of Information Act doesn't apply to the private information you have no business prying into. And it's Randolph, my name is Randolph." His pale face was becoming red.

Sophie's eyes darted from Mabel to the medical examiner.

Mabel thought he was more upset with her calling him Randy than protecting his findings.

Randolph cleared his throat. "Dear, dear Mabel, you may have changed in looks from our childhood days. But I see your temperament is as childish as ever." He looked down his nose at her and continued. "Mrs. Frazer died of old age." He jabbed a finger in the air with each word.

"Oh, really? As my mother pointed out, no one dies of old age. They die from something." Mabel crossed her arms, childish indeed.

"The woman died of natural causes, plain and simple. Satisfied?"

"No, I am not. For a number of reasons: One. Mini was to meet my mother for a game of bridge and was found dead in bed. And two, the woman never locked her door, but it was locked the night of her death. How do you explain that?"

Randolph's knuckles whitened as he curled his fingers into fists. He took a deep breath and then exhaled. "I've seen many elderly people just like Mini Frazer die at home. The woman was in her eighties. She felt unwell, locked her door and went to bed. End of story."

"If Mini was feeling ill, why didn't she phone me and tell me she was cancelling the bridge game?" Sophie asked.

Randolph unclenched his hands and placed them flat on his desk. "My dear Mrs. Schonberg, how would I know? I don't know what went through the poor lady's mind. I can only report on the facts. Now, if you will excuse me, I have more important things to get on with."

Mabel sat up straight in her chair and lifted her chin. Looking over her granny glasses at Randy, she said, "You said Mini died from natural causes. What does natural causes mean? It could mean anything."

Randolph stood. "I have been more than generous with my time," he said, his voice icy. "Good day."

MABEL FUMED ALL THE way back to Glenhaven. "What a pompous ass. Old age, natural causes. That is a cop-out. I don't think the man did his due diligence. I think he saw an old woman lying in a bed, dead. And he signed the death certificate and then went on his way. She pulled up the driveway to the manor.

"Now, dear, there is no need for foul language," Sophie admonished. "But I am disappointed in the boy. He was so good at ferreting out information when he was a child. You would think this job would suit him to a T."

"I think he's a lazy ass." Mabel glanced at her mother. "Sorry, but like I said, the man just sees an old woman and can't be bothered to look any further." She stopped behind a red Volkswagen Golf parked in front of the entrance.

"That's Gemma's car, isn't it snazzy?" Sophie beamed. "It's a Volkswagen Golf."

Mabel wrinkled her nose and frowned as she took in the little red sports car. "Really? Since when have you taken an interest in cars?"

"The name is on the car, silly. And this isn't Gemma's only car. She has a lovely silver car too. I can't remember the name of it, but it is very nice."

"Two cars. Besides ferrying all you seniors around town, what does Gemma do?" Mabel asked as the tall woman opened the passenger side door of her car. Homer Murphy struggled out.

"I think Gemma's husband was well off. Freda told me her husband died young and left Gemma with a lot of money. That's why she can volunteer. Bless her." Mabel gave her mother a sour look.

"Thanks for the drive, dear. I'm sorry our investigations came to nothing. But it was a nice day out, even though we ate at that fast food place. I hope I don't get indigestion." Sophie leaned over and kissed Mabel on the cheek. Then she popped out of the car, walking briskly up to the entrance of the building.

Mabel sighed; it seemed that her mother was quite capable of opening her car door when it suited her. And it also appeared that the wonderful Gemma was more of an attraction than her daughter.

Gemma opened the trunk and took out Homer's walker. To Mabel's surprise, Sophie passed by Gemma and hugged Homer, and the old man seemed to return it.

The front door of the condo burst open, and Charlie Sweeny ran out onto the steps. "Get your cars the hell out of here. The ambulance will be here any minute."

Chapter Nine

Mabel hopped out of her car and shouted. "Where? Maybe I can help."

Gemma set Homer's walker beside him and asked, "What's happened?"

"She's fallen down the stairs. I think she's dead," Charlie said, waving his hands in the air.

"Someone has died. Who is dead?" asked Gemma as Homer took hold of his walker.

"Well, I'm not sure she's dead. But you guys better move your cars." Charlie jumped from foot to foot, his thin hair flying in the breeze, revealing his liver-spotted bald head.

"Maybe I can help," Mabel called.

"No, get back in your car and move. The ambulance is on the way, just move your damn cars."

"Who fell?" asked Gemma as she shut the trunk of her car.

"Freda. Move it, move it," Charlie shouted, bouncing about in the condo's doorway.

Mabel popped back in her car, waiting for Gemma to move her shiny red sports car. Sophie scurried past Charlie into the vestibule, followed by Homer, who moved at a surprisingly fast pace with his walker. Mabel parked her old Pontiac in the visitors' parking lot alongside Gemma's sports car. She grabbed her purse, slamming her car door shut.

"This is terrible; I hope Charlie is wrong; I hope Freda is okay," Gemma said, pressing the key fob to lock her car door.

"He said Freda fell down the stairs. Maybe she is just knocked out."

"I hope so. Freda is such a lovely lady." Gemma slung her big yellow purse over her shoulder.

Two ravens perched on the Gravenhurst sign appeared to look curiously at the ambulance and the firetruck as they drove up the driveway to the condo, sirens blazing. The lights flashing the ambulance and the fire truck parked in front of the entrance. Two paramedics, one carrying a medical kit, raced into the building.

Charlie, following the paramedics, exclaimed, "I don't know how long she's been there lying in the stairwell. Jody is with her."

"Do you see the tall paramedic with the big black bag? He's my brother, Paul," Gemma said proudly. She put her arm around Mabel's shoulders. Her tall, imposing figure made Mabel feel diminished.

"Who's Jody?" Mabel asked. "Charlie said Jody is with Freda."

"That will be Jody Harris; Jody is a home care worker. Some of the residents require someone to help them now and again."

Two firemen rushed past the women as they entered the lobby.

A small, skinny fireman opened the door to the stairwell; Mabel could see Freda's feet and Gemma's brother, who was crouching over the woman, his medical kit lying open by his side.

A young woman with green-streaked hair had her hand cupped over her mouth. She stood holding the door open for the paramedics and the fireman. A fireman turned and looked at Mabel, who was creeping up to the door. "Move along," he instructed.

"Sorry, come along, Mabel," Gemma said, taking Mabel by the arm and escorting her into the lounge.

"I'm not a child," Mabel muttered angrily.

"Of course not, sweetie," soothed Gemma.

The term sweetie grated on Mabel's nerves, and she wrenched her arm from Gemma's grasp and joined her mother, who was talking with Charlie.

"The paramedics shooed us all in here," exclaimed Sophie.

"Before the paramedics came, did you see Freda?" Mabel asked.

"No, Jody wouldn't open the door for anyone."

Just as well, Mabel decided, a bunch of looky-loos would not have helped Freda. She watched a small man with silver hair and slippers on his feet edge closer to the door of the lobby. Farley, leaning up against the fireplace, was eyeing everyone in the room.

A woman with curlers in her hair seated on the couch in front of the fireplace complained loudly. "Move, you big lug; I'm trying to watch TV. I'm missing Jeopardy."

"Look over my head; I'm not that tall," snarled the gangly man in overalls, moving a few inches to the side.

"I called the ambulance," Charlie said importantly. "But I didn't phone the fire station. I don't know why they came."

"They're all volunteers, the fireman, and the paramedics. Someone got their wires crossed, I guess." Gemma patted the man on the shoulder. "You poor man, you found Freda. How awful for you."

"No, not me; Jody found her, and she hollered to me to call an ambulance."

"Is Freda conscious?" Gemma asked, setting her big yellow bag on a side table.

"I don't think so," Charlie said sorrowfully. "Jody, and I think Freda is dead."

"I'm glad Jody was with her," Linda, Charlie's wife, said.

"She's a home care worker, not a nurse. The woman scrubs floors," Gemma said with a dismissive shrug.

"A paramedic has wheeled a stretcher into the lobby," called the slipper-footed man from the lounge doorway.

"Home care workers aren't house cleaners. Jody comes to help old Mrs. Angus," contradicted Linda.

"My dear, you misunderstood me; what I meant was she's not a nurse."

"And Mrs. Angus should be in the care home. Gravenhurst Manor is no place for her. She never gets out of her apartment," Charlie added.

"Mabel, make us some coffee, please," requested Sophie. "And tea, that would be nice too, dear."

Mabel shrugged and went into the kitchen, setting her purse on the counter; she filled the kettle and placed it on the stove, turning on the burner. Then rummaged through the cupboards and found the coffee and a canister of tea. *This is typical of my mother,* Mabel thought resentfully as she spooned coffee grounds into the filter of the coffee pot. *While Gemma, her mother's precious friend, is busy chatting, I have to make coffee.*

Mabel leaned on the half counter, watching the residents mill about, gathering in clusters around the open lounge door. Charlie was waving his arms about, conversing with her mother and Gemma. Little bent Hannah sidled up to Homer, tugging on his arm, whispering into his ear. Farley moved from the TV, edging his way into the lobby. The slippered man left his post by the door and shuffled back into the lounge as Jody, a big girl with short, spiked green hair, came from the stairwell. Elbowing her way past the residents, the flushed girl with a multitude of colourful tattoos on her arms and a nose ring plunked herself down on a chair.

"How is Freda?" Charlie asked. "Is she dead?" Jody shuttered.

Eager to find out about Freda. Mabel abandoned the coffee pot and hurried out of the kitchen.

"Has Freda regained consciousness?" Gemma asked as she knelt before the girl; she took Jody's pump-ringed fingers in hers. "Is Freda going to be okay?"

Jody bit her bottom lip and shook her head. "I don't think so; Freda just lay at the bottom of the stairs; she never even moaned. I think poor Freda is dead. I tried to take her pulse." Jody's voice trembled. "I don't even know why I did that, and what good would knowing what Freda's pulse is?

Even if I knew how to take it." She shivered. "And now I'm cold and I don't know why."

Mabel took an afghan off a loveseat and wrapped it around Jody's shoulders. "Someone, please, get her a hot cup of sweet tea."

All heads swivel to the entrance as the paramedics wheeled the stretcher out, a blanket covering Freda's body from head to toe. Farley was holding open the door.

Chapter Ten

The late morning sun shone down, but it was cool. Gusts of wind shredded leaves from the tall old maple trees, scattering the dried leaves across the gravestones. Bare branches scraping against a dying tree made a mournful sound. Mabel turned up the collar of her coat and shivered. She and her mother had joined the small group of mourners gathered for the graveside service of Freda Jilvontee.

The fake bright green carpet spread on either side of the grave threatened to blow away. But the casket held firm as it hung over the open grave, waiting to be lowered.

Mabel thought of Ichabod Crane as the tall, gaunt minister's long black robe flapped in the stiff breeze. The minister held a bible in his bony white hand; the pages fluttered. Helen Graham, dressed in a heavy black woollen coat, placed her hand on the page. The minister smiled his thanks and began to read a psalm in a harsh, raspy voice.

Alfred, Freda's nephew, stood next to the minister, the little farmer tugging at the black jacket of his ill-fitting suit. It's strange, Mabel thought, Alfred's wife Ruth was not among the mourners. It was Gemma who stood beside Alfred at the graveside of his aunt. She had looped her arm with his. The portly farmer looked uncomfortable. Mabel couldn't decide if it was because of his closeness to Gemma. Or the shiny black suit that looked like the seams were about to burst at any moment.

MABEL DROVE HER CAR slowly down the gravel road leading to town from the graveyard, listening to her mother critique the graveside service.

"I'm disappointed at the turnout for Freda's funeral," Sophie said, opening her purse. She took out a small pink and white compact, powdering her nose and cheeks. "Hardly anyone from our condo was there. I know she wasn't the most popular person in the manor, but still, I think it shows a lack of respect."

"And only forty or so people from the town came to the funeral. You're right; it is a sad turnout for someone who's lived their whole life in Glenhaven. But maybe it's because it was an outside service; it is kind of chilly this morning," suggested Mabel.

"Well, no wonder people didn't show up. There is no lunch; imagine they aren't even serving lunch. This funeral is a cheap affair; there is no church service and then no lunch. Are you taking me out for lunch?" She closed her compact, tucking it into her purse.

"Sure. We can go to Pam & Ally's café. But remember, they don't have a menu, only the daily special," Mabel cautioned, slowing her car down. Dust and gravel stones were whipping up from the vehicles proceeding her.

"I don't care, at least it won't be like the fast-food joint you took me to in Kegsworthy."

Mabel gave her mother a sidelong glance and sighed. "Why do you think Freda was so unpopular with the residents of the manor?"

"Freda was a bit of a busybody." Sophie shifted in her seat, straitening the skirt of her black dress.

"Really, people didn't come to her funeral because she was a busybody? Half the town would fit the same description. Everyone knows everyone's business in Glenhaven."

"I suppose so," Sophie conceded.

Mabel, following the slow-moving line of cars from the funeral, steered her car off the gravel road onto the paved road leading into town. "Aren't you surprised Hannah wasn't there?"

"No, I'm not surprised."

"Why not? I saw them working on a puzzle together. I thought they were best mates."

"Hannah hates puzzles."

"Then why was she doing a puzzle with Freda?"

"Well, I guess I don't know that for a fact, but I could tell," defended Sophie.

Mabel shrugged.

"Mini sure didn't like her."

"Mini didn't like Hannah?"

"No, Freda, she didn't like Freda."

"Why was that?"

"I told you Freda was a busybody, and, and well, I suppose it doesn't matter since Mini is no longer with us."

"What doesn't matter?"

"Mini might have had a bit of a gambling problem. Before Mini moved to Gravenhurst, she said she took trips to Carlyle and stayed at the Bear Claw Casino and Hotel. She went to play the slots, and from what she told me, there were lots of trips." Sophie gave her daughter a sidelong look. "Don't go blabbing this about."

"I won't say anything. Even if your friend liked a game of chance, I doubt she gambled away her life savings. Or did she?" Mabel pulled the car up in front of the café and parked.

"I think money was getting tight. Once, when I visited Mini, I heard something as I opened her door. I overheard Mini telling Gemma she needed money. I don't know if Gemma was going to lend Mini money. They stopped talking as soon as I came in. But I do not doubt that Gemma would help her. Gemma is such a generous person."

"Okay, let's say Mini gambled."

"Mabel."

Mabel held up her hand. "Okay, maybe she gambled."

"She did, she told me she did."

"Right, sorry. But that doesn't explain why she would dislike Freda. If she disliked her?"

"Well, she did; I know that for a fact," Sophie shot her daughter an impatient look.

"But why?"

"You don't listen. I said Freda was a bit of a busybody. I even heard her taunt Mini about her gambling. Mini had a reputation to uphold. She was a piano teacher."

Mabel hid a grin. "A regular pillar of society, was she?"

Sophie looked over at her daughter. "Don't be snarky, and please open my door."

Mabel sighed, got out of the car, and walked around to open the door for her mother. "A few skeletons in the closets of the old gals."

Sophie's eyes narrowed. "I told you about Mini in strictest confidence."

"Yes, yes, I won't blab about the piano teacher." Mabel held the car door open.

"But something bothers me about Freda falling down the stairs." Sophie wrinkled her forehead as she got out of the car.

"What is that?" Mabel closed the car door.

"Freda had an arthritic hip. That's why she never went dancing. And she never took the stairs. Even if the elevator was busy, she would always wait, no matter how long it took. So, I wonder why did she take the stairs?"

Chapter Eleven

Mabel kicked off her shoes and flung her jacket over a kitchen chair, went to her wall phone, and dialled Violet's number. Waiting for her friend to pick up her phone, Mabel carried the receiver with her to her fridge and opened the door. She stood looking into her refrigerator. Nothing appealed to her. But since she had a big lunch, maybe a light supper of soup would do.

"Hello, back from the funeral."

Violet's voice interrupted Mabel's thoughts. She shut her fridge door, trapping her phone cord. "Darn." She jerked the door open and freed up her phone.

"Pardon me, what's wrong?"

"Nothing, I just caught something in the door. No worries." Mabel heard a loud rattle and a clatter and then a clang. It sounded like Violet was banging on pots and pans.

"What's new? You're back from the funeral. Were there many people there?"

"No, a small gathering; I guess Freda was not very popular."

"Really."

Mabel heard another thump and a bang; the bang sounded like a door slamming shut. "What the heck are you doing? What's all the clanking and banging about?" Mabel leaned against her cupboards, absently flipping the phone cord like a skipping rope.

"Neville did dishes last night. And he decided to move my pots to the cupboard by the fridge. Can you imagine! By the fridge."

Mabel could hear the exasperation in her friend's voice. Violet was a bit of a neat freak, everything had a place and needed to be in that place. She chuckled; her friend had rearranged her stuff once. Now Violet would know how it felt. "So why didn't you stop him? It's your house?"

"I wasn't here. I was off helping Helen Graham; she and the mayor's wife are organizing a drama festival."

"I gather Neville surprised you?"

"You could say that." Violet's voice was sharp.

"Where is dear Neville now?" Mabel asked.

"He's out in the yard, raking leaves. At least he can't rearrange my yard," Violet huffed.

Mabel grinned. Neville had crossed a line, and if he didn't watch what he was doing, he would wear out his welcome. She heard what she thought might be another cupboard door slam. The sooner the smarmy man pulled up stakes, the better. She needed to check him out, and she'd do a search on the internet for him again tonight. This time, she vowed she wouldn't go down the rabbit hole. Plopping on a chair, she pulled another one out from under the table with her foot, putting both feet up on it.

"There, everything is back where it should be," Violet said. "So, did your mom go with you to the funeral?"

"Yes, she did; Mom was the one who wanted to go. Freda was a neighbour of hers at the condo. You know, this is the second funeral for a resident of Gravenhurst Manor that I have attended. I hate funerals."

"Of course you do. Everyone does. If you liked funerals, that would be really weird."

"And two funerals from the manor in a month. It's a tad suspicious if you ask me. Oh, just a minute, Gertrude is howling at the door." Mabel let her cat in and returned to her chair. "Okay, I'm back, Gertrude; wanted in."

"Okay, what are your suspicions based on? Besides that, Freda wasn't popular."

"By the sounds of it, Freda was no angel. And neither was Mom's friend Mini." Mabel related the information she gleaned from her mother. She finished and asked, "What do you think? Do you think something is going on at the condo too? Or is it just Mom and me?" Mabel wasn't sure when she started to be on her mother's side. It might have been when Randy the rat pooh poohed her mother's concerns. But the more she thought about the events the night of Mini's death, the more she suspected foul play.

"I'm not sure, but things don't add up. Mini's door was locked, and your mom couldn't open the stairwell door to get back on that floor. And your mom just told you Freda had a bad hip and never took stairs. But she did, and she fell, very odd."

Mabel was pleased Violet agreed with her. Violet was level-headed; she trusted her opinion. Mabel didn't like to admit it. But sometimes, she did jump to conclusions. Although she assured herself most of the time, she was right.

"You went to see the coroner; what did he say about Mini's death?"

"Randy the rat, that pompous little twit. I grew up on the same street as him. He used to spy and report on us when we were kids. Now, he couldn't find an elephant in a phone booth. He's got a comfortable little fiefdom that doesn't involve him doing any work. Other than going out looking at a dead body and saying, case closed." Mabel got up to run water from the kitchen tap and pour it into a bowl for Gertrude.

"Maybe you're a little prejudiced against him from your childhood."

"I am not," Mabel hotly denied.

"Okay, so, if there are one, or maybe two, suspicious deaths? Who's your prime suspect?"

"Gemma, she's too good to be true. She's a young woman who hangs around old people, running errands and whatnot. It just doesn't ring true." Mabel sat back on her kitchen chair. Gertrude jumped up on her lap.

"You sure you're not just a tiny bit jealous?"

"Me jealous?" Mabel scoffed. "Why would I be jealous of Gemma?"

"Your mother has taken quite a fancy to her."

Mabel pursed her lips, stroking her cat; finally, she said. "Okay, maybe a little, but I wouldn't let my feelings get in the way of, well, I wouldn't, that's all."

"Does Gemma have an alibi for the night Mini died?"

"I don't know, but I'm going to find out. Oh."

"Oh, what?"

"I do know where Gemma was when Freda did a header down the stairs. She was hauling old Homer around. I'll have to take her off my list."

"A header down the stairs, really, Mabel."

"Okay, fell or pushed down the stairs, happy?"

"I'm not happy she fell down the stairs."

"Geez Louise, you know what I mean. Anyway, Gemma was carting old Homer around. She parked her car at the condo just as Mom and I arrived back from Kegsworthy."

"Maybe she dropped him off at some appointment and beat it back to the condo to push Freda down the stairs."

"Good thinking. I wish you were with me on this." She missed Violet, her wingman. "When is Neville going back home?"

"I'm not sure."

"He's been here a month. You should ask him how long he's staying."

"I guess I should."

"Violet, you need to be more forceful; you're just too darn polite." Mabel scratched Gertrude under her chin. The cat began to purr, stretching her neck out for more attention.

"No, I'm enjoying his visit."

Mabel rolled her eyes; Violet was fooling herself. But she was a grown woman. And as long as Neville wasn't scamming money from her friend, she would mind her own business. Violet wouldn't thank her for interfering.

"Never mind about Neville," Violet said. "Let's get back to Mini and Freda. What is the motive for killing these old ladies? Think about it: what enemies could these ladies have at their age? And I doubt they have buckets of money. And even if they did, how would anyone get their hands on it?"

"You've hit the nail on the head. Money. Money has to be the motive. Maybe these ladies were too trusting. Scammers are always after seniors, trying to rip them off, and sometimes succeeding too. These women must have had money, maybe not a bucket full. But they sold their houses to move into that condo. A low-life hustler could be taking advantage of some of these seniors in Gravenhurst Manor. And even if this scammer just takes a few thousand, or even a few hundred at a time, it would still mount up."

"You think someone is getting into their bank accounts?" Violet asked.

"It's possible."

"If what you say is right, why would they kill the goose that lays the golden egg?"

Chapter Twelve

Mabel looked up at the early morning sky as a flock of Canadian geese flew overhead in their familiar V formation. Honking their way south for the winter. She paused in front of the local café. Sitting in the back seat of a car, Hannah Huston was tapping on the window.

She looked at Hannah through the car's closed window. "Hi, Hannah, how are you today?"

Hannah's teeth clicked as she shouted, "I'm locked in. Can you open the door for me?"

It must be terrible to be this old and need help to open a door, but one day, this could be her, Mabel thought as she tried to open the car door. The door was locked. "Unlock the door, Hannah."

"I can't, and there is no button in here to unlock the dumb thing."

"Are you sure?"

"Would I be sitting here if there was?" Hannah curled her lips in a mutinous pout.

"Whose car is this?" Mabel asked, wondering how the little woman got locked in the car.

"It's Charlie Sweeny's car. He and Linda drove me down here for coffee."

"They are here in the café?"

"Where else? They're drinking coffee while I sit out here." Hannah huffed.

Mabel entered Pam & Ally's café and looked around for Charlie and his wife. The little café's decor had never changed from the seventies. Down the middle of the restaurant, two rows of dark green Formica tables and matching chairs and a row of booths lined one wall.

It was a well-known fact if you wanted to get the lowdown on the happenings in Glenhaven, Coffee Row was the place to go. Pam & Ally's café used to be the only café in town. But the new potash mines had breathed new life into the town. A housing boom and new businesses and new restaurants were popping up. But the locals remained loyal to the little café.

Mabel trotted to a booth where Charlie and his wife Linda were having coffee.

"Enjoying your coffee?" Mabel asked, a mischievous grin on her face.

"Yes, thank you, we're going shopping after. There is a sale at the hardware store. I need a new toaster," replied Linda. "Our toaster is acting up, white bread on one side and burnt on the other."

"Yeah, what a dumb appliance. It's got one job. Once a day, make toast. It should last a heck of a lot longer than it did," complained Charlie.

"I think Hannah would like to join you for coffee."

"Hannah." Linda's face flushed in embarrassment. "Oh, my lord, I knew we forgot something. Charlie, go get Hannah."

"Why doesn't the blame woman just come in, for heavens' sake?" Charlie set his coffee mug down on the table with a thud.

"Because you've locked her in the car," Mabel replied with a twinkle in her eye.

The café erupted in laughter as a red-faced Charlie hurried out the door.

Alice Woodstock, a tiny bird-like woman with frizzy orange hair, bustled to the Sweeny table. Poor Linda, thought Mabel. Alice was always after gossip. Mabel went to the coffee station and poured herself a cup of coffee and dropped a loonie into a dish. It was the honour system, and if the coffee pot ran dry, the patrons made more. Pam and Ally, the café owners, were in the kitchen preparing lunch. She passed tables where groups of men dressed in coveralls and hardhats sat drinking their coffee; she didn't know any of them. But said good morning to them, anyway. Some of the men replied, others just nodded. Mabel assumed the nodders were from the city. In small-town Saskatchewan, you said good morning to everyone. She then greeted the seniors sitting at the two tables at the front of the café. The women sat at one table, and the men sat at the other table closest to the door.

Mary Woodhouse, a cheerful, plump woman with salt and pepper grey hair and flushed cheeks, waved her over to the women's table. "Welcome back. How was your trip to Egypt?"

Mabel pulled out a chair beside Mary and placed her coffee mug down on the table. "It was fabulous. But I've been back for some time. I just got back from visiting my daughter Melina. I have a new grandchild."

"Oh, my wonderful, what did she have?" asked Helen Graham, a thin woman with a white complexion, her lips covered with a thick layer of red lipstick.

"A girl, 7 pounds and six ounces. Rene Mabel," Mabel said proudly. "I have pictures." She tapped her phone to display the photos. As Mabel showed the baby pictures, the comments of 'oohs and ahhs and *so adorable and sweet. And look at the hair.*' Erupted around the women's table.

Alice Woodstock returned to the table and sat across from Mabel. "Long time no see," she greeted.

"I have been home for a while. I guess I've been busy."

"Now that you travel to far-off places. You're too busy for your friends. It must be nice to have enough money to travel like that. Or did dear Violet pay your way?"

"Not that it is any of your business. But I pay my own way." Mabel sat on the chair, picking up her coffee mug, she glared at Alice. She wasn't surprised by Alice's snide remarks. She and Alice had a long history, and none of it was friendly.

Alice's nostrils flared; she tightened her lips.

"Weren't you scared? It would scare me to go to Egypt." Helen said. She tugged up the zipper on her sweater. Helen was always cold, even in July.

"You're scared of your own shadow," commented Alvin from the other table. The short, tubby man with a dour disposition was Mary's husband.

"Alvin," Mary scolded.

"Helen has a delicate condition," defended Helen's husband, Mike.

Helen beamed at her husband.

"Anyway," Mary intervened, "how was your trip? Do you have any pictures?"

"I do, but I left them at home."

Charlie entered with a disgruntled Hannah in his wake. He ignored the hoots of laughter from the men and scuttled to his table.

"Can you imagine? They even forgot I was in the car." The small, bent woman tottered to the counter and poured herself a cup of coffee. Still grumbling under her breath, Hannah went to sit with Linda and Charlie in the booth.

"I bet your mom is glad to have you home," Helen said.

"She is," replied Mabel.

"I heard while you were gallivanting off in a foreign country your poor Mom had to move into Gravenhurst Manor all by herself." Alice's lips had a disapproving scowl.

Mabel's eyes darted around at the seniors. Did everyone in town feel the same way? Did everyone think she had neglected her mother?

"The manor is such a nice addition to the town," Mary said. "I'm sure your mom is happy there."

"Gravenhurst Manor, another new building. Glenhaven has changed since that mine opened up. I don't know half the people in town anymore. I liked it the way it was before," grumbled Mike. "It used to be you could walk down the street and say hi to everyone you saw. Now there are a bunch of strangers." The sloped-shoulder man turned his chair, dragging it over to the women's table.

"Shush," admonished Mary, glancing over at the workmen.

"The potash mine brings employment, and it's pumped new life into this town." Alvin followed Mike, his chair screeching on the tiled floor.

The door from the kitchen opened, and Ally, a small Asian man with thinning jet-black hair, paused in the doorway. He surveyed the patrons enjoying their coffee. Wiping his hands on his long white apron, he sauntered over to the coffee machine.

"But Mike, you still know the best people," Helen said brightly. "The people right here at this table."

Everyone grinned and agreed.

Ally looked in the loonie dish and then turned with a disgusted look on his face. "So, all the best people, eh? How come you drink my coffee, and you do not pay?" There was a loud chorus of voices declaring they'd paid.

Ally held up the empty bowl, turning it upside down. "No one paid." He glowered at the people sitting at their tables with their full cups of coffee.

Mabel looked across the café at Hannah. She knew the bowl was nearly full when she paid.

"You want coffee, you must pay." Ally shook the empty bowl.

Charlie looked across the table at Hannah, his lips in a thin line. He reached into his pocket and took out two loonies. "I already paid," he said.

"So did I," Alice said, her back stiff. She glowered at Ally.

"I know we all did." Mike's head swivelled to stare at Hannah.

"I'll pay for everyone, my treat," Hannah said, rolling her teeth in her mouth and making an odd clicking sound. "Put your money back in your pocket, Charlie." She opened her purse and looked around the room. Smiling at everyone, she dropped the exact amount of coins into the dish.

Ally scowled at his customers. He took the dish into the kitchen with him and returned with a small bell. He set the little brass bell beside the coffee machine. "You ring the bell, and I pour the coffee, then you pay." He turned on his heel and strutted back into the kitchen.

"Whoever took that money makes us all look bad," lamented Helen.

"No worries, I think Ally knows it wasn't any of us. Whose table did he go to first? Not ours; he knows who took the money." Alvin leaned back in his chair, crossing his arms over his potbelly; he nodded his head.

"Hannah took the money," Alice whispered. "Why else would she pay for everyone's coffee?"

"Alice, we mustn't pass judgment. No one saw Hannah take the money," Mary cautioned. "And even if she did, she paid it all back. Let it go."

"We will just be more careful next time when that woman comes in," agreed Helen.

Alice looked across the café at the small, hunched woman and hissed, "From now on, we watch that old girl like a hawk."

"She's not from here. I told you these new people moving to town wasn't a good thing. This proves it," snorted Mike.

"Don't be silly; you can't blame everything on the new people," intervened Mabel.

"This time, I can." Mike slammed his fist on the table, his wife Helen jumped.

"No, Hannah isn't a newcomer; she and her husband Jed had a farm out on Bingo Road. A half-section, if my memory serves me," Alvin said.

Mike glowered. "Whatever. She took the money."

"Let's not dwell on a little lapse in judgment. We all make mistakes." Mary swirled the coffee drags in her cup.

"A lapse in judgment?" snarled Alvin. "A thief, more like."

"It's not like she stole the crown jewels; it's a few coins. Let it go, for goodness' sake," Mary admonished her husband. "Let's talk about nice things." She turned to Mabel. "I've heard good things about the manor. Nice, new, and designed for seniors."

"Yeah, it's a really nice place," agreed Alvin. "I've been up to visit old Homer at the condo. Although I don't know why I bother, he is such a cranky old guy. But he was a friend of my dad's, so I kind of feel obligated. He's sure got a nice unit."

Mabel took a sip from her coffee and hid a grin. Alvin, a strong-minded man, was almost as cantankerous as Homer.

"I've visited a time or two. I don't know how seniors can afford that place. It must cost them a fortune." Alice wrinkled her nose as if she had smelt something bad.

"They sell their houses and probably still get to bank a good coin or two," commented Mike, arranging his thinning white hair over his pink scalp.

"What about the inheritance for their children?" Helen asked.

"Let them make their own money." Alvin folded his arms and nodded to his wife. "I heard two condos are up for sale. Mary and I are thinking of selling our house and buying one of them. There will be less upkeep. I'm tired of mowing the lawn in the summer and shovelling snow in the winter."

The Coffee Row seniors exchanged surprised looks.

"You're going to move?" Mike set his elbows on the table and leaned forward.

"It's not for sure." Mary gave her husband a sidelong look. "We are just thinking about it. I like running my bed and breakfast. But Alvin isn't as keen."

Alvin got to his feet, went to the coffee machine, and picked up the coffee pot.

"One of the condos must be Mini's. I was at Mini's funeral," Helen piped up. "I didn't know her very well, but I thought I should go."

"You go to every funeral," guffawed Alice.

"It's respect. I do it out of respect for the deceased and the family." Helen tilted her chin and crossed her arms over her chest.

"Mini attended my church," Mary said. "But she's not from here. I can't remember where she moved from. Mind you, there are so many new faces in town. There was a time when I knew everyone. But not anymore."

"That's what I said; too many new faces in town," Mike growled, setting his empty coffee cup on the table.

"Mini was from down by Carlyle; that's where that big casino is." Alvin returned to fill everyone's cup.

Mabel held her cup out for a refill. Her mother might be right. Maybe Mini gambled.

Mary put a hand over her cup. "Do you think you should pour coffee, Alvin? Ally said to ring the bell."

"We paid, and you get seconds free. I'm not ringing that damn bell." Alvin continued around the table, pouring coffee.

"I saw you at Freda's funeral." Helen smiled across the table at Mabel.

"Yes, I was there with my mom."

"It looks like we have two funeral groupies," Alice smirked.

"I went because my mother wanted to. Freda was my mom's neighbour."

"I heard Freda's funeral was quite nice. Not like poor Mini's. Mini's funeral started out very badly. The priest was saying a prayer, then some ignorant person's cellphone rang and rang. The ring tone was disgusting. It disrupted a very holy part of the service." Alice looked at Mabel with a knowing smile on her face.

"A nice funeral. What a weird thing to say," mocked Alvin.

"Never mind, Mini's funeral was nice until that cellphone blurted out *Staying Alive*," Alice said indignantly.

Helen nodded her head as Mike and Alvin grinned. Mary glanced at Mabel, then ducked her head. There was a slight smile on her lips.

Avoiding Alice's malicious smile, Mabel looked down at her coffee cup.

"Freda had a nice graveside funeral, simple but nice. Although not many people were there. I'm glad I went." Helen looked defiantly at Alice.

"Freda wasn't well-liked. Even her nephew Alfred kept clear of her." Alice sat back in her chair, folding her arms, she arched an eyebrow. "I heard his wife Ruth didn't even go."

Mabel hated to ask Alice, the know-it-all. But she wanted answers, and it diverted the conversation away from the phone incident. "Why do you think people disliked Freda?"

"Well, I'll tell you." Alice folded her hands on the table and leaned forward, her eyes sparkling. "It seems Freda was a big snoop. She spied on everyone."

The men snickered. Alice was one of the worst gossips in town.

Ignoring the men's snickers, Alice said, "Not a nice trait."

"But that could be said of a lot of people," Alvin said, exchanging a snide look with Mike.

Alice glanced briefly at the men and continued. "True, but Freda used the information she found about her victims to her advantage."

"Victims?" Mabel's eyebrows shot up.

"Yes, victims, unless they helped her in some way. She would threaten to tell the whole community what they had been up to. She had a talent for ferreting out dirty little secrets."

"This is like the pot calling the kettle black," snorted Alvin.

Alice bristled. "Are you referring to me?"

"If the shoe fits."

"I may relay news, and that I don't deny. And okay, and sometimes I'm wrong, I don't deny that either. But I have never tattled about someone's indiscretions. You name me once where I've done that." Alice stuck out her chin.

Alvin twisted his lips, and snorted, "Oh, I can think of a few times you told tales."

"I can think of more than just a few," sneered Mike.

"I am not a gossip," Alice snapped.

Alvin and Mike threw back their heads, laughing.

"I just relay the news. People tell me things." Alice's eyes narrowed. "And I might add, all of you are quite happy to hear anything I have to tell." She sat back in her chair with a smug look on her face.

The Coffee Row seniors exchanged looks, knowing Alice was right.

"Why didn't you say anything about Freda?" Mabel asked.

"Say what? That Freda blackmailed people? She never asked for money, just favours. And if I did, I would be betraying the confidence of friends."

Mabel gave Alice a skeptical look. She found it hard to believe that anyone would confide in Alice, of all people. But when she looked around the table, she saw Mary taking a great interest in her nails. And Helen was zipping and unzipping her sweater at a furious pace.

Chapter Thirteen

Mabel strode up the sidewalk to Violet's house, unzipping her fleece. It was unusually warm for an October evening. She tucked the bottle of wine under her arm and rang the doorbell, then waited. Usually, after ringing the bell, Mabel would have just entered. But now, with Neville staying with Violet, she was uncomfortable with the idea.

"Welcome, welcome, come in, come in," Neville greeted, opening the door. "Let me take your jacket. Violet is busy in the kitchen."

"Thank you." Mabel knew where to hang her jacket, but she smiled and gave it to Neville. Apparently, Neville decided he was more of a host than a guest. She had to admit the man did look very smart, dressed in a dark navy blue suit. Suddenly, Mabel felt self-conscious. Is this a party? She glanced down at her jeans and straightened her long-sleeved t-shirt.

She slipped past him, taking her wine into the kitchen. Violet had on a dark green dress with a green and white pinstriped apron over it. She had the oven door open, taking the turkey out of the oven.

"Everything smells wonderful," Mabel said, feeling underdressed, she set the bottle of wine on the counter. It was awkward, her best friend's home, and yet, it was as if she was visiting for the first time.

"Thank you, turkey and all the trimmings, as they say. I can't go wrong," Violet replied modestly. "Do you want to open the wine? You know where I keep the wine glasses."

Mabel was as familiar with Violet's cheerful yellow and white kitchen as she was with her own. She opened a white cupboard door and took out three wine glasses.

"You should let the wine breathe before pouring it," Neville said, taking the wine bottle from Mabel. "Oh, it has a screw top."

"I chilled it." Mabel snatched the bottle out of his hand, twisting off the top.

"I'm a big fan of white wine, and the wine will go well with the turkey." Violet arranged the wine glasses in a row. "You pour, dear, and we'll take our wine into the living room. The turkey has to rest before I carve it; I've set the timer. Everything else is ready."

"I'll carve the turkey," Neville said, arching one eyebrow as he watched Mabel.

Mabel poured the white wine into each glass, then bent, eyeing the levels. She added a few more drops of wine into one glass, making sure each glass had the same quantity. Her friend was more comfortable if everything was even.

"No, Neville, I'll carve, I always carve." Violet accepted the wine goblet from Mabel.

"Yes, you're a guest, Neville," Mabel said, offering him a glass of wine.

"I'm going to carve the turkey. I'm more than a guest here," Neville asserted. He lifted his glass, turning it, scrutinizing the wine.

Violet smiled and led the way into her living room.

Mabel glanced at Violet. She knew her friend well, and this smile was not genuine.

Violet's living room was as neat as the rest of her house. The sofa and loveseat in the living room were in soft, muted browns, as was the area rug in the middle of the hardwood floor.

"A new TV," Mabel said, admiring the new plasma screen TV mounted on the wall. "When did you get your new TV?"

"We went shopping in Regina for it a week or so ago. Neville thought I could do with a new one."

"It's very nice and very big. And you've got a new coffee table too. You have been on a big shopping spree." Mabel ran a finger over the dark redwood grain of the new coffee table. She sat on the loveseat and took a sip of her wine. She was out of the loop. Violet hadn't even bothered to mention it.

"Do you like my new coffee table?"

"It's beautiful, you have excellent taste." She did admire Violet's taste, but it bothered Mabel that Neville seemed to have a great deal of influence on her friend.

"Thank you."

"So, what have you been busy at?" Neville put his arm on the back of the couch, just behind Violet's head.

"I went down to the Co-op Lumberyard and ordered a two-by-four."

"A two-by-four? Only one piece of lumber?" Neville looked at her curiously.

"Oh, I'm just getting the two-by-four in case I need to fix something." Mabel swirled the wine in her glass.

Violet rolled her eyes and shook her head. "You won't need it, I promise you."

Neville looked from woman to woman. "Am I missing something here?"

"Never mind, Neville, Mabel likes to tease. What else have you been doing besides visiting the lumberyard?" Violet took a sip of her wine.

"I went to Coffee Row."

"Coffee Row? Where is that?" Neville asked.

Violet chuckled. "It's a term, not another tourist spot for you to visit. It's a group of people who gather for coffee and share the latest news. And sometimes a little gossip. Our Coffee Row gathers at Pam & Ally's Café."

"Ah, that quaint little seventies café downtown." Neville tasted his wine. He wrinkled his nose and set his wine glass on the coffee table.

Violet slipped a coaster under the glass.

Mabel took another sip of her wine. What a snob. There was nothing wrong with the wine.

"I assume you visited Coffee Row for gossip." Neville arched an eyebrow and ran his forefinger over his pencil mustache.

Mabel's face reddened. She had been in search of gossip, but she didn't like Neville pointing it out.

"Mabel is looking for information. Coffee Row is a great source."

"Of gossip, you mean," Neville corrected and snickered.

Mabel's eyes narrowed.

"You are sort of right, but they know where the bodies are buried, so to speak." Violet looked over at Mabel. "What did you find out?"

"Mini lived in or near Carlyle, that's where there is that big casino. Mom said she thought Mini gambled. I think she could be right."

"But even if Mini gambled, that wouldn't make her a target for murder. There aren't any loan sharks in Glenhaven," Violet reasoned.

"No, I guess not," Mabel conceded. "Anyway, Alice was there."

Violet laughed. "Alice, well, you'd find out lots from her."

"Alice?" asked Neville.

"Never mind, she's not important. Or is she?" asked Violet, sipping her wine.

"I take everything she says with a pinch of salt. But she knew stuff about Freda, or so she said."

"Stuff?" Neville asked.

Violet waved a dismissive hand at Neville and asked, "What did she say?

Neville sat back on the couch and crossed his arms over his chest.

"She said Freda was a snoop." Mabel grinned as Violet laughed out loud.

"Seriously, Alice said that? She's the biggest gossip in town."

"I know, but listen, she said not only was Freda a snoop, but she used her information to gain favours. I don't mean money. But apparently, if you didn't do what she asked, she threatened to reveal whatever dirty little secret it was."

"Do you think someone pushed Freda down the stairs in retaliation?" speculated Violet.

Mabel shrugged. "Or maybe to prevent some indiscretion from coming out?"

"Really, ladies, this scenario of yours is preposterous." Neville snorted. "Some little old lady knows a piece of gossip so dangerous that she is murdered? Ridiculous."

"That depends on what she knew, doesn't it?" defended Mabel.

"Mabel is right. Maybe what Freda knew wasn't gossip. Whatever she knew could well have been something damaging. But first, we should find out if what Alice says is true."

Neville frowned. "We? You're not getting involved in this goose chase, are you?"

"Pardon me? What I get involved in is no concern of yours, Neville." Violet's voice was sharp.

"Sorry, Violet, please don't take offence. I would hate it if you ended up looking foolish because of some fool errand Mabel is on."

"My friend is not a fool. And whatever errand Mabel is on, I will be on as well," snapped Violet.

Mabel raised her wine glass in a salute. Violet was standing up to Neville. She had been afraid her friend was too enamoured with the man to think for herself.

"Sorry, Violet, I don't think Mabel is a fool. I'm sorry it came out that way. And, of course, you will do whatever you can to help your friend. And I'll help too."

Mabel doubted he meant a word of his apology, and if he could prevent Violet from helping her, she bet he would.

The buzzer from the kitchen sounded. "Time to carve the turkey," Violet said.

Chapter Fourteen

Mabel parked her car in the visitor's parking lot and looked across the car park at the gabled porch entrance to the Gravenhurst Manor. The big glass doors of the condo swung open. And Gemma, wearing a long yellow dress with a white shawl draped over her broad shoulders, came out.

Mabel took off her sweater and threw it into the back seat of her car, then strode to the condo. It was October, and the weather was hot, July hot. Global warming?

"I'm waiting for my ladies; I'm taking the old dears to the fall supper," Gemma said by way of a greeting. She was holding open the manor door.

Three elderly ladies emerged from the condo and stood on the step. Gemma's yellow dress skirt flared out as she sprinted to her little red sports car, opening the doors. Her shawl slipped off her shoulder, dropping onto the ground. Her big brown purse fell as she stooped to pick up her shawl.

Mabel retrieved the purse and offered it to Gemma.

"Thank you, sweetie; I wasn't sure you were coming for your mom," Gemma said, shaking the dirt from her white shawl; she slung the purse over her shoulder. "I'm so glad you are here to take your mom. I've got a full car. But I told your mom I would make a special trip back for her. I don't want her to miss out on the Fall Supper."

Mabel pressed her lips together. Gemma always seemed to use the term sweetie when she addressed her. But she was good to her mom, so she shook off her displeasure. "That's very kind of you," she said, standing back as the stooped figure of Hannah Huston shuffled her way to the car.

Gemma dashed over to offer a hand to Hannah. "Come along, sweetie. It might be a little crowded, but there is room in the back seat." The shawl slipped to the ground again; this time, a gust of wind blew it under the car.

So, it wasn't just her that Gemma called sweetie, but it felt demeaning. "You can come with Mom and me if you want, Hannah," Mabel offered; kneeling on the ground, she pulled Gemma's shawl from under the car.

Hannah plopped down on the back seat. She was scrunched, her knees were almost touching her nose.

"Nonsense, Hannah wants to come with me, don't you, sweetie?"

"I might as well ride with Gemma; I'm in the car now," Hannah said, yanking on the seat belt. Gemma took the shawl from Mabel and rolled it into a ball, tossing it to the driver's side seat. Mabel dusted the dirt off her knees.

"Move, sweetie," instructed Gemma. Sweeping past Mabel, she hurried to help a tall woman with iron-grey hair. The woman walked like she had bad hips. Gemma helped her into the passenger seat. The tall woman's knees were jammed up against the dashboard. Then Gemma turned back, racing to offer her arm to a tiny, thin lady who seemed agile on her feet. The little woman brushed the help off and scooted around the car to squeeze in the back beside Hannah.

"What's wrong with these dumb things," Hannah said, fumbling with the seatbelt.

Gemma shifted her bag back up over her shoulder. Each woman seemed to have the same problem with the seatbelts as Hannah. Gemma scooted from one lady to the other, fastening their seatbelts for them. "We will see you at the supper, Mabel," she said, hurrying to the driver's side of her car. "And remember, sweetie, the supper is at the Lion's Hall. And don't be late; there is always a big turnout for the Fall Supper." Gemma smiled and closed her car door.

"It's always held at the Lion's Hall," Mabel called as the sports car sped down the driveway. "I'm not senile, and I've lived here a lot longer than you," she muttered. Entering the vestibule, she pushed the button to her mom's suite.

"Who is it?" Her mother's voice came over the intercom.

"It's me, Mabel."

"Mabel?"

"You know, Mom, the longer you fool around, the higher our number will be; you do want to eat supper?"

"I'll be right down."

As Mabel waited for her mother, more residents came out the door. Each acknowledged Mabel with a smile or a nod before rushing to the parking lot. Mabel suspected they were all going to the community supper at the Lions Hall. The last one out the door was Farley, with a canvas tool bag slung over his shoulder.

"Working on a Sunday, Farley."

"Yep, these condo owners are a mollycoddled lot. They used to take care of a house and yard. Now they won't even screw in a light bulb. Pampered bunch," Farley grumbled as he ambled out the door.

Sophie emerged from the elevator wearing a light blue jacket over a white blouse with a big bow at the neck. A flared blue skirt in the same colour as the jacket completed her outfit. She trotted over to the door. "Not dressed up, dear? Didn't you have time?"

Mabel tugged on her T-shirt, ignoring the little jab her mother gave her; she took her car keys out of her jeans pocket. "You just missed Gemma and her crew. You should have seen her running around like a ringy dingy rabbit, shoe-horning those women into her sports car. Those poor ladies are packed in there like sardines in a can."

"Don't be snarky, dear. Gemma is godsent to us all."

"Yes, so you keep telling me."

Chapter Fifteen

Mabel stopped in the lobby of the Lions Hall at a tiny booth with a half-moon plexiglass window. The small grey-haired man took her money and gave her two blue tickets with numbers at each end. Fred Granger, a small man with sandy hair and a bushy mustache of the same colour, ripped the tickets in half. One half of the ticket, he dropped into an empty ice cream bucket. The other half he gave to Mabel. "I paid, Mom; put your wallet away."

"Thank you, dear," Sophie said, tucking her wallet back into her purse.

Mabel escorted her mother through a doorway into the large hall where black metal chairs, set up in rows, covered worn hardwood floors. The old Lions Hall was well maintained; the smell of fresh paint filled the air. At the far end of the hall, a raised platform with big heavy burgundy curtains hung open, revealing a cavernous stage. A large crowd of people already seated chatted. Their conversations and laughter filled the hall as they waited for their number to be called. Mabel spotted Violet and Neville sitting four rows down. "Come on, Mom, there are two empty chairs next to Violet." They hurried, stepping around a milky brown puddle. "Someone should clean that up," she said.

"Some child probably spilt their milk," commented Sophie, following Mabel down the aisle.

"I hope that is what it is and not something worse," Mabel muttered.

"Hello, Sophie," greeted Violet. "This is my friend Neville. Neville, this is Mabel's mother, Sophie Schoenberg."

Neville rose from his chair and smiled charmingly at Sophie. "So please to meet you," he said. Beaming, Sophie sat next to Neville.

Mabel grinned; she could see Neville had captivated her mom, and she suspected it was his English accent. She sat beside her mother and said, "The place is filling up fast. What's your numbers?"

Violet checked the numbers on her ticket. "I've got 209. What's yours?"

"We just got here. But our numbers are only ten behind. We might get to sit together."

"I don't really understand the concept of this supper. We pay money for our supper, and we get these tickets with numbers?" Neville looked at the ticket in his hand. "And now, we sit in this hall with everyone else who has done the same thing. Waiting to be called by the number on our ticket?"

"Yes, then we go downstairs for a wonderful home-cooked meal."

"But why do we have to sit here? We paid; can't we go for our meal now?" Neville asked.

"I'm sorry, I should have explained. You can see by the number on our ticket there are way too many people to feed all at once. It's for charity. It's a way to raise money. I think this year, the money is for the swimming pool."

"I understand the fund-raising part of this. But when do we dine?"

"When our number is called. No worries. There will be lots of food, and all the food is home-cooked, including turkey and all the trimmings and homegrown garden vegetables. And pierogies," assured Violet.

"Pierogies?"

"I won't explain them to you, but once you taste them, you will be hooked," assured Violet.

"And the homemade pies, the variety will blow your socks off," Mabel's mother said enthusiastically.

Mabel glanced at Neville; the man didn't look very enthusiastic. He was squirming in his chair, crossing and uncrossing his legs.

"Look, there's dear Gemma. She's brought a carload of ladies from the manor. I could have come with them," Sophie said, waving.

Mabel felt a surge of jealousy as she watched the tall, auburn-haired woman usher the three ladies to the stairway leading to the basement below. "Ah, yes, Miss Goody Two Shoes," she muttered.

"Don't be snarky dear, it doesn't become you," reprimanded Sophie. "I don't know what we would do if we didn't have Gemma."

Fred Granger, rattling the ice cream bucket, came tearing through the door. "Son of a Gun, we're being robbed," Fred yelled, stumbling; he slid into a row of chairs.

A man wearing a black balaclava carrying a shotgun ran in after Fred; he pushed the small man into another row of chairs. More chairs fell over as people jumped up, shrieking and shouting, scrambling over the fallen chairs.

The shotgun-carrying man shouted, "Everyone, shut up and stay where you are, and no one will get hurt."

The crowd's frightened cries became low, with worried mutterings, as they watched the balaclava man wave his shotgun. Fred held the ice cream bucket in front of him like a shield as the man backed him further into the room.

"We are only after the money. There is no need for anyone to get hurt over money." He glanced over his shoulder and yelled out the door. "Get a move on it, hurry up."

"What the hell do you think I'm doing? I've got to tie this old guy up," a muffled voice yelled back.

The balaclava man closed the door and turned to the crowd. "If no one calls the cops, no one will get hurt."

He was too late. Everyone in the hall had their cell phones. Numbers were being punched. The RCMP was being called.

Mabel bit her lip. The men would be long gone by the time the police arrived. And with them, the money raised from the fall supper for the new pool. She got up from her chair and staggered down the aisle, coughing and gagging.

"Hey, you, stay where you are, sit down, don't come any closer," the masked man yelled.

Mabel kept stumbling, weaving her way toward him. "I'm sick, I'm going to throw up," she gasped, making more gagging sounds.

The tall, skinny balaclava man waving the shotgun jumped back. Mabel, retching and coughing, stepped into the milky brown substance. She slid, crashing into the robber. He fell to the floor, his shotgun flying out of his hands. As he reached for his shotgun, Mabel's head came up, connecting with his.

"Crap," shouted the man, rubbing his head.

His shotgun lay on the floor in the pool of brownish liquid. Sam Peebles, a tall, gaunt farmer, snatched up the weapon. Mabel scrambled away from the ski-masked man, stumbling into Fred.

As the skinny robber scrambled to his feet, Alvin Woodhouse leapt over a chair, slamming into the robber. Throwing him down on the floor face-first into the milky substance. The Balaclava man gagged.

Sam, with the slimy shotgun in his hands, stood close to the wall just inside the door. He held up a finger to his lips. "Quiet, everyone." His foot nudged the robber on the floor. "Tell your friend to come here."

Alvin ripped off the man's mask, revealing a teenage boy with blond hair. Alvin pushed his head down toward the mucky pool on the floor.

Looking frightened, the young boy gasped, "Okay, okay." Alvin grabbed the boy's long blond hair and yanked his head up.

"Come here, come here quick," the boy yelled.

"What the hell? Can't you handle a bunch of old farmers? I've got the money; hurry up," a muffled voice called from the other side of the door. "Come on, quit fooling around. We've got to get the hell out of here." The door opened, and a man wearing a ski mask stuck his head in.

Sam brought the shotgun up, sticking the barrel under the robber's chin, he pressed it into the man's neck. "If you have a gun, drop it now. My trigger finger is slippery, and I will blow your head off."

There was a loud clunk as the pistol hit the floor.

"Get in here," ordered Sam. "Lay down beside your buddy and don't move a muscle."

The man paused, looking at the mess on the floor, then he looked at Sam holding the shotgun. Sam had a nasty grin on his face. The masked man dropped a plastic bag, sunk to his knees on the floor, and cautiously laid down.

"Has anybody called the RCMP?" asked Sam as he kicked the gun away from the ski-masked man.

"There was a course of yeses and a round of applause.

"You might as well call the next numbers for supper, Fred. Me and Alvin here will keep these jerks right here until the police arrive." Sam kept the shotgun trained on the two robbers, who were gagging and trying to keep their faces off the mess on the floor.

Alvin ripped the mask off the second man, revealing a boy who didn't look much older than the first. He scooped up the bag the robber had dropped. "Here's the money," he said, triumphantly holding the bag up for all to see. There was another round of applause and much cheering. "You lowlife stealing from the charity. I hope the judge throws the book at you two." His foot prodded the boys.

"Can't we move? This is gross," the first boy begged.

Sam grinned. "Nope, you can just stay right where you are."

Chapter Sixteen

"Numbers 150 to 200, you can go for supper; there's room at the tables," Fred yelled. A round of hand-clapping greeted his announcement.

Violet was out of her chair and into the aisle before anyone else. She whipped out a package of alcohol wipes from her purse and handed the package to Mabel. "Geez, Louise Mabel, you just never learn."

Mabel pulled out a handful of wipes from the package and wiped her face and hands where the milky brown liquid had splashed up. "I guess we should get moving; we're blocking the aisle," she said, leading the way. "Fred called out numbers."

Sophie grabbed her daughter's arm and gave her a hug. "No, he didn't call our numbers, dear. You should sit down," she urged.

Mary scrambled over some fallen chairs and confronted her husband. "Alvin, why on earth did you tackle this man? That thug could've hurt you."

"Nah, I'm fine; me and Sam have everything under control. Go for supper, Mary," Alvin said, directing traffic away from the boys, who were stretching their necks, trying to keep their faces off the floor.

Reluctantly, Mabel sat on a nearby chair, scrubbing at the knees of her jeans with Violet's wipes.

"I don't know what you were thinking. Running down the aisle toward those villains. You could've been hurt or even killed. The man had a gun," Sophie scolded her daughter.

"Nonsense," Mabel said. "And I didn't run, I staggered."

"You did that on purpose, didn't you?" Violet smiled admiringly at her friend.

"My word, did you plan that?" Neville asked. "That was quite extraordinary."

Mabel thought she detected a touch of admiration in his tone. "I didn't plan on running into the robber if that's what you mean. I only wanted to distract the man by pretending to gag. I hoped someone would overpower him. Stepping into that mucky mess was just an accident."

"That was plain foolish, Mabel. Next time, you stay sitting in your seat. I forbid you to act..." Sophie's voice trailed off. She grasped Mabel's hand.

Mabel gently squeezed her mother's hand. "I'm sorry, Mom, but I really didn't think about doing anything; one minute, I was sitting, and the next minute, I was in the aisle."

"Then think. And don't do this again." Sophie returned the hand squeeze.

"There is room for 30 more, tickets 200 to 230," Fred called out.

"That's us; let's go for supper; bringing down robbers always gives me an appetite." Mabel stood, scrunching up the wipes and putting them in her pocket.

"I wouldn't say you actually brought down that would-be robber," Neville said.

Violet gave him an annoyed look. "She certainly helped."

"Accidentally helped," Neville insisted. "She just said she didn't plan her actions."

"I made a joke, Neville; of course, I didn't bring down that robber," Mabel said. "Sam and Alvin are the real heroes."

"But you did help," Sophie defended. "And I'm sure the police will want to talk to you. Maybe you should stay here."

"What for? As Neville said, I accidentally ran into that scummy little delinquent. I'm starved; let's go for supper."

"Mabel's right; we should go for supper; the police will know we're downstairs eating. If they need Mabel, they can call her up or come get her." Violet put the near-empty package of alcohol wipes back in her purse.

As Mabel made her way to the stairs leading to the basement, she was greeted with handshakes and pats on the back. Some people laughed and said, '*Good show. Others said Way to go, Mabel.*' Each time, Sophie proudly said, "She's my daughter."

Mabel smiled at her mother's comments as she followed the crowd down the stairs, where the enticing aroma of roast turkey wafted up.

The large basement walls were painted in dark gold tones with blue and gold tiles on the floor. A table laden with an assortment of jellies and salads followed by containers of roast turkey, mashed potatoes, pierogies, meatballs, and various hot vegetables lay before them. At the end of the long table, trays of homemade buns, salad dressings and bowls of cranberries, sour cream and sauteed onions. Along one wall was another long table with a variety of pies laid on small plates. Women and men scurried back and forth from the kitchen, filling up the chafing dishes with more hot vegetables and carved turkey.

"There is lots of food and room for you folks to dig in and enjoy," greeted a man with a large bowl of gravy, skirting around them.

Long tables with blue and gold plastic tablecloths filled the rest of the room. At each table, people were eating their supper or enjoying their pie and coffee. Mabel could hear snatches of excited conversations and descriptions of what happened with the would-be robbers.

Violet, motioning for Neville to get in line at the buffet table, picked up two paper plates and handed one to him.

"Paper plates? Are we expected to eat with these strangers?"

"Yes, this is what a fall supper is, Neville. You'll enjoy it," Violet encouraged.

"And just where are we supposed to sit? And with whom?" Neville's mustache wiggled as he turned his lips down.

"There is lots of room, look." Sophie gestured with her empty paper plate.

"Mom is right. There are plenty of empty chairs scattered throughout the room. We may not all get to sit with each other, but we'll find a spot to sit, no worries. They wouldn't have called our ticket numbers if there was no room." Mabel prodded Neville. "Move, people are lining up behind us."

"Seriously, I have to sit with strangers? It's alright for you, you know these people, but I don't," Neville grumbled, spooning salad onto his plate.

"Don't be so prissy; you'll get to know them." Mabel poked him and urged him to move down the food table.

"Prissy? I'm not prissy. What the hell is this?" Neville curled his lip as he held up a spoonful of jellied salad with shredded carrots in it.

"You'll like it; it's my friend Helen's specialty," encouraged Violet.

Neville dubiously added the jelly salad to his plate. By the time he had finished going through the hot buffet line, his plate was overflowing.

"There's Mary, and there are empty chairs by her," Mabel said, leading the way down an aisle between two of the long tables.

Mabel set her plate down beside Mary. Violet, Neville, and Sophie sat across the table from them.

Neville unwrapped his cutlery, and he looked askant. "We eat with these little plastic forks and knives?"

"Please don't be so picky," requested Violet. "Just hush up and eat."

Mabel grinned as Neville did as he was told. She turned to Mary. "Alvin is the hero of the day, jumping up to help Sam apprehend that hooligan. You must be very proud of him." Mabel took her plastic fork and knife and began attacking the turkey on her plate.

"I am, but he should be more careful. He's always taking chances. One time, he chased a thief off our property with just a baseball bat. But what can I do? Alvin is Alvin; he is a law unto himself, as you well know." Mary dabbed her lips with her napkin. "I'll get the kitchen to make him and Sam up a plate. I doubt the men will get down here for supper. The RCMP will want to know all the details. And I bet they will want to talk to you too."

"I doubt it. I just accidentally knocked the shotgun out of his hands, and it fell into that slimy mess on the floor. Isn't this delicious?" Mabel took a bite of turkey topped with cranberry sauce.

"If you wouldn't mind, please stop talking about, well, you know what. We're trying to eat." Neville dipped his fork into the jelly salad; the heat from the turkey gravy had melted the jelly, and it slid off his fork. He grimaced.

"He's right, dear, poor Neville, and I have a delicate constitution," Sophie said, scooping up a forkful of mashed potatoes and gravy.

Mabel grinned, her mother's delicate constitution? The woman's appetite could put a truck driver to shame. She turned back to Mary. "I couldn't help but notice you were kind of upset, well maybe not upset. But when Alice told us the other day about Freda. I got the feeling you already knew. Had you already heard about Freda's conniving ways?"

Mary's face flushed, and she set her fork down.

"Mabel," Fred called from the bottom of the stairs. Fred threaded his way past the long tables. He stopped, waiting as three small children carrying pies on small plates paraded past him.

"The RCMP officers want to talk to you, Mabel," he said loudly.

Everyone at the table stopped eating, forks in the air, as they eyeballed Mabel.

Embarrassed at the attention, Mabel dropped her napkin on her plate. "I don't know how long. I'll be, Mom."

"I'll give her a lift home," a voice from behind Mabel said.

Mabel looked over her shoulder at Gemma, who stood smiling at Sophie. Sophie beamed happily back at Gemma. "That would be lovely, thank you."

"Mom, Gemma's car is full," Mabel reminded her mother.

"If Mabel isn't back by the time we finish supper, Neville and I will take you home."

Gemma shrugged. "Do what you like, my dear little Sophie. I just wanted to offer."

"Thank you, Gemma. I know I can always count on you, but Mabel is right; your car might be a tad crowded."

Always count on Gemma? Mabel felt a surge of jealousy as she left the table and followed Fred up the stairs.

Chapter Seventeen

A teenage girl with a teapot and a boy with a coffee pot stopped at the table.

"Neville, do you want coffee or tea?" Violet asked.

"Tea, I guess."

"Me too," agreed Sophie, holding up her cup.

As the girl stopped to fill the Styrofoam cups, Neville looked sideways at Violet. "Styrofoam?"

"Neville, don't say a word," Violet cautioned.

"But Styrofoam, really?" Neville asked, ignoring her warning.

Violet sighed, reluctantly, acknowledging that Neville was a bit of a snob; he was in her town, and she wished he'd mind his manners.

Sophie leaned close to Neville and whispered, "Just because our customs are different in Glenhaven, it doesn't make them wrong."

"It's not the customs, it's the cups." Neville's lips turned down.

"I'll go get us a slice of pie," Violet said, steering the conversation to a safer topic.

"That would be lovely, dear, lemon pie for me, please, if they have it," requested Sophie.

Neville brightened. "Do you think they would have rhubarb pie?"

Violet rose. "I'm pretty sure they do." She walked down the aisle toward the dessert table. And paused as a small lady in a scarlet velour suit, carrying two overflowing paper plates, passed in front of her. Hobbling along behind her, a hunched little man dressed in a yellow and black checkered suit. The woman set the plates down. Gravy spilled off a plate onto the table. Violet quickly grabbed a handful of napkins from a nearby table and, reaching around the scarlet-suited woman, she mopped up the gravy. The woman gave her a grateful smile and sat down. Violet held the chair for the old man, who dropped onto the chair and immediately dug into his food. A hand reached out and touched her on the arm. She turned; it was Alfred Jilvontee from the table across the tiny aisle, tugging on her arm.

"Hi Alfred, are you by yourself? Where's Ruth?" she asked.

"Ruth is working in the kitchen. Can I speak to you for a moment?" he asked.

Violet pulled out an empty chair and sat next to him. She deposited the soiled paper napkins on an empty paper plate. "I'm sorry about your aunt; I missed the funeral. I should have been there."

"No worries, it was a graveside service; my wife Ruth didn't even go. And I have to ask you a big favour." He dug into his jacket pocket and pulled out a set of keys. "I'm supposed to clean out my aunt's unit at the Manor. We're going to sell it. But I hate to touch her lady things. And Ruth won't set foot in Aunt Freda's condo; my wife." Alfred paused, then said, "My wife, she didn't get along with my aunt. And I don't know who else to ask. It's not like Aunt Freda had any close friends. I guess you could say she was not the easiest person to be around. She seemed to rub everyone the wrong way." Alfred chuckled. "Even me, if truth be told. I never always got along with her, either. But she was my aunt."

"I see."

"I know it's not good to speak ill of the dead, but there it is."

"You want me to pack up her condo?"

"If you would, please. Like I said, I don't want to touch her lady things."

Mabel will be pleased, Violet thought. A good old snoop through Freda's things might offer up a clue. "Sure, no problem, I'll do it for you. Do you want me to deliver the boxes to your farm?"

"No, give her clothes and such to Good Will. Just tell me when it's done and return the keys," Alfred said, handing her a set of keys. "The big key is to get in the building, and the small one is for her condo," he explained.

Violet accepted the keys and pocketed them. "No problem, I'll get Mabel to help."

Alfred dug into his pie. "Thanks," he said, his mouth full of pie, a dribble of cherry juice dripped down his chin.

I bet Mabel didn't think of a key? Violet happily mused as she made her way to the pie table. No one would have had to be buzzed into the building if they had a key. Farley, the weird man who looked after the building, certainly had a key.

She'd seen the ring of keys hanging off his belt. And Jody, the home care worker, could have a key. And Gemma, did she have a key? According to Mabel, she was always at the condo. And who else?

Chapter Eighteen

Mabel stepped on her brakes. The car skidded to a halt in front of the sign on the lawn of Gravenhurst Manor. "Would you look at that," she huffed. The *'nhurst'* part of the sign had been blacked out. And the word 'yard' was sprayed in with red spray paint. The sign now read, *'Graveyard Manor.'* A skull and crossbones completed the graffiti.

Neville, who sat in the back seat of the car, peeked out over the pile of empty cardboard boxes. "Pranksters."

"More like idiots," Violet said. "It's not even Halloween."

"Morons," muttered Mabel, putting her car in gear, continuing to the parking lot. But then, her suspicious instincts kicked in. Pranksters? Or a warning? Maybe some nutbar was killing seniors, and there was no motive for the murders. This was a scary thought. Her mother could be in danger. No, she was probably wrong with her suspicions. Mini's death had to be natural, and Freda's death was just a terrible accident. Yes, she had to be wrong; her mother was safe.

"Speaking of morons, who were those morons who tried to rob the Fall Supper?" Violet held open the car door for

Neville as he struggled out of the back seat with a load of boxes.

"I don't know their names, but they are from Kegsworthy," Mabel said, stacking cardboard boxes beside the car.

Each took a stack of boxes and trudged to the front door. Violet, using Freda's key, opened the door and held it open as Mabel and Neville carried the boxes inside. Once inside, they piled the cardboard cartons beside the elevator, and Violet pushed the button for the elevator. As they waited, Mabel's suspicions of murder came back. She recalled her mother's account of the busy elevator and the blocked door. And Freda, who never used the stairs, fell down them.

"How long do you think this will take?" Neville asked. He stepped back as the door opened, and Homer came out, and his walker pushed against the cardboard boxes.

"Look out," protested Homer, barreling his way through. "What the heck is going on here?"

"We are cleaning out Freda's condo," Mabel said.

Violet held the elevator door open. "How are you today, Homer?"

"Why the hell do you always want to know how I am." Homer thumped past them, boxes flying as he went.

Mabel, stacking her pile of boxes inside the elevator door, said, "That man could start an argument even if he was in a room on his own."

"I think he is just a very unhappy man," Violet said, helping Neville pick up the scattered boxes.

"Homer works at being unhappy." Mabel glared at the small man's back as he tromped with his walker into the lounge.

They stacked the boxes in the elevator, and the door closed. It was cramped.

When the door opened on the second floor, Farley was standing with a vacuum cleaner hose slung over his shoulder, ready to board.

Neville, the first one out, offered his hand to Farley. "Good morning," he greeted.

"Morning," responded Farley. "Moving in?"

"No, we are just helping Albert Jilvontee move his aunts' belongings," Neville replied.

"I'll help you carry those boxes," offered Farley, dropping the vacuum hose. "Do you want me to open her door for you?"

Violet smiled warmly at the caretaker. "No, Alfred gave me the keys, but if you help us carry the boxes to the door, that would be great."

Farley revealed tobacco-stained teeth as he grinned back. The lanky man pulled up the sleeves of his coveralls and scooped up a pile of boxes.

Mabel eyed the tall, thin man with suspicion. Did he take a happy pill? His disposition certainly had changed. "Did you see the sign out front?" she asked.

"Yep, I'm not senile like some of these people in here," Farley snapped, dropping the boxes in the hallway by Freda's door.

"Are you going to clean that graffiti off?" Mabel persisted.

"I am when I get to it," Farley snarled and stomped off. The man's good humour had disappeared.

"I only asked," Mabel said to his back. She held the door open to Freda's condo while Neville and Violet toted in the cardboard boxes. The suite was a mess. Drawers in the kitchen cabinet were half-open, and the cupboard doors were ajar. Mabel stepped to the side as Mabel and Neville piled the boxes by the cupboard.

In the living room, seat cushions on the oversized brown couch were askew. The doors under the stand that held the TV set were wide open. And magazines, pictures, and letters scattered across the carpet. "I don't think this is a sign of poor housekeeping," Mabel mused.

"Oh, someone was looking for something, alright," Violet said, following Mabel into the living room. "I wonder what?"

Neville leaned up against the cupboard and crossed his arms. "What would this lady have that would be valuable?"

"More to the point, who was doing the searching?" Mabel entered the bedroom. The signs of a search continued. The bed covers rolled up in a ball on the floor, and the mattress shifted half off the bed. The dresser drawers were pulled open, and Freda's undies lay on the floor. The closet doors were also wide open, and her clothes were in a jumble at the bottom of the closet. "Whoever did this search was either in a hurry or just plain sloppy. Freda's apartment has been turned over, as they say in the movies."

Neville stood in the doorway. "Do you think they found what they were looking for?"

"Maybe not; everything looks like it has been pawed through. So, we pack up everything, no matter if it looks like junk. We can go through it all later. I'll take the bedroom; you take the living room, Neville. That leaves the kitchen for you, Violet."

"So, you're the boss here?" Neville asked.

Mabel, looking over her granny glasses at the man, asked, "Do you want to go through her underwear?"

"Good lord, no." Neville turned on his heel.

Violet grinned and followed him out of the bedroom and set a box on the kitchen counter, taking a tea towel from a drawer and folding it neatly.

"Violet, please just put stuff in the boxes," pleaded Mabel, picking up a cardboard carton. "We'll be here all day if you do that."

Violet sighed and grabbed a handful of towels and dishcloths, tossing them into the box. A small black book dropped to the bottom of the carton.

Chapter Nineteen

Mabel opened the oven door to check on her turkey and reached for her turkey baster. "This bird is browning nicely," she said proudly.

"It is indeed, and everything smells wonderful," Violet agreed.

"More turkey? What is it with you, people, and turkey?" Neville pulled on one end of Mabel's grey-topped chrome kitchen table, and Violet tugged on the other, pulling the table open.

"It's Thanksgiving." Mabel closed the oven door. "I always roast a turkey for Thanksgiving."

Neville picked up a table leaf and placed it in the opening. "I thought your Thanksgiving Day was in November?" He pushed on the end of the table, closing it.

"That's our American cousin's. This is Canada, and our Thanksgiving is in October. Anyway, it means the same thing. It's about being grateful for what you have." Violet unfolded a big snowy-white linen tablecloth with tiny ivy leaves embroidered on the hem.

Neville sighed. "And more turkey." He grabbed the end of the tablecloth, helping Violet to spread the tablecloth evenly over the expanded kitchen table.

"How many place settings do we need?" Violet asked, giving the tablecloth a final tug.

"There are eight adults. You two, me and Mom. My brother Cyril and his wife, Jessie. They're picking Mom up from her place. And, of course, Grant and Susan. I've borrowed a highchair for Sammy, he is two. Do you think he'll sit in one?"

"I do hope so. This is such a nice tablecloth. And toddlers his age are very messy eaters.

Neville, please bring the chairs from Mabel's living room."

"Who are Grant and Susan," Neville called from the living room.

"Grant is my son, Susan is his wife, and little Sammy is my grandson; they're coming from Edmonton, Alberta."

"Yes, I know where Edmonton is." Neville placed a wooden chair between two red padded chrome chairs.

Mabel put a stack of snowy-white linen napkins on the table. "The family is staying with me for the weekend," she said, bustling back over to her cupboard and taking out her dinner plates.

"New dishes, I don't remember these; I love the design," Violet said, admiring the white plates etched with tiny white leaves.

Mabel placed the white china on the white linen tablecloth. "Mom gave me these when she moved to the condo. This china didn't match her new decor." She grinned. "Her new dishes have little pink flowers."

"Your table is very white; it looks almost sterile," commented Neville, stroking his mustache.

"Why, thank you," Mabel said proudly.

Neville rolled his eyes.

Mabel gave Neville a questioning look. Then the doorbell rang, and she rushed over to answer it. "It's Mom, Cyril, and Jessie," she announced, holding the door open.

"Hugs all around," Jessie greeted, her blonde hair glistening with hair spray.

Hugging the tall, thin woman was like hugging a coat rack, and her sister-in-law smelled of gardenias. The perfume was overpowering. Mabel sneezed.

Jessie planted a kiss on Mabel's cheek, then swooped over to give Violet a hug.

Sophie unbuttoned her coat and offered up a cheek for Mabel to kiss. "Take my coat, dear."

Cyril, a small, portly man with unruly white hair, wore a blue pinstriped suit. He gave Mabel a bear hug.

She grinned. "I should have known you'd wear a suit. I'm sure you wore a three-piece suit in the sandbox when you were little," Mabel teased.

"Don't be silly," Sophie scolded. "Don't pay your sister any mind. You look wonderful. It wouldn't hurt you, Mabel, to dress up for the occasion." Mabel shrugged. Her joke had fallen flat.

Cyril laughed as he ruffled Mabel's white hair. "You're just jealous because I'm the good-looking one," he teased.

"Don't tease your sister; you know how sensitive she is." Sophie tugged on her son's arm and smiled at him.

"Just teasing, Sis, you look great." Cyril smiled apologetically.

Mabel grinned back. He was the golden child. There was no use trying to compete with Cyril. And she didn't want to; she thought the world of her older brother.

"Neville, this is Cyril, Mabel's brother and his wife, Jessie. Neville is a friend; he's visiting me," introduced Violet.

Mabel took her mother's coat and waited for Jessie to remove hers.

Cyril bounded over, hugged Violet, and shook Neville's hand. "Mom told me you're visiting from England."

"Yes, I am. And I'm quite enjoying your little town."

"Oh, we're not from here; we live in Winnipeg," Jessie explained as she shed her coat.

"Winnipeg?" Neville questioned.

"Winnipeg, Manitoba, the province to the east. Winnipeg is about a four-hour drive from here," explained Cyril.

Mabel watched the exchange. Neville knew about Edmonton but not Winnipeg. Something was fishy about this man. She needed to google him again.

"That's quite a long drive," commented Neville.

"Yes, a long drive, that's why we're staying overnight. That is. If it is okay with you?" Jessie handed Mabel her coat.

"Of course, it's okay with Mabel. Where else would you stay?" Sophie said cheerfully.

Mabel draped the coats over her arm and looked at her brother and sister-in-law. It would have been nice to have been given notice, but they would make do. "There is the spare room downstairs in the basement. It's clean; I just have to make up the bed."

Jessie sighed with a grimace on her face. She said, "I saw the motel as we drove in. But I really don't want to stay in that old dive. I guess we can rough it in your basement for one night."

"It's a bedroom; I'm not making you sleep in a storage room." Mabel's brow furrowed as she shifted the coats on her arm.

"It will be fine, thanks, Sis," Cyril assured her.

There was a rapid tattoo on the back door, and when it opened, Mabel's son and daughter-in-law burst in, bringing with them a whiff of frosty air. Her small, curly-haired two-year-old grandson ran across the kitchen floor to hug Mabel. Mabel handed the coats to Violet and scooped the little boy up in her arms, showering him with kisses.

Chapter Twenty

"Call me when you want the turkey carved," Grant hollered from the living room.

"Are you sure I can't help?" Susan, a tall, slender woman with close-cropped, inky black hair, stood beside the kitchen table with a glass of white wine in her hand. Her son was making zoom; zoom sounds with his tiny red car as he ran in circles around her legs.

Mabel smiled over at her beautiful daughter-in-law. "You have your hands full with Sammy. We'll visit later. Besides, Violet knows where everything is in my kitchen. We're used to working together."

Sniffing the air, Gertrude poked her head out from under the table.

"Kitty," Sammy yelled.

Gertrude's fur ruffled, her back arched, and she crept back under the table.

"Kitty." Sammy's face beamed, and his brown eyes sparkled. The little red car fell to the floor as he dropped to his hands and knees and ducked under the tablecloth after Gertrude. Loud yowling and hissing, followed by a high-pitched meow, emanated from under the table.

Mabel squatted and lifted the tablecloth, scolding her cat. "Gertrude, behave yourself."

Susan set her wineglass down and crawled under the table, pulling her son out from under it just as Gertrude darted away. The big orange cat's ears were flat to her head. Her tail flicked back and forth.

"Kitty, kitty." Sammy struggled in his mother's arms.

"I guess you're right, Sammy can be a handful. I think he thinks Gertrude is a new toy." Susan firmly planted the squirming little boy on her hip. She picked her glass of wine off the table and retreated to the living room.

"You don't mind me volunteering you, do you?" Mabel asked Violet.

"Don't be silly, you know me; I like to organize things," replied Violet.

The two women bustled around Mabel's kitchen in perfect harmony. In short order, the preparations were done. The platters were readied, condiments were on the table, and homemade buns and cranberry sauce. Vegetables drained, ready to be put into the waiting bowls. The turkey was set on a cutting board, ready for carving.

"You're up, carving time," Mabel called to her son. There was no answer.

"I'll go and round him up, but I could carve the turkey if you like?" suggested Violet, looking hopeful.

"And I know you would do a fine job, but Grant did offer." Steam wafted up as Mabel took the lid off the potato pot and added milk and big daubs of butter. Opening the utensil drawer, she removed a metal potato masher and began mashing the potatoes.

Violet disappeared into the living room, returning minutes later with Grant.

"You're missing the football game." Grant leaned down to kiss his mom on the cheek.

"Your brother is trying to explain Canadian football to Neville." Violet giggled.

"Who's winning?" Mabel asked, adding more milk to the potatoes in the pot.

"Not your team, and you don't want to know the score; it's not pretty." Grant grinned as he washed his hands in the kitchen sink.

Mabel gave her son a side-long look and bent to her task, attacking the potatoes with even more vigour.

"It's not that bad. Your team, the Riders, still have a chance. And your mom is cheering them on. Meanwhile, Jessie is showing pictures on her iPhone of her daughter's ballet performance to your daughter-in-law." Violet chuckled. "Every other word is about Marie dancing with the Royal Winnipeg Ballet."

Grant picked up the carving knife and sliced a drumstick off the turkey. "Mom, you should go and rescue Susan. I know you're dying to hear how smart and talented Aunt Jessie's children are."

Mabel rolled her eyes at her six-foot-tall son. He was the spitting image of his dad, with curly blond hair and dark brown eyes. "And who is going to finish the supper preparations? I'll visit with your aunt later. Anyway, supper will be served as soon as you do your carving."

With quick, steady precision, Grant expertly carved the turkey as Mabel stirred the gravy in the roasting pan on the stove.

"There you go," Grant said, placing the last slice of turkey on the platter. He turned on the kitchen tap, washing his hands.

Violet placed the vegetables into bowls as Mabel poured the gravy into a gravy boat.

Gertrude came out of her hiding place, the smell of turkey overcame her caution about Sammy.

"You did a nice job of carving, dear," Mabel complimented as she picked up the turkey platter.

Sammy darted into the kitchen and around the table. "Kitty, kitty," he yelled happily, grabbing the big orange cat by her tail.

Gertrude let out a yelp and scrambled between Mabel's legs. "Gertrude," she shrieked, stepping on the discarded toy car spinning around. "Oh, no," she yelled. The platter tipped in her hands. The turkey slid off the plate onto the floor, landing under the table. Gertrude's greed overcame her fright, and following the turkey, she dug in.

"I'm sorry, I'm sorry," Grant said, scooping Sammy into his arms out of harm's way.

"Oh, my gosh," Violet said, lifting a corner of the tablecloth. The cat was greedily chewing on the turkey.

"Sorry, Mom," Grant apologized, holding firmly onto his wriggling son.

Sammy continued to squirm. "Kitty, kitty," he chanted.

The family appeared from the living room. They looked horrified at the cat gnawing on a drumstick.

"Oh my gosh," cried Susan.

"Not the turkey," murmured Cyril.

"That furry little beast has the turkey. This is a disaster," Jessie said in a shocked voice.

Sophie brought her hand to her mouth, looked at the cat, and then at Mabel. "What will you do now?"

Neville laughed and squatted down to watch Gertrude, who gave out a warning snarl. "Well, I, for one, am sick of turkey. How about a hamburger?"

The family stood hushed as they looked at Neville and then Mabel.

Mabel shrugged and ruffled Sammy's curly black hair. "I agree, burgers for all. We'll order out and have a Burger King Thanksgiving," she said with a chuckle.

Chapter Twenty-One

One lone light lit the living room. It was long after midnight; Cyril and Mabel were the only ones up. Violet and Neville had taken Mabel's mom home, and everyone else was in bed for the night.

"This is a Thanksgiving we won't soon forget." Mabel looked over at Gertrude, licking her paws. The cat had a self-satisfied look on her face.

"Thanksgiving supper was fine; we had all the trimmings sans turkey." Cyril chuckled. Taking off his suit jacket, he folded it neatly on the back of the big grey armchair.

Mabel kicked her shoes off, put her feet up on the grey tweed sofa and stuffed a navy blue cushion behind her back.

"We need to have a talk about Mother," Cyril said, loosening his tie and leaning forward; he rested his forearms on his knees.

"Really, what about?"

"You don't think Mom is losing it, do you?"

"No, she's sharp as a tack. What makes you think she is losing it?"

"Mother confided in me. The way she put it, there was some funny business going on with her bank account."

"Funny business? Does she need money?"

"No, nothing like that."

"That's good, so what is it she is worried about? She hasn't said anything to me."

"Nothing?"

"No, nothing. What exactly did Mom say to you?"

"She can't account for large sums of money withdrawn from her savings account."

"Money is missing from Mom's account?" Mabel swung her feet down on the floor. "How much?

"And that's not the weirdest thing."

"That's not the weirdest thing? Mom's money gone missing."

"The weird thing is the money was withdrawn, then redeposited back into her account."

"So, Mom just mixed things up and doesn't want to admit it." Mabel settled back on the couch.

"That could be. That's why I asked if you thought Mom was losing it."

"How much money are we talking about here?"

"Her savings account was the only account with the weird transactions. I looked at all her accounts and checked all her bank statements." Cyril shook his head and grinned. "Mom still gets paper statements in the mail."

"So." Mabel didn't see anything funny in bank statements coming in the mail.

Cyril arched an eyebrow. "Anyway, as I said, I checked her statements. I checked the chequing account, and there were no errors, no odd withdrawals, or deposits. It was her savings account where the unexplained entries were. The first withdrawal was for a hundred dollars. Then, the monthly withdrawals were a thousand. Mom doesn't use the savings account. Or so she says."

Mabel frowned.

Cyril crossed his arms and leaned back in his chair and continued, "Mom said she had no idea what the withdrawals were for. She showed me her notebook with all her expenses, the date she paid them, and the amount and the number on her cheques. It was when five thousand was withdrawn, Mom said, that was when she got a little worried."

"Well, I would think so." Mabel's feet were now planted firmly on the floor, her back rigid, her eyes narrowed in worry.

"Like I said, I looked back over the last six months. The withdrawals started with a hundred, then climbed to a thousand and then, the five thousand was withdrawn."

"You've seen her furniture; everything is new in her condo."

"I know, but she has the cancelled cheques to show where and what she paid. Even for all that lovely furniture." He grinned. "Can you believe her decorating? Whatever happened to her taste? Pink everything, her condo looks like the inside of a Pepto-Bismol bottle."

"I know it's awful, but she loves it, so that's all that matters."

He lifted an eyebrow. "Right, back to her accounts. As I said, she has cancelled cheques for all her purchases. And the point is she does not have any outstanding debts. She bought her condo when she sold the house."

"And you saw the ledger and the cancelled cheques?"

"Yeah, her little notebook. And the accounting errors, or whatever this is, has all to do with Mom's savings account."

"So, what would be the reason for this weird accounting? Banking error? Or Mom is getting mixed up?" Mabel wrinkled her brow. Mini gambled. Was her mom gambling too. She looked at her brother. Should she say anything about gambling? No, not until she found out for sure.

"I don't know, and I can't stay to sort out this banking issue. I've got a big conference coming up on Tuesday. So, you will have to deal with this accounting problem."

"I'll go to the bank and sort this business with her savings accounts pronto." Mabel crossed her arms. And she would have a long chat with her mother.

"They probably won't tell you a thing because it's Mom's account. You'll have to get Mom to go with you."

"Oh, that will be easy. Not."

"Anyway, like I said, the weirdest thing is, the money has returned. Deposited back into Mom's account in one lump sum. And Mom says she has no idea where the money went or how it all came back."

"First, the money is gone; now it's back. You're right; that is the weirdest part." Maybe her mom was losing it. Or maybe she was gambling. She'd find out. No more secrets, Mom, she vowed.

Chapter Twenty-Two

"What a mess, and I'm the one who has to get rid of this stuff," Violet said, standing with her hands on her hips, surveying her garage. Piles of cardboard boxes from Freda's condo were stacked along the garage wall. "I should never let myself be persuaded to store these boxes," she grumbled. Sighing, Violet picked up two cartons and set them on the steps leading to her house. Perching on a small wooden stool, she put on a pair of rubber gloves and began to rummage through a box, muttering. "Odds and ends, cracked ornaments, old slippers, and VHS tapes. What am I supposed to do with all this stuff?" There were twenty-some boxes to go through. She pulled her phone from her pocket and tapped Mabel's number. If she had to go through this junk, she wasn't going to do it on her own. As she waited for Mabel to pick it up, she opened the other box and took out a paperback book, a Western. She grinned; the carton was crammed full of old cowboy novels.

"Hello." It was Mabel.

"Is this Burger King?"

"I suppose you want fries with your next Thanksgiving dinner?"

Violet chuckled. "I'm starting to go through Freda's junk. Are you coming to help, or is your family staying for a few more days?"

"Cyril and Jessie left at the crack of dawn, and Brian and his family are going to Susan's parents' house in Estevan. Where is Romeo?"

"His name is Neville, and he is out with Alfred; he's taking him hunting."

"You know, Violet, we should take lessons."

"Lessons for what?"

"Shooting lessons in our line of work would come in very handy."

"We do not have a line of work."

"Yes, we do; we are detectives. And we should get guns; we could take lessons and—"

"We are not detectives, for heaven's sake. We bumble around and discover a few clues that does not make us detectives. And certainly not with guns." Violet snorted.

"We don't bumble, we detect."

"Have it your way, but I draw the line at guns. Gun-toting grannie's, what a ridiculous idea."

"We might be grannies, but we could—"

"No guns, and that is final."

"Okay, okay, no guns, it was just an idea. Speaking of guns. Neville can't hunt, can he? He won't have a hunting license."

Violet flipped through the paperback. "No, he's dressed up in one of those tacky orange suits. But he's just an observer, or so they said."

"Alfred has taken quite a shine to your boyfriend."

Violet's lips formed a thin line; she didn't like the term boyfriend. He was a friend. "It is kind of nice Alfred has taken an interest in Neville."

"You mean you're glad he's not underfoot all day."

Violet sighed. If Neville would just stop trying to reorganize her house, things would be fine. She wondered if she should tell Mabel about the trip Neville suggested. A trip to the Nordic countries and Russia. Russia had always been on her bucket list of places to visit. She'd read about the fantastic palaces the Tsars lived in. It would be amazing to see. But Mabel made it clear she wasn't a fan of Neville. So would Mabel want to go if Neville was included? She'd think about that later, first things first. Get Freda's belongings out of her garage. "Regardless, I'd like to have all this stuff of Freda's sorted by the time he comes home."

"I'll be over in a half-hour or so; Brian is outside now, loading up their car."

"As long as you come, I'm not going to be stuck going through all this old stuff by myself. By the way, did you know Freda was a cowboy fan?"

"No, I didn't, why do you ask?"

Violet crammed the book back in the box and set the VHS tapes to the side. "No reason, I guess. You know this is kind of creepy, snooping through her stuff."

"You're not snooping your detecting."

"If you say so."

"I do, and don't forget that woman blackmailed people. That could be the motive for murder."

"You said she never asked for money. Do you think it's blackmailing if you don't ask for money?"

"It's blackmail in my books, and somebody searched her suite; someone was hoping to find something. We need to find what they were looking for."

"Maybe they found it."

"Stop being such a pessimist. I'll be over shortly. My boy is coming to say goodbye; see you soon."

Violet tucked the phone back in her pocket. The books she would donate to the local library. And garbage for the old VHS tapes. She set another box full of Christmas ornaments on the steps next to the carton of western paperbacks. The decorations could go to a church rummage sale.

Violet sorted and piled. The boxes of junk became as high as the boxes for recycling. Old clothes filled most of the boxes, those she would donate to community living, along with the old dishes. What a shame Freda had no family who wanted the dishes; they were in perfect condition. But Alfred said to get rid of all of Freda's things. She stood, stretching her back, looking around at the cardboard boxes she piled near the garage door. At this rate, she'd be done before Mabel even came.

She dropped another box on the floor, sat on the stool beside the box, and opened the lid. More junk, an old cookie jar full of odd buttons, spools of thread in many colours, jammed beside the jar a small wallet. Violet opened the wallet and found a few dollars and credit cards. She set the wallet to one side to give to Alfred. The next box was full of dishtowels and dishcloths. At the bottom of the box, a little black book caught her eye. It looked to be a diary. She opened the small notebook and perused the spidery writing.

"Mabel will be interested in this," Violet said aloud. She took the little book into her house, removed her gloves, and sat on a kitchen chair, reading. The doorbell rang, and Mabel walked in.

"Sitting down on the job, I see. It's hard to get good help," Mabel quipped.

"Sit down. I may have hit the jackpot." Violet held up the little black notepad.

Mabel undid the zipper on her fleece and pulled out a chair. "I'm all ears."

"This is Freda's diary, or you could call it a gossip journal. I just started reading it. That woman was a nasty snoop. Some of these entries go way back. Do you remember the way Mary looked at you at the Fall Supper when you asked her about Freda?"

"I do; she got a little flustered when I asked her if she knew about Freda's scheming."

"This entry, dated September 6, 2010, explains it. I'll read it from her diary. Freda wrote *I have found out how dear Mary won first in the baking contest. Mary is a cheater. I saw her at the bakery in Kegsworthy, she came out of the bakery with a triple-layer cake.*" Violet glanced up from the notebook and added. "Freda has written in brackets. *I see a lot of good homebaking coming my way from Miss Goody Two Shoes.* And she underlined those words."

"Poor Mary, that isn't much of a scandal, but she'd be so embarrassed she would do the baking for that foul woman," Mabel said, sheading off her jacket.

"There are lots of other entries. I won't go into them all. But Ruth, Alfred's wife, is mentioned. Do you want to know why?"

"No, well, maybe, it can't be anything too serious. After all, this is Ruth. What did she do, buy frozen TV dinners and pass them off as her own?"

"Ruth had a boyfriend."

"We all had one at some point. You have one now, for goodness' sake."

Violet pressed her lips. Mabel never got tired of teasing her about Neville. "We never had a boyfriend while we were married. Ruth had her boyfriend five years ago."

"Seriously, Ruth? Who would have thunk it?"

"Freda caught them out at the old bingo hall."

"Eew."

"She has the month and the date and the where. I remember Alfred saying his wife, Ruth, wouldn't have anything to do with his Aunt Freda. So, Freda had a hold over Ruth."

Mabel's eyes brightened. "A motive to kill Freda. Maybe Freda was threatening to tell Alfred. Or Ruth was just tired of having that threat over her head."

"But Ruth, a killer?" Violet wrinkled her brow.

"She's a suspect, we can't rule her out." Mabel leaned forward in her chair. "We don't know where she was the day of Freda's so-called accident, falling down the stairs."

"Helen Graham's name is mentioned too. But it's a silly thing; well, also not nice. Helen kicked a dog."

"Helen kicked a dog? Whose dog?"

"Fred Granger's dog, Pokey," Violet read.

"Oh, no, not little, Pokey. Why would she kick that little white terrier? He is such a friendly little guy."

"I know, hard to believe. But Freda has it written down with the date and everything."

"What did Helen have to do to keep her quiet?"

Violet read the page, then looked up at Mabel. "It doesn't look like Helen had to do anything. Maybe Freda just likes to taunt her."

"Anyway, I doubt Helen offed Freda because of a dog kicking incident."

"This list goes on, more names, but it is all small-minded nasty things. Like parking in a no-parking zone and fender benders. Loads of silly stuff like that. Do you want me to read her list?"

"No, it makes my skin crawl. And if someone did push Freda down the stairs, it's not because of a triple layer cake, double parking or fender benders."

"Right. I'll skip up to when Freda moved into the condo. Aha, Hannah is in here. She's a kleptomaniac, at least; that's what Freda has written down here."

"Mom said she thinks Hannah is light-fingered. I think she might be. I'll tell you about that later. What else has Freda written down in her book of shame?"

"Freda has the date. She caught Hannah stealing and what she took. She has written, *I think Hannah is going to be my new best friend.*"

"So, Freda kept up with her scummy ways. But I don't think old Hannah pushed her down the stairs. Hannah can barely hobble along."

"No, I don't think so either." Violet turned the page, and her eyes widened. "Freda has a new notation and a date. When did Mini die?"

"I don't know. But Mom would. Lend me your phone."

Violet punched in Sophie's number and handed Mabel her phone. Mabel held the phone so Violet could hear her mom, and they waited for Sophie to pick up.

"Hello," Sophie said.

"Mom, it's me, Mabel, and I have a question to ask. When did Mini die?"

"Well, that is a great way to greet your mother."

Mabel looked at Violet and shook her head. "I'm sorry, Mom, But Violet and I are trying to solve Mini's unexpected death for you. So it would be a great help if you could just give me the date."

"Oh, I see. It was September tenth."

"You're sure?"

"Of course, I'm sure. She was my friend. Do you have any information?"

Violet shook her head at Mabel.

"No, not yet. But knowing the date will help. I've got to go. I'll pop over and visit soon. I have lots to talk to you about."

"Okay, dear, Homer has just come by. I'll say hello for you,"

Mabel handed Violet back her phone. "Homer visiting Mom. You just never know, do you? Homer is the last person I would have ever thought Mom would strike up a friendship with."

"I'm more interested in the date Mini died. Your mom said September tenth." Violet smiled. "The date fits; Freda has written September 10. And beside it, she has written. *I'm in the money now, no more penny anti crap. I've hit the big time. I saw her block the stairway door and jam the elevator door open.*" Violet glanced up at Mabel. "Your mom was right. The elevator was blocked when she tried to use it." Violet turned the page, then flipped back.

"Go on, who? Who?"

"She doesn't say."

Mabel sat back and sighed. "Darn it, why didn't she put the name?"

"Hold on." Violet turned the page. "Freda has another entry. It reads, *My cell phone has picked up everything, including her going into Mini's suite. I'm going to enjoy how she tries to explain this.*" Violet looked with excitement at Mabel. "A mobile phone with pictures, or maybe even a video."

"But still no name."

"Nope, but the evidence we need is on the phone."

Mabel jumped up from her chair. "Right, we search those boxes. I didn't see one when we cleaned out her place. You'd think one of us would have seen it.

"Maybe it got scooped up with a load of junk. We didn't see this book either. Come on."

Chapter Twenty-Three

"At least we got the rest of Freda's stuff sorted," Violet said, pulling off her rubber gloves.

"We've double-checked every box, and we've come up empty-handed. We could have been a lot faster if we didn't have to sort that junk," Mabel complained as she washed her hands at the kitchen sink.

"Never mind, it's done. Do you want a cup of tea?" Violet waited until Mabel dried her hands and filled her kettle with water.

"I'd love one; I'm parched," Mabel said, slumping on a kitchen chair.

Violet turned the burner on under her kettle and opened and shut a cupboard door. "Maybe Neville has the cell phone and has forgotten to tell us."

"Why don't you go to his bedroom, or whatever room he sleeps in, and take a look."

Violet took china cups and saucers from her cupboard and placed them on her table. She gave Mabel an amused look. "Subtlety isn't your long suit. Why don't you just come out and ask me if I'm sleeping with Neville?"

Mabel shrugged and said, "It's none of my business."

"Right, it isn't. But to settle your curiosity. Neville is sleeping in the guest room at the end of the hallway."

Mabel raised an eyebrow and grinned.

Violet folded her arms across her chest. "You can darn well stop your surmising right now."

"I wasn't. Okay, maybe a little. Regardless, go and search Neville's room."

"I will not. He's a guest in my house. That would be downright rude," Violet said, opening and closing cupboard doors.

"Okay, I'll do it for you." Mabel jumped up from her chair.

"No, you will not. I will not condone you poking around in Neville's room." Violet gave Mabel a stern look, then turned back to her cupboards, opening two more cupboard doors and then closing them. An irritated frown appeared on her face.

"Okay, what if I went to use your washroom and I got lost? I could be misdirected and wander into his room accidentally."

"And accidentally search his room? We are going to wait until Neville gets back and then ask him if he has the phone." Violet opened another cupboard door and then slammed the door shut. "And ask him where the heck he put my teapot. That man has no business moving things in my kitchen."

"What if he denies it and lies?"

"Why would he lie about where he put my teapot?"

"Not your teapot, the phone. What if Neville lies about having Freda's phone?"

"Get real, why would Neville lie about the phone." Violet cupped her chin and tapped her lips with her index finger, staring at her cupboard doors.

"Because it would be a free phone. Instead of racking up charges on his phone, Neville might be using the phone to call home to England."

"You're way too suspicious."

"And you are way too trusting. What do you know about Neville? How long has he been here? He's like the man who came to dinner."

"Who came to dinner?" Violet opened and shut another cupboard door, looking puzzled.

"*The Man Who Came to Dinner*. With Monty, somebody. It's a movie, an old movie."

"An old movie. What does that have to do with the missing phone? Or my teapot, come to that?"

"Nothing; I'm sorry I brought it up."

Violet took her phone out of her pocket and tapped on the screen. "I'm going to ask Neville what the heck he's done with my favourite teapot."

"I thought he was out with Alfred?"

"Yes, he is. He's got his phone with him, so there, I hope that settles your suspicions. And you know you should have your phone with you too."

"Why would I bring my phone? I was only coming here."

"What if I wanted to tell you something?" Violet asked as she went into her dining room.

"Like what?"

"I don't know, but if I did?"

"What would be so important you couldn't wait? It only takes a few minutes for me to get here. Back in the day, we didn't carry a phone everywhere."

Violet tapped her foot as she waited. Neville didn't pick up. She pocketed her phone and marched into her dining room. "One day, you'll be happy you have a cell phone. That is if you ever bothered to carry it with you," she called from her dining room.

"Forget about my phone. The point is that Neville is taking advantage of your good nature. What do you know about the man? Has he told you anything about his life back in England?"

"It's rude to pry. Ah-ha," Violet called. She came back into the kitchen and triumphantly held up her teapot. "Neville put it in my china cabinet."

"You mean you haven't found out anything about him? What do you talk about? He's been here forever. There is politeness, and then there is foolishness. I've always thought you were very rash to invite a strange man you meant on holiday to your home."

"It hasn't been forever, and we do find things to talk about." And they did talk. They talked about taking a trip together. Violet turned her back to Mabel, rinsing out her teapot with hot water. "I'm not going to give Neville the third degree. What is it with you? Do you think he is some kind of international criminal on the run?"

"No, but he might be a con man after your money."

Violet laughed. "Money, me? I'm not a wealthy widow. You're silly." She put two tea bags in her teapot and poured hot water from her kettle into the pot.

"Am I really? Men take advantage of lonely women all the time."

Violet put a yellow-flowered tea cozy over the teapot. "I'm not a lonely woman," she said, setting the pot on a matching trivet.

"I searched for him on the internet, and I couldn't find hide nor hair of him, isn't that strange?"

"Strange?" Violet scoffed. "Unless he is famous or some kind of crook, you wouldn't find him on Google. So, your strangeness has just proved that Neville is just Neville. He's not some English con artist here to take advantage of an innocent colonial." She set a yellow-flowered cream pitcher and a matching sugar bowl on the table. Now definitely wasn't the time to tell Mabel about Neville and Russia.

"Has Neville ever asked you about your finances?"

"What is it with you and finances? I'm not an idiot, for goodness' sake." Violet placed two white embossed cloth napkins beside each teacup. "I'd certainly would know if he was trying to withdraw money out of my account. I've never lent him my bank card, nor has he asked for it."

"Violet, you've hit the nail on the head."

Violet poured tea into a china cup. Relieved, they had finally gotten off the subject of Neville. "Glad to hear it. Now drink your tea."

"The motive, it's the motive. I think Gemma was ripping Mini off. And Mini found out, and Gemma killed her."

Chapter Twenty-Four

"Gemma ripped off Mini? How do you come by this wild theory?" Violet went to her cupboard and opened a drawer. And took out two teaspoons and returned to the table.

Mabel took a teaspoon and added sugar to her tea. "It's not wild. Let me tell you about Mom. And I've got a bone to pick with my mother."

"You're confusing me. What has any of this got to do with your mom?"

"I'll explain. Last night, Cyril informed me Mom has been keeping secrets from me." Mabel huffed, stirring her tea.

Violet arched an eyebrow. "Secrets, really?"

"Yes. There have been a bunch of irregularities with her bank account. And she didn't tell me anything about it."

"Irregularities?"

"Like, thousands of dollars' worth of irregularities."

Violet's eyes widened. "Oh my gosh, thousands of dollars. How did this happen?"

"The money was withdrawn from her savings account in drips and drabs. From what Cyril said, it had been going on for months. But Mom apparently didn't get worried until a lump sum of five thousand was withdrawn."

"I would think so."

"But get this, strangely, all of a sudden, all the money, every last dollar, was deposited back into her account. And in one lump sum."

"That is peculiar. What is your mom doing, playing the stock market? Or God forbid gambling?"

"Mom and the stock market? No, but gambling has crossed my mind. I don't think she has. But how would I know? Mom never tells me anything." Mabel's eyes narrowed, and she continued. "But Mom confides in Cyril. She told my brother the whole story. He's an accountant, you know." Mabel snorted and pursed her lips.

"This is very strange. Are you sure your mom just didn't forget?"

"Mom swore to Cyril she didn't withdraw the money."

"Your mom swears you don't visit her, and you do. So, maybe she did forget."

"Mom is playing a silly game. She is as right as rain."

Violet gave Mabel a sidelong glance and rolled her eyes. "So, this money withdrawn was then suddenly redeposited. And your mom doesn't know why?"

"Yes." Mabel took a sip of tea and then set her teacup down. "Did you change tea brands? This tea tastes different. Good, but different."

Violet sighed. "Neville helped with the shopping."

"It's nice, but I like your brand better."

Violet brightened.

"Anyway, back to the money, I'm sure it is somehow connected to Gemma. I think that woman got access to Mom's account. And took the money."

"Whoa, that's a stretch."

"Why do you think it's a stretch? That woman is always hanging around. Mom told me she drives residents from the condo to their appointments. And even gets their mail for them. She could have spied on them when they used their bank cards."

"You can't steal five thousand dollars with a bank card?"

"Maybe not, but I don't trust her. What if she is stealing from the people she is supposedly helping? What if she stole from Mini, and Mini found out? And Gemma killed her?"

"I still think this theory of yours is a big leap."

"It is not. Mom was missing money, and she didn't know where the money went?"

"For one thing, you're jealous of Gemma; it's fogging your reason. Just because someone is nice to old people, that doesn't mean they are a crook. And the money is back. I know you don't want to think this, but your mother could have gotten confused. She withdrew the money, then redeposited it, and just can't remember doing it."

Mabel swished the tea in her teacup and looked across the table at her friend. "Okay, I admit I'm a wee bit jealous of the fuss Mom makes over Gemma. And I can't explain the in, and the out money. But I will get to the bottom of this money business. I'll take Mom down to the bank, then we'll know for sure what went on."

"Good."

"Now, back to Freda's little black book. We now know Mom was right. Someone jammed the elevator and blocked the stairway door. And why would someone do that if they weren't up to no good? And from her notation in her little black book, Freda took pictures or a video."

"Agreed."

"And Freda wrote 'her' in the notebook, not 'he.' So, a woman blocked the elevator and the door, so we know the killer is a woman."

"Right." Violet opened the little black book and read, "*I'm going to enjoy how she tries to explain this.*"

"My guess is, Gemma."

Violet closed the notebook and gave her a sidelong glance. "Evidence, dear, evidence. Remember Ruth? She had a motive. Just because you don't like Gemma, it's not a reason to—"

"Okay, I might be wrong. I agree; the woman could be Ruth or even Jody. Jody said she found Freda, but maybe she pushed her. Mind you, after she found Freda. She was shaken up like she was in shock." Mabel topped up her cup with tea.

"Jody may well have been in shock. The woman is a home care worker; it would not be easy to kill someone. It's not like a hitman in the movies. And she does have access to the condo. Either a resident lets her in, or she has a key."

"Gemma might also have a key. Mom said Gemma was her key holder."

"Yes, but Judith would have taken Mini's key back. They have the condo on the market. They would have to have the keys."

"Yes, but I bet some trusting soul has given her one."

"Maybe, but we don't know if she has. Jody is certainly strong enough to do the deed, but so is Ruth." Violet paused, wrinkled her forehead, and passed Mabel the sugar bowl. "Then, of course, so is Gemma. Anyway, one wouldn't have to be a strong man to push someone off balance down the stairs. Especially if the victim is elderly."

"You're right. But you agree, both deaths are suspicious."

"I do, Freda's notebook tells us that." Violet tapped her fingers on the little black book. "So, what's our next move?" She spun the notebook around on the table.

"Well, since you won't let me search Neville's room. We wait until he comes home and hope he has that phone. Notice I didn't make a crack about Neville." Leaning back in her chair, Mabel grinned.

"I noticed." Violet rose, taking the little black book with her to her cupboard. "I'll put this book somewhere safe. I guess we're not going to show it to Constable Robert until we get the pictures off Freda's phone."

"Right, I don't think Freda's gossip log is enough proof. Don't forget, Randy, the rat, our wonderful coroner. Declared Mini's death as natural. His version will carry more weight than ours. We need that phone."

Violet opened a drawer and slipped the book under some dishcloths.

"Your dishcloth drawer. Do you think the book will be safe there?"

"Why would anyone come here to look for it? Even if they did, whoever searched Freda's place didn't look in her tea towel drawer. I didn't even see the book when I cleaned out her kitchen."

Chapter Twenty-Five

Violet felt the crunch of the dry leaves underfoot as she walked alongside Mabel on their way to the senior's condos. There was a bite to the frosty air.

"Do you still have Freda's keys?" Mabel asked.

"Last night, I gave the keys and some things I thought the family might like to Alfred when he brought Neville home."

"Does Neville have the phone?"

"I asked him, and he said no."

"Hum."

"Then I did something I'm kind of ashamed to admit."

"You searched Neville's room," Mabel guessed.

"Yes, I'm ashamed to admit I did. I waited until Neville left this morning, and then I searched his room."

"Oh, wonderful, I'm so proud of you." Mabel grinned happily up at her friend.

"You certainly are taking a lot of enjoyment from my dishonesty."

"You're not dishonest; you're just snoopy."

"How come I'm snoopy when I search, and when you do it, you call it investigating?"

"Snooping or investigating, did you find the phone?"

"No, sorry, and I investigated high and low. Freda's phone is not in his possession." Violet tugged up the collar of her coat. A stiff breeze was blowing.

"Darn, so where is dear Neville today?"

"His buddy Alfred is taking him to an archery compound. Apparently, Neville is a crack shot with a bow. Suppose that's what you call it when you shoot arrows. Poor Neville told me he tried to shoot Alfred's rifle and darn near shot Alfred's truck."

"He shot Alfred's Truck." Mabel giggled.

"No, almost. I think the bullet pinged the antenna. Anyway, Neville is determined to redeem himself with his expertise with a bow. He belongs to an archery club back in England."

"Neville and Alfred have really hit it off, haven't they?" Mabel increased her steps to keep up with her friend's long stride.

"I'm just glad he's finding stuff to do. As you know, he rearranged my pots and pans, then moved my teapot. This will keep him busy." Violet picked up her pace. She was feeling guilty. Last night, she and Neville had poured over online travel brochures for Russia. She should tell Mabel.

"Would you slow down? I'm not jogging to Gravenhurst Manor, for goodness' sake."

"Sorry." Violet slowed.

"So, when is Neville leaving?"

"I never said he was leaving."

"It's quite obvious he has worn out his welcome. When are you going to serve him his walking papers?"

"No, he's fine. He likes to organize things, is all. It's a minor irritation." Violet increased her stride. She needed to tell Mabel about the trip. Should she tell Mabel now?

"It didn't seem minor when you were talking about it," Mabel said, rushing to keep up.

"Neville is really a good houseguest. He cleans up after himself and does his own laundry. He's okay, other than his reorganizing tendencies."

"I'm sorry. I think Neville is a moocher, or a con man, or both. You're too darn nice."

Violet decided to wait. She had to change Mabel's opinion of Neville, or she'd never go on the trip. Then, of course, there was Mabel's mother. Would Mabel even want to go? They needed to solve these unexplained deaths before she broached the Russia plan to her. "Forget about Neville. We have a mystery to solve."

"Okay, you're a big girl. I guess you know what you are doing."

"Good, let's get back to Freda," Violet said, relieved. "It stands to reason whoever pushed Freda down the stairs took the phone. That is if someone pushed her."

"Please stop saying that. We know for sure Freda was planning some kind of blackmail. She had pictures or a video on her phone. I bet she confronted the killer and boom, the killer pushed her down the stairs. And Freda wrote the words she and her. So, the killer is a woman."

"Yes, we've already decided it was a woman, but who?"

"My money is still on Gemma."

"We had this discussion yesterday. No jumping to conclusions as to who done it. Just because you dislike Gemma, it doesn't make her a killer."

"Maybe not. And I don't think whoever pushed her has the phone. Someone searched her room. My money is on the killer."

Chapter Twenty-Six

As they walked up the driveway to the Gravenhurst Manor. A stiff wind picked up, swirling the dead leaves around in an eddy, and Mabel hunched into her red fleece. "I can't wait to have this little chat with my mom. Imagine! She never even mentioned it to me. Oh, no, she has to wait until the golden boy comes home," Mabel huffed.

"I think you're more upset your mom confided to your brother than you are about the money."

"I am not," Mabel hotly denied.

Violet looked at Mabel and raised her eyebrows. "You're not going to argue with your mom about why she told Cyril and not you, are you?"

"No, of course not."

"Promise."

"I'm not jealous." Mabel opened the door to the condo and paused in the doorway. "Okay, maybe a little," she admitted. "I guess the main thing is, someone has access to her accounts. Or the bank screwed up royally."

"Good." Violet smiled approvingly.

Three black ravens swooped off the portico's roof, startling the women.

Ravens, weren't they an omen of danger? Or was it death? Mabel shivered, opened the door, and pressed the intercom button. "Hi, Mom, it's Violet and me."

"Violet and who?" her mother replied.

"Ha ha, very funny, open the door."

The door buzzed open, and they entered the foyer. Mabel looked across into the lounge. Tables were set up in rows; at one end near the kitchen, there was a tall table with a microphone and a large plastic globe full of bingo balls.

"Oh, oh, we might have picked the wrong day," Violet said.

The elevator doors opened, and a tall, gaunt man with a droopy mustache came out; he smiled and nodded. Trailing behind the man was a small tubby woman wearing black tights and a blouse with bright red poppies. "Hurry up, Jimmy," the woman said, hurrying past Mabel and Violet. The man smiled again and followed the tubby poppy woman into the lounge. Mabel stepped into the elevator, then stepped back.

Homer elbowed his way out and grunted.

"Hello, Homer." Mabel made room for him to pass. He grunted again, thumping past with his walker, following the thin man and tubby woman into the lounge.

Mabel stepped back into the elevator. "That man could do with a personality transplant," she muttered as the elevator doors closed.

Violet pushed the button for the second floor. "He's probably in pain, and pain makes people cranky."

"I guess, but I personally think the man was born a curmudgeon."

The doors opened on the second floor, and Sophie rushed into the elevator before they could exit. Sophie gave Mabel and Violet a peck on the cheek. "You're just in time; it's bingo today. What fun, you can join me." She jabbed at the elevator button. "We need to get down there before all the good cards are gone."

"Good cards?"

"Of course, dear, some cards are luckier than others. Get your money out, only fifty cents a card, or three cards for a dollar. I always play twelve cards. It's for charity, so don't be a piker." Sophie tapped her foot impatiently as the elevator descended to the lobby.

"We can come back another time," suggested Mabel.

"Nonsense, dear, it's great fun. You might be lucky; it's cash prices, you know."

Mabel and Violet gave each other a helpless look as they rode down the elevator. When the elevator stopped at the main floor, Sophie surged out. Mabel slowly followed. Her mother was very keen to play bingo. Was her mother a secret gambler?

"You play for money?" asked Violet.

"Yes, dear, you could win five, ten, or even twenty dollars." Sophie tugged on Violet's arm.

"We don't have bingo markers. Maybe we should come back another time." Violet stopped in the doorway.

"Don't worry, dear; you can buy bingo cards and markers from Helen; come along, you two. You'll enjoy it."

Mabel shrugged and reluctantly stood in line. Her friend Helen was at a small table, taking the money for the bingo cards. The last thing she wanted to do was play bingo, but she needed to ask her mother about the money in her savings account. So, she'd stick it out until the games were over. The line came to a standstill. A blue-haired woman wearing a lilac pantsuit was sorting through the pile of bingo cards.

"What is taking her so long?" Mabel whispered to her mother.

Sophie tapped her toe on the floor and then shifted impatiently. "That's 'Lucky Sally Raybould.' She wins a lot; she knows which cards to pick."

Mabel gave Violet a sidelong glance and grinned. No wonder Sally was lucky. The blue-haired woman left with a fistful of bingo cards.

Helen Graham looked up at Violet and Mabel in surprise. "You're here for bingo? I've never seen you here before." She smiled at Mabel. "But it's nice you are here with your mom."

"It's our first time," Mabel said, recalling the dog kicking incident. She paid Helen for the bingo cards and markers. She suspected Freda's take on the incident was flawed. Why would Helen kick a harmless little dog like Pokey? "Maybe one of us will be lucky," she added cheerfully.

Leading Mabel and Violet to a table near the fireplace, Sophie scoffed, "I doubt you'll be lucky. You only bought six cards each."

Mabel took her place at the table. Looking at her cards, she wrinkled her forehead. "How you can play more cards and keep track of the numbers called is beyond me."

"I think six is enough for me too," Violet said, setting her cards in a straight row.

"You do have to be sharp; I grant you that." Sophie spread her cards on the table. "But Gemma doesn't call fast, not like some."

Mabel pursed her lips and looked across the room at the bingo caller's table. Ah, the wonderful Gemma. Gemma stood at the table, her well-manicured hands turning the handle on a clear plastic drum. The bingo balls began to spin.

"Is everyone ready?" Gemma called out.

There was a chorus of yeses and enthusiastic applause.

Gemma smiled. "We will start with four corners." A bingo ball popped out of the spout of the spinner. She held it up and called. "B 6." She paused and called the number again, then placed it into a small hole in the large mechanical bingo board on the table beside her. Gemma waited patiently as the bingo crowd searched their cards for the number called.

"Bingo," shouted Homer.

The bingo players laughed.

"Homer, behave yourself," Gemma scolded, with a smile on her face.

Sophie chuckled. "Homer is such a comical man."

"Since when?" Muttered Mabel, placing a coloured marker on the B 6 number on her card.

"That's not a corner, dear," Sophie corrected.

Violet grinned, placing her plastic marker on the B 6 in the corner of her bingo card.

Mabel sighed. It was going to be a long afternoon.

A loud, shrill cry, followed by a thump and a heavy thud. The sound came from outside of the lounge.

Chapter Twenty-Seven

Mabel's eyes darted to the lobby.

Some of the bingo players glanced up, while others concentrated on their cards.

The thud was followed by a loud scream, then silence.

"What the heck?" Violet stood.

Gemma dashed from her bingo table to the lobby, followed by Mabel and Violet.

Gemma paused in the lobby, looking around. She went to the front door. "No one is here," she said.

"It sounded like someone fell," Charlie Sweeny said from behind Mabel.

"You're right." Gemma hurried over to the stairway door and opened it. "Oh, no," she gasped, her face ashen.

Mabel pushed past Gemma and entered the stairwell. Hannah Huston lay on the stairs, her eyes wide open, her mouth in a silent scream. Mabel knelt and felt for a sign of life. There was none.

Violet tugged on Mabel's shoulder. "Come on, there is nothing we can do for her." She ushered Mabel out and closed the door behind her. Taking her phone from her pocket, she dialled 911. Violet spoke on her phone in a hushed voice and walked to the entrance.

The elevator door opened, and Farley, with his canvas tool bag slung over his shoulder, stepped out. "What's going on? What's all the excitement?" he asked, looking at the bingo players gathered behind Mabel.

Mabel turned from the door to face Farley and the curious crowd of seniors. "There has been an accident," she said.

"Move people, move," Gemma said, her arms flapping as if she was shooing chickens. "Back into the lounge."

The bingo players muttered to each other and edged closer to Mabel and the stairwell door.

Gemma tapped on the handyman's shoulder. "Come along, you too, Farley."

Ignoring Gemma, Farley strode toward the stairway door. Mabel stepped in front of the door and folded her arms. Farley's eyes narrowed. He dropped his tool kit to the floor, crossed his arms, and stared a mutinous stare back at her.

"Did someone fall? Is someone hurt?" asked Charlie Sweeny's wife, Linda.

"Who fell?" Sally, the blue-haired woman, scurried up beside Linda.

"Who is it?" Mabel's mother asked from beside her shoulder.

"It's Hannah. She's fallen. Come with me, my dear." Gemma put her arm around Sophie. Sophie shrugged off Gemma and looked curiously at the door.

"Fallen down the stairs? Hannah?" Charlie asked.

"Yes, yes, down the stairs. Come along, there is nothing to see here; go back to the lounge," Gemma urged, making more shooing motions. No one budged.

"Hannah fell down the stairs! What the hell?" muttered Homer.

"What the hell?" echoed a scrawny little man.

"Is she hurt?" asked Jimmy, the droopy mustache man.

"Of course, she's hurt; the woman fell down the stairs," Charlie stormed.

One of the bingo players crowded in front of Mabel reached for the door handle to the stairway. Mabel slapped the tall man's hand.

Withdrawing his hand, the man glared at Mabel and said, "Someone should do something."

"Someone is. Violet is calling an ambulance," assured Mabel.

A large woman in a bright green sweater wormed her way to the front of the collection of seniors. "Has anyone called an ambulance?" she asked. "Someone should call an ambulance."

"I just said Violet is calling for an ambulance." Mabel raised her eyebrows.

"Yes, everything is well in hand; back to the lounge. You all know that Hannah fell down the stairs. There is no need to stand about out here." Gemma exhaled noisily through pursed lips and grabbed Charlie by the arm.

"I can't believe Hannah fell down these stairs?" Charlie shook off her hand.

"We should take a look," demanded Farley.

"I forbid you." Gemma's voice rose an octave.

"Who made you, king?" Farley snapped.

"She's a woman, not a man," the poppy blouse woman interjected.

"What the hell does that mean?" growled Farley.

"You mean who made you queen," she explained.

"Who the hell cares, king or queen?" Charlie intervened.

Violet pocketed her phone. "I called the emergency number, and they're sending someone out."

"People, people listen to me. Everything is being taken care of. Please, everyone, get back to the lounge," Gemma urged, her voice shrill.

The bingo players ignored her.

"Get out of the way, woman," Farley said, nose to nose with Mabel.

Maintaining her place in front of the stairway door, Mabel looked at the man over her granny glasses. "No, I will not; you are not going in there to gape at poor Hannah."

"Why not?" snarled Farley. "I can help her."

"No, you can't."

"Why not?"

"Because Hannah is dead," Mabel said bluntly.

"Dead? Oh my god," wailed Helen.

"Poor dear Hannah," exclaimed the tubby woman.

Gemma shook her head, "Really, Mabel? Did you have to tell them?"

"When the paramedics get here, everyone will know," defended Mabel.

Gemma raised her hands. "Please, everyone—"

"Oh, my gosh, just like Freda," interrupted Linda. "Charlie, did you hear that?"

"First Freda and now Hannah. What kind of place have we moved into?" thundered Charlie.

"Oh, no, poor Hannah," gasped Sophie.

"Are you sure? How do you know Hannah is dead? Someone should be with her," demanded a short, squat woman with a pinched face.

"I'm a retired nurse, and I assure you Hannah is dead," Mabel said forcefully, feeling guilty for leaving Hannah alone in the stairwell.

"I want to go sit with Hannah. This is absolutely shameful to leave her behind closed doors all alone," insisted the pinched-faced woman.

Gemma stamped her foot and shouted. "Would you people listen to me?"

The mumbling amongst the bingo players ceased, and heads swivelled. They looked at Gemma in surprise.

Gemma, her face red, lowered her voice and said, "You are not doing any good out here; soon, the paramedics will be here. We mustn't get in their way."

"We need to call a meeting; let's go to the lounge. The building inspector needs to be called," expounded Charlie. "Those stairs are a death trap. Two deaths in what, a month? We should sue."

Gemma's lips turned down in a sulk as the seniors returned to the lounge. "They listen to Charlie and his ridiculous lawsuit but not me," she mumbled.

"Lawsuits?" Farley picked up his tool bag and marched out the front door.

"Don't worry, it won't come to that," Gemma called as the door swung shut. "And besides, you're just a janitor," she said to the closed door.

"Are we going to play bingo?" Sally, the blue-haired woman, asked.

Sighing, Gemma followed Sally into the lounge, where the seniors were gathered around Charlie. Violet and Mabel remained in the lobby.

"What do you think?" Violet asked in a hushed tone. "I think this is a suspicious accident."

"Yes, it's suspicious. Two people have died on these stairs. I heard a cry, a thump, then a scream. Hannah did not fall down the stairs. She was pushed, just like Freda." Mabel paced back and forth in the lobby. "I am so angry I could scream. There is a lunatic running around here killing off seniors."

"Calm down, for goodness' sake," urged Violet.

"Calm down? In all the history of being told to calm down. Has anyone ever calmed down?" fumed Mabel.

"At least keep your voice down," cautioned Violet, glancing at the lounge.

Mabel stopped pacing and dropped her voice. "Why didn't Hannah take the elevator? She even hobbled on a flat floor. Why on earth would she attempt the stairs?"

Violet whispered, "I know, I know, it's suspicious, but we have no proof the fall was anything more than a tragic accident. And if Hannah's death is not an accident, it does rule out one suspect. We are your prime suspect's alibi."

The sound of Homer thumping his way across the floor from the lounge brought their conversation to a standstill.

He came to a stop beside Mabel. She smelled garlic on his breath. She stepped back, ready for a rude remark on his part.

"It weren't an accident. I can tell you that much." He looked at Mabel with his red, rheumy eyes.

Mabel held her breath and took a step toward him. "What do you mean?"

"You fool woman. Hannah. It weren't no accident. What do you think I mean? Has anyone else fallen down the steps today?" snorted Homer.

"Homer, Homer," Gemma called from the doorway of the lounge. "Come away from there; come back to the lounge; there's a good fellow."

"I'm not a dog," snarled Homer.

Gemma hurried to his side. "Oh, my dear Homer, you are such a funny little man; of course, you're not. But the ambulance will be here shortly. You mustn't get in the way. You too, ladies, come along."

"I'm not a funny little man," Homer snapped, thumping his way back to the lounge.

Mabel planted her feet and crossed her arms. "Don't worry about us. We'll wait here for the paramedics."

VIOLET HELD OPEN THE condo door as the firemen and a paramedic carrying a medical kit filed past.

Mabel opened the stairway door. "In here," she said.

Moments later, Gemma's brother, a tall man with curly auburn hair, came panting in behind them. "I was at work,"

Paul puffed. "Someone should've stopped to pick me up." The freckle-faced man stormed into the stairwell.

Before the door closed, Mabel heard one of the men growl. "You got the alert; drive yourself, man. It's vital we get here as fast as we can."

Mabel exchanged a look with Violet as they retreated to the lounge doorway. In this case, speed wasn't vital at all. Hannah was dead.

"It's a disgrace." A tall, thin reed of a man stood and pounded his fist on a table. Bingo cards fluttered to the floor.

"George, what exactly do you mean a disgrace?" Linda Sweeny asked. The tall, willowy, white-haired woman knelt to pick up the bingo cards from the floor; sitting at the table, she stacked them.

Charlie sat beside his wife. "He means Hannah, falling down those stairs. First, Freda fell, and now Hannah. Like I said before, those stairs are a death trap. The building inspector should be called."

"And the manager should get over here right now. Something has to be done before some other poor soul trips on these infernal stairs and dies." The reedy man, George, pounded his fist on the table again.

Linda placed her thin blue vein hand over the bingo cards as they fluttered on the table. A round of applause followed his announcement.

"What about bingo? Aren't we going to play?" Blue-haired Sally Raybould asked again as she arranged her bingo cards. Bingo chips were in her hand.

"Please put your bingo cards to the side for a moment," Gemma's sharp voice over-road the hubbub of arguments that followed Sally's request for bingo. "I think George is right. Those stairs are a safety issue."

"You think? There is no doubt about it. There is something very wrong with the way those stairs are constructed," spoke up Charlie.

"I'll put in a request for the manager to come," offered Gemma.

"A request?" sputtered George. "No, a demand."

There was agreement throughout the room.

Paul, Gemma's brother, came into the room. "I heard what this gentleman said." He nodded to George. "There is something about those stairs. Maybe the step distances are not even. The building inspector must have missed it. Whatever the reason, those stairs are dangerous. So, everyone, please avoid those stairs."

"It weren't no accident," Homer muttered loud enough for Mabel to hear.

Chapter Twenty-Eight

The large crowd of people returning from the graveyard where they had laid Hannah Huston to rest crowded into the church hall. Mabel held the door open for her mother. The church hall attached to the church had long, curtainless windows. Sunlight streamed in, highlighting the children's pictures tacked on the white walls. The pictures, painted in bright primary colours, depicted scenes from the bible. At the room's far end hung a large brass cross. Above the cross, a blue banner with instructions in gold lettering advises believers to remember to be thankful for God's blessing.

Mabel and her mother enter behind two women who were disagreeing about flowers left at the graveside. "A waste of money," the tall, smartly dressed woman murmured.

"A sign of respect," defended the other woman, who came up to the shoulders of the smartly dressed woman.

Mabel edged by, ushering her mother past the two long tables laden with trays of sandwiches, dishes of pickles, and large fruit platters. And plates of homemade cakes, cookies, and muffins.

"Everyone." The minister tapped with a spoon on a water glass to get everyone's attention. "Please take a seat at a table," he requested. "We will say grace before going to the food tables."

Sophie scooted toward a table near the kitchen. Mabel clutched her mother's elbow. "let's go sit with Homer. You and Homer are friends, right?" If she could stop herself feuding with the old goat, maybe she could find out about his odd comment about Hannah and the stairs.

Sophie tilted her head and gave Mabel a broad smile as they neared Homer's table. "Yes, I am, dear. Homer's bark is worse than his bite. He's really a tender-hearted soul."

Tender-hearted? Mabel doubted that, but Homer might have information. The women paused as a woman with a tray full of sandwiches hurried out of the kitchen, placing it on the food table.

Sophie took the only empty chair at the end of the table. She looked up at her daughter. "Where are you going to sit, dear?"

"Don't worry about me." Mabel quickly darted to a nearby table and grabbed a chair. Dodging around people lining up for places at the tables, she dragged it back to where her mother and Homer were sitting. Pushing her way in next to Homer, she plunked down the chair and grinned at him. "How are..." She stopped, remembering that he hated anyone enquiring how he was. "How is your nephew, Pete." Pete's knee had been broken by a thug one summer and had never mended properly.

"Better," Homer said. "I gave him my old house; it's a darn nice house; I wish I still had it. This damn condo is jinxed."

Before Mabel could reply or ask any questions, the Minister took up a position by the food table. He instructed everyone to bow their heads in prayer. Mabel stood fidgeting. The minister's prayer was long and rambling, and as soon as he pronounced amen, the rush to the food table began. Mabel followed Homer, remembering not to offer any help. The last time she did, she ended up wearing a salmon sandwich.

Sophie sat at the end of the table, daintily eating a sandwich she'd broken in half. Mabel returned to the table, squeezing in between Homer and a large, muscley woman with a silk shawl over her bare shoulders. The woman introduced herself as Gwen Horseman; her plate was filled with an assortment of dainties and one lone pickle.

Mabel felt squished; Homer's stooped shoulders rubbed against hers. She was sure he knew something about Hannah's so-called accident. She gingerly reached for a sandwich on her plate. "So, you think the condo is jinxed?"

"Jinxed? You think Gravenhurst Manor is jinxed?" Gwen grinned; her polka-dot shawl slipped down her arms, revealing a colourful tattoo of a bird in the grasp of a snake. Or was it a snake in the grip of a bird? Mabel averted her eyes.

"Homer suggested that not me." Mabel took a bite from her sandwich, her elbows clamped to her side.

"Why do you think it is jinxed, Mr. Murphy?" Gwen tugged on the strap of her bright yellow sundress and smiled at Homer. She picked up a large piece of chocolate cake. Licking the icing off, she popped the rest into her mouth.

"Because people die like flies there." Homer's response was muffled by the sandwich he had stuffed into his mouth.

Alice Woodstock, sitting next to Gwen, shook her head. Her frizzy orange hair poked out from under her large green felt hat. "Their old people, sorry to say that so bluntly, Homer, but it's true. Old people die."

"You're a barrel of cheer," Mabel said, carefully snaking her arm out to grasp her Styrofoam cup.

Sitting across the table, a man in an ill-fitting navy blue suit remarked, "It's a funeral; one is hardly expected to be cheerful at a funeral."

"What a life Hannah had. After her husband left her, the poor woman lived all by herself." Gwen selected another dainty from her plate. Licking the icing off the cake, she shoved it into her mouth.

"I know; look at the head table with the family; I would be hard-pressed to put a name to any of them. I bet they never came to visit poor old Hannah," agreed Alice.

"That's the trouble with funerals. They don't come to your birthday party, but they show up for your funeral," mumbled Homer.

"Hannah and Tom lived on the farm next to mine for many years. I don't think Hannah was lonely. I used to see her and Freda Jilvontee downtown together; I think they were good friends," said the blue-suited man, stirring his coffee with a brown plastic stir stick.

Alice smirked at the man and shook her head, her bonnet shifted on her head, tilting to sit at a jaunty angle.

Homer snorted and chomped down on a slice of hard cheese. A piece of the cheese flew up into his cup; he stuck his index finger in the Styrofoam cup, fished it out, and popped it into his mouth.

Mabel looked at Homer out of the corner of her eye. Did Homer know about Freda's blackmailing ways?

"And Hannah's passing is a blessing," Alice pompously said, rearranging her hat.

"Death a blessing? Are you nuts? The woman fell down the stairs," Homer snarled, licking his finger off. "How is falling down the stairs a blessing?"

"The funeral card said Hannah was 87. Who wants to live to be that old?" Alice asked.

"Someone who is 86," answered Mabel.

Glaring at Mabel, Alice folded her hands around her cup.

Popping another piece of cheese into his mouth, Homer grinned at Mabel.

"Hannah was not the first person to fall down those stairs." Mabel set her lukewarm cup of coffee down. "Freda fell down the stairs last month."

"Yeah, I heard that. That's not right. It's shoddy construction." The blue suit man burped and continued. "I'd sue the condo managers if I was the family."

"Maybe Homer is right, and the place is jinxed." Alice pushed her small paper plate with an uneaten dainty away. "Mind you, old people don't negotiate stairs all that well. The poor old dears probably just missed their step."

"Don't you want your cupcake?" Gwen asked.

Alice curled her lips and shook her head.

Gwen scooped up the cupcake, licked the icing, and peeled back the paper, and the cupcake quickly disappeared into her mouth.

Gemma stood at the head table; she cleared her throat and said, "Family and friends of Hannah, I'd like to say a few words about..." Gemma's words were lost as people continued to eat and chat amongst themselves.

"People, people." Gemma tried again. A few mourners looked at her curiously; others continued to eat and visit. Gemma cleared her voice. "Ahem, ahem, ladies and gentlemen." Few paid any interest, and the chatting persisted.

A sudden loud bang brought everyone to attention, and all chatter stopped.

Sitting opposite Mabel and Homer, the man in the blue suit banged his shoe on the table once more for good measure.

Gemma gave the man a surprised look, then a weak smile. The man grinned at her and put his shoe back on.

"I'd like to share a few memories with you of our dear departed friend." Gemma began by reciting how she came to know Hannah, recounting the many ways she helped the elderly woman.

Mabel wished the man had kept his shoe on. The speech reminded her of the eulogy Gemma did for Mini, which was more about Gemma than the deceased. But the annoying woman was no longer a suspect. She was calling bingo when they heard Hannah falling down the stairs. Mabel glanced over at her mother, who appeared to listen with rapt interest.

Okay, she admitted to herself, she felt a little jealous, but something about the woman didn't ring true.

A loud snore erupted from Homer. He appeared to be asleep, but he was sitting upright. Mabel bit her lip. She had a feeling the old man was faking. Everyone looked around to see who was snoring. Mabel grinned. Laughter ensued as Homer snorted and snored even louder.

KICKING OFF HER SHOES, Mabel sat on a kitchen chair and propped her feet on another, waiting for Violet to answer her phone.

"Hello."

Mabel grimaced; it was Neville. "Hi, Neville."

"Oh, it's you, Mabel, what do you want? Are you still poking your nose into those unfortunate deaths at the Manor?"

Mabel's hackles rose. "May I speak to Violet?" she asked between clenched teeth.

"I don't want you dragging Violet into your cockamamy schemes."

"So, you're not going to let me speak to my friend?"

"I never said that. I just want you to leave Violet alone."

"I see." Mabel smiled; a plan was forming. She'd fix his little red wagon. "Have you bagged any good trucks lately?"

"What?"

"Have you shot any more trucks?"

"I never shot a truck," Neville defended.

"You couldn't even hit the truck? Neville, you really are a poor shot," Mabel mocked happily. She'd gotten under his skin. Grinning, she flipped her long telephone cord back and forth. Gertrude jumped off a chair, her head swivelled back and forth, watching the black cord.

"I was not aiming at the truck."

"No, of course not. I bet you'd be way better at cow tipping."

"What the hell is cow tipping?"

"It's a sport we country people are very good at. As you know, cows are big animals with long, skinny legs. But what you may not know is they sleep standing up. It's great fun to sneak out in the middle of the night and see how many cows you can tip over. I believe Alfred, your buddy, holds the record."

"Really."

"Yes, by the way, did you know you are the talk of the town?"

"I am? Why?"

"It's a small-town Neville, everyone knows. You're now known as wild shot Neville," Mabel teased. Gertrude leapt at the cord. Mabel chuckled as the cat, standing on her hind legs, pawed at the swinging telephone cord.

"Good lord," stormed Neville.

"Who is it?" Mabel heard Violet's voice in the background.

There was a moment of silence, and then Mabel heard Violet on the phone. "What did you say to Neville? He stormed out of the house; he said he was the talk of the town. But he'd show them all."

"I was just teasing him; never mind, it's nothing." Mabel continued to swing her telephone cord.

"I'll bet."

Mabel detected skepticism in her friend's voice.

Gertrude leapt up, attacking the cord. The phone tumbled out of Mabel's hand onto the floor. The cat jumped sideways, her tail twitching; she hissed at the black phone receiver.

Snickering at the cat, Mabel picked up the phone. "That gave you a fright, didn't it?" The cat slunk out of the kitchen, the fur on her back sticking up.

"What? I'm not frightened. What was that noise?"

"I dropped my phone; Gertrude knocked it out of my hands."

"Ah, okay. Did you find out about the banking irregularities with your mom's savings account?"

"No, not exactly."

"So, did you ask your mom about her bank account?"

"No, not yet."

"Are you afraid to ask your mom about the money?"

"No, I haven't found the right time."

"Really, you were with her at Hannah's funeral. You had time then."

"A funeral really isn't the time to talk about money matters," defended Mabel.

"If you say so," pooh-poohed Violet. "Speaking of the funeral. I guess I should have gone, but I didn't know Hannah, and I don't know Hannah's family either. Were there lots of people there?"

"There was a good size crowd, a lot of people from Kipling. That's where Hannah was originally from. Hannah had no kids, only a brother still living. I didn't see him. But lots of nieces and nephews at the funeral. But what I called to tell you is that Homer and I are now best friends."

"Oh, yeah, right," scoffed Violet.

"I'm serious. I just figured out how to handle the old goat."

"I'll believe that when I see it."

Mabel flipped the long cord of her phone and looked out the corner of her eye for Gertrude. The cat was nowhere to be seen. "You'll see, you'll see. That is, if you can tear yourself away from the sharpshooter?"

"Hum, I'm beginning to see what upset Neville."

"Yes, I confess I did tease him," admitted Mabel, chuckling. "Anyway, do you think you can come out and play? Now that I am on Homer's best friend list, we can go and have a chat with Homer. He knows something about Hannah, I'm sure of it. He said the oddest thing to me the day she fell."

"I hate to leave Neville alone."

"Oh, Violet, what is up with you? You're being all submissive. This is very un-Violet."

"I mean, I don't want to leave him alone in the house. God knows what he'll move or change. he's starting to drive me crazy."

Mabel grinned. Neville's days were numbered.

Chapter Twenty-Nine

"Well, Farley has finally painted over the graffiti on the Gravenhurst sign," Mabel remarked as she parked her car in the visitor's parking lot. She looked across the nearly empty parking lot at the front entrance. "I wish we could park in front like that truck."

"I don't think you are allowed to park in front of the condo entrance," Violet said, buttoning her fluffy blue down-filled jacket before opening the passenger side door. "I'm sure it's a pick-up and drop-off point. That truck shouldn't be allowed to park there."

"I think you're right, but we're not the traffic police." Mabel opened her car door and hunched her shoulders into her fall jacket; snow flurries swirled overhead. Stuffing her hands in the pockets of her red fleece. She made a bee-line across the windswept parking lot. Violet quickly passed Mabel and opened the condo doors.

Mabel burst in the doors, shivering. "I hope this isn't a sign of an early winter."

"Me too. We should ask your mom about parking." Violet ran her finger over the names on the brass plaque and pressed the call button to Sophie's suite.

"I'm not asking Mom about parking spots. I've got other fish to fry."

Violet pressed again, holding her finger on the button.

"I'm going to question my mother about her dodgy finances. I want to know what is up with her bank accounts."

Sophie's voice came over the intercom. "You're going to question me, are you? It's none of your darn business what I do with my money."

"Ops." Violet looked sheepishly at Mabel and took her finger off the button.

Mabel jabbed the button on the intercom. "Why did you tell Cyril about your accounting problem? Why not me?"

"Mabel, you don't want to argue over the intercom with your mom," intervened Violet.

They waited, but the door latch did not release. Violet raised her eyebrows and looked at Mabel. "Your mom is mad at us. So, now what?"

"Thanks to you and your lead trigger finger on that damn buzzer." Mabel pressed the button again.

"Is this the Auditor General?" asked Sophie.

"I'm sorry, Mom, can we come in?"

"If you behave yourself." The door buzzed and then opened.

"Would you look at that?" Across the lobby, a sign hung on the stairwell door. The sign read '*Out of order.*'

Violet grinned. "I didn't think stairs could be out of order."

"And I bet there is nothing wrong with those stairs," muttered Mabel.

"I know, but how to prove it?" Violet pushed the call button for the elevator.

The door opened, and Jody, dressed in a scarlet top and black leggings, stood in the opening. Her ringed fingers held a large floral tote bag.

"Hi Jody, how are you?" Mabel took a step back and let the big girl exit the elevator.

"Hi," she replied. Jody's spiked hair was now tinted purple. She hitched the strap of the canvas bag over her shoulder.

Mabel looked at Violet for help. Jody was a suspect; she might have a key to the manor. They should question her.

"I'm glad you're here; I need your help. Mabel has just told me that she feels weak." Violet put her arm around Mabel and nudged her.

Violet was on the same wavelength. What a great idea. It was a perfect delaying tactic so they could question the home care aid. But how did one look weak? Should she faint? She settled for swaying, drew her forearm to her forehead, and mumbled, "Help me; I feel weak."

Violet rolled her eyes. "Oh, dear, she does look weak."

Mabel let herself sag. Violet stumbled under the unexpected weight, and Mabel slid to the floor, dropping to her bum, her legs splayed. She softly moaned, fluttered her eyelashes and peered up at Violet. Violet glowered down.

Jody's flowered tote bag slid down her tattooed arm, falling to the floor. Grabbing hold of Mabel's arm, she yanked, pulling her upward. Mabel hung down like a rag doll.

Violet bit her lip and stared wide-eyed.

Mabel moaned again. This time, she was in real pain. It felt like the girl was going to pull her arm out of her socket.

"You do know, I'm not a nurse," Jody said, shifting her hands under Mabel's armpits. "What do you want me to do with her?"

Violet's eyes darted furtively to Mabel. "Ah, help me get her to the lounge."

"Okay, no problem. I'm used to lifting old people, even chubby old people like your friend." Mabel slipped from Jody's grasp and fell back onto the floor with a thud.

"Old?" Mabel's chin jutted out; her eyes glittered as she rubbed her bottom.

"I've got her," Jody said, grabbing Mabel under the armpits again. "I'll get her into the lounge and call a doctor. She don't look well at all."

Mabel's foot became caught under the leg of the leather chair by the elevator. She glared at her friend as Jody yanked her arms. The chair moved with her foot. Call a doctor? Violet and her great idea.

Jody tugged, then shook Mabel up and down; Mabel's head flipped back and forth. The term whiplash coursed through Mabel's brain. If she didn't get free of Jody, she really was going to need a doctor. Mabel jerked her foot out from under the chair. "I just need to rest. No, doctor, please," she said between clenched teeth.

Jody wrapped her arms around Mabel's waist, dragging her into the empty lounge.

Mabel bounced up and down as her feet skittered across the carpet. "Ow, ow, ow," she cried.

"You'll be fine," encouraged Violet, following behind.

Jody dropped Mabel on the couch; Mabel groaned, rubbing her bum, she shifted her sore shoulder. Violet swung Mabel's feet up onto the couch, then pushed her head down on the sofa. She picked up Mabel's hand, patting it. Mabel glared, shoving her away.

"I'll call an ambulance," volunteered Jody. She dashed back to the lobby, grabbing her large tote bag. Digging out her phone, she returned to Mabel on the couch.

Mabel sat up, swinging her feet down onto the floor. "Ow, ouch," she cried. Her butt hurt. "I feel much better now."

Jody put a hand on Mabel's chest and shoved her back down on the couch. "You can never be too careful, especially at your age." Holding up her phone, Jody tapped on the screen.

"My age?" Mabel struggled to sit up. "How old do you think I am? No, don't answer that." She snatched the phone out of Jody's hand.

Jody grabbed it back and shoved Mabel back down. She swung Mabel's feet up on the couch and stuffed a cushion under her head. Mabel looked up at Violet helplessly.

Violet put her hand on Jody's shoulder. "Really, she'll be fine. The poor old thing does this all the time. She didn't eat breakfast."

Looking confused, Jody stuffed her phone in her pocket.

Mabel's eyes shot Violet a dirty look. Poor old thing? Glowering, she elbowed her way back up to a sitting position, swinging her legs off the couch.

"It's her blood sugar levels. I'll see if they have any orange juice in the kitchen; you stay here with Mabel and have a little chat with her; that will make all the difference." Violet sped across the lounge into the kitchen.

Jody plopped down beside Mabel and awkwardly patted her hand. "I thought maybe you guys thought I was a nurse. I'm a home care worker, not a nurse."

Mabel smiled weakly, withdrawing her hand. Jody's pats started to smart. "Yes, I know you are a home care worker." Mabel looked across the room at Violet, who was opening the fridge door. And grinned. "It's Violet who needs help. She wants to talk to you about home care. She's finding it hard to do her housework."

Violet stopped her search for orange juice, her hand on the open fridge door. Her eyebrows rose as Mabel continued.

"Yes, she isn't as young as she once was."

Violet slowly closed the fridge door, her eyes narrowing.

"Really?" Jody looked over at Violet, standing stock-still with a carton of orange juice in her hand.

"Oh, I know she looks fit, but the poor old dear is having issues," Mabel said, stressing the words 'old dear,' her eyes twinkled as she continued. "I've been trying to get her to accept help. That's why I am so happy she asked you."

"Ask me? She didn't ask me about home care. She said you were weak, weren't you dizzy?"

"Ah, ah, I was," sputtered Mabel. "But I guess you could say that this is a happy circumstance. I'll be as right as rain. That is, if poor Violet can find me a glass of juice." Mabel's eyes gleamed with deviltry. "It's Violet that needs help."

Violet opened a cupboard door, took out a glass, then slammed the door shut.

"You have such a good reputation as a home care worker," continued Mabel.

"I do?" Jody's eyebrows shot up in surprise.

"I've heard good, ah, good reports about your, your cleaning, and whatnot," Mabel finished lamely.

Jody brightened. "Oh yeah, yeah, the residents like me; they like my work, and I'm in demand."

Violet marched back into the lounge with a large glass of orange juice in her hand. Giving Mabel a cold stare, she gave her the glass of juice.

"Yes, I'm quite in demand," Jody repeated. "I'll look at my schedule to see what I can do for you, Violet."

Violet's body was rigid as she crossed her arms. Her lips were in a thin line. "For me?"

"Yes, dear, for you. You're not as young as you used to be," Mabel interjected. "You know we've talked about this. All your housework is playing you out. Don't deny it; you know it's true." She held up her glass of juice, grinning over the glass at her friend.

Arms folded, Violet looked down at Mabel, tapping her toe on the rug.

"Like I said, I'm in demand," Jody said importantly. "So, I'll have to check my schedule, but we will work something out for you, I promise,"

"Isn't this great, Violet? I bet Jody is a whiz with organizing. I bet she can re-organize your house in no time."

Violet's eyes widened in alarm. "Mabel," she warned. The speed of her toe-tapping on the rug picked up, becoming an angry tattoo.

"I'm self-employed; I don't normally do heavy housework. But for the right price, I could do some housecleaning for you." Jody's eyes gleamed as she smiled at Violet.

"Do you have a lot of clients in this condo?" Mabel took a swig of the orange juice. She licked her lips. It was very sweet. It was some kind of powdered orange drink; she could see undissolved crystals floating in the glass.

"I've quite a few clients, and I do light housekeeping for them. I vacuum, wash the floors, and stuff like that. And then there is old Mrs. Angus, that old lady needs a lot of help. If you ask me, she's six breaths away from death."

Mabel and Violet's eyebrows rose as they exchanged looks.

"And just between you and me, the rest of these people don't really need me. They just don't want to do housework." Jody chuckled. "But I'm sure not going to refuse the money."

Mabel raised an eyebrow. So much for client confidentiality. "Do you come to the condo every day?" She set the glass of orange juice on an end table.

"Not on weekends. I keep those open for me." Jody giggled. "A girl has to have a little fun."

"I heard Mrs. Angus is almost bedridden." Violet picked up Mabel's glass and returned to the kitchen, rinsing the glass under the tap. "It must be hard for her to get to the intercom to let you in the condo." She set the glass in the sink.

"Yes, how do you get into the building?" Mabel arched an eyebrow.

"Oh, Mrs. Angus gave me her spare keys." Jody took a package of gum out of her purse.

Violet, returning from the kitchen, asked, "Keys?"

"For the condo and her suite. It makes life way easier for her and for me." Jody stuck a stick of gum in her mouth. "I'd offer you one, but it's Nicorette gum. I can't smoke in here."

Mabel lowered her eyes. This girl had access to the condo. Did she kill Mini? And if she did? It would follow she killed the other two as well. "I remember you were the one who found Freda at the bottom of the stairs."

Jody grimaced, chomping rapidly on her gum. "It was awful; I'd never seen a dead body before."

Violet placed a hand on Jody's shoulder. "Lucky you didn't find Hannah when she fell," she consoled, patting the girl's arm. "To find two women at the bottom of the stairs, dead. Would've been dreadful."

"Were you here when Hannah fell?" Mabel asked.

Jody chewed vigorously on her gum, paused, wrinkled her brow, then nodded her head. "Yeah, I guess I was. I was giving Mrs. Angus her bath. I never heard a thing about it until after they took poor old Hannah away."

"I thought you two were coming up to see me." Sophie entered the lounge and glowered. "I'm waiting for the inquisition."

Chapter Thirty

"Inquisition?" Jody gave Sophie a puzzled look.

Mabel jumped to her feet. "Mom is just teasing."

"Mabel had a turn," exclaimed Jody.

Sophie wrinkled her brow. "A turn?"

"Yes, a kind of a turn," stammered Violet. "But luckily, Jody was here to help her out."

With a worried look on her face, Sophie turned to her daughter. "Help her?"

"Never mind, Mom, I'll tell you all about it in a bit," Mabel interjected hurriedly, then turned to smile sweetly at Jody. "Thanks for your help." She was eager to check out Jody's alibi with Mrs. Angus. But first, somehow, she needed to get her mom to tell her about the irregularities with her bank account.

Jody rose, gathering her bag. "I'll phone you, Violet, and let you know when I have an opening."

"Ah, yes, okay, thank you," Violet stumbled over her reply.

Jody opened her bag and pulled out a package of cigarettes as she exited the condo.

Mabel tilted her head, smiling innocently up at Violet.

"An opening?" Sophie asked, perplexed.

"Your daughter has been so helpful." Violet glared at Mabel. "She told Jody I needed home care."

"You started it with the frail old lady thing."

"You got your information, don't complain. It's me that has to get out of this home care business. You laid that on kind of thick. I feel bad, fooling Jody."

"What have you two been up to? It sounds like shenanigans to me," Sophie said as she pushed the call button for the elevator.

"All part of our investigations."

"Is this about Mini?" Sophie asked.

"Yes, Mini. And Freda and Hannah. We don't think they fell down the stairs accidentally," Mabel said.

"Someone pushed Freda and Hannah down those stairs? Why would someone kill them? They were old ladies." Sophie's face flushed. "I mean, senior ladies."

"Mini was a senior, and you seem to think someone killed her," reminded Mabel.

"Well, yes, I did, but I have decided I was making too much of it; Mini was old. And I have to accept that," confessed Sophie as the elevator doors opened.

"But you were with Mini that night. You told me there weren't any signs she was ill. And remember the busy elevator that wasn't busy? And the blocked door?" Should she tell her mom about Freda's diary? "And Freda—"

"Never mind about Freda," Violet said, giving a small shake of her head as she entered the elevator.

Mabel nodded. They didn't have the evidence to back up the diary.

Sophie followed. "Yes, Violet is right; forget about Freda and Hannah. It's hard to believe someone would be killing off my friends."

"Your friends? I seem to remember you didn't have a very high opinion of Freda or Hannah."

"Never mind that. It is just silly to think we have a serial killer here in Gravenhurst Manor. Like in those Hollywood movies? You're letting your imagination run away with you?" Sophie turned to Violet, "And Violet agrees with me, don't you, Violet?"

Violet glanced at Mabel. "I think the deaths of all three women are suspicious."

"If you say so, dear."

Mabel rolled her eyes. Her mother took Violet's opinion but not hers.

"And please stay away from those stairs. Those stairs are dangerous," Violet cautioned, pushing the button to close the elevator door.

A hand reached out and stopped the door. "Hello, hello," greeted Gemma cheerfully.

Mabel's eyes narrowed as the well-groomed woman swept into the elevator. What did that woman hear?

"How is everyone today? It's a little nippy out, but it is November. We're lucky we've had no snow yet."

"A few flakes were falling when we came."

Ignoring Mabel, Gemma leaned down and gave Sophie a peck on the cheek.

Sophie smiled happily up at Gemma.

Violet pressed the button for the second floor.

Feeling diminished by Gemma's presence, Mabel moved closer to her mother.

"I heard your warning to my dear little Sophie about the stairs." Gemma undid the buttons on her long black woollen coat. "You'll all be happy to know I've phoned the condo manager with the resident's concerns."

Mabel pasted a smile on her face. Who made this woman the spokesperson for the condo? She didn't live here. But she might as well have; the woman was always here. She thought uncharitably.

"The condo manager told me a building inspector is coming to look at the stairs today." Gemma loosened the long, burgundy silk scarf from around her neck. "It's outrageous that those two women had to die before anything is done." Gemma shook out her burgundy scarf, folding it, she tucked it into her large matching handbag. "I've always said these steps are too steep for seniors."

"I don't think these stairs are all that steep," disagreed Mabel. "The steps are wide. And there is a sturdy handrail."

"You've used the stairs?"

"No, but I have looked at them."

"Well, maybe they're not too steep for you, you're young. Not all the seniors who live here are as agile as you. Nor do they see as well as you do. One missed step. And look what happens. It's best to let the experts decide." The door opened, and Gemma stepped out into the hallway.

Mabel followed. "All I'm saying is it's strange. This building has been occupied for over a year. And now, suddenly, two women die falling down the stairs in less than a month."

Gemma gave Mabel a long, hard look as she hoisted the strap of her large purse over her shoulder. "Don't you worry yourself, sweetie. The inspector will get to the bottom of it." She gently patted Sophie's shoulder and smiled kindly down at her. "But I am so happy for you, my dear Sophie. Your daughter has finally taken an interest in where you live." She hurried off down the hallway and rapped on a door. She looked back at Mabel and smiled. The door opened, and Gemma entered, closing the door behind her.

Mabel's mouth hung open. That woman had just insinuated that she was a neglectful daughter.

"Gemma is always dressed so stylish," Sophie said, opening the door to her suite. She arched an eyebrow as she looked at her daughter. "It wouldn't hurt you, dear to take more of an interest in how you dress."

Mabel's face reddened, conscious that she was dressed in jeans and had an old sweatshirt on under her red fleece jacket. Her mom didn't seem to see Gemma had basically said that she neglected her. Instead, her mother was comparing fashion attire.

"Don't just stand there, dear, come in." She ushered the women into her suite. "I made tea while I was waiting for you girls. It's been steeping. It should be ready to pour now," Sophie said cheerfully.

Mabel's lips formed a thin, tight line as she unzipped her fleece.

Violet didn't look at Mabel or Sophie as she removed her blue jacket and draped it over the back of a kitchen chair.

Sophie bustled into the kitchen, on the countertop, and set an oval-shaped glass tray with china cups and saucers. The design of the little pink flowers on the cups matched the teapot. She opened her fridge, took out a small pitcher of cream, and set it beside the matching sugar bowl on the tray.

"I'll carry the tray for you," Violet volunteered.

Mabel debated whether she should voice her grievance that Gemma had slammed her. But she had a sneaking suspicion her mother would side with the odious woman. But then maybe Gemma's parting statement wasn't a slam. Was her jealousy getting in the way? She had to admit it irked her, the way her mother fawned over the tiresome woman. She could be making too much of an off-hand remark. Or maybe what caused Gemma to make that comment was her mother's silly joke that she never visited.

Sophie, carrying a china plate with cookies on it, followed Violet into her living room. "Cookie, dear? There you're favourite, chocolate chip."

Ignoring the offer, Mabel flung her coat on the back of the couch; plopping down on it, she sank into the cushions.

Violet set the tray on the coffee table. She took a cookie, carefully sitting on the edge of the couch.

Mabel stuck out her chin and crossed her arms over her chest. "I didn't abandon you. I was in Egypt."

"Whatever are you talking about, dear?" Sophie poured tea and passed the cup and saucer to Violet.

"And when I came back, I went to Edmonton to be with Melina when she gave birth to little Rene. I had to be with her." She struggled forward until her feet touched the floor.

Sophie poured another cup of tea. "Yes, dear little Rene, I haven't seen her yet."

"I have a daughter too."

"Yes, dear, you do. Whatever are you rambling about?" Sophie handed Mabel the cup of tea. The tea sloshed over on the saucer.

"You do know she's your granddaughter, and she gave birth to your great-granddaughter?"

Sophie passed her a napkin. "Mabel, what is the matter with you? Of course, I know who Melina and Rene are. I'm not senile."

Mabel mopped up the spilled tea on her saucer. "Then, you do realize I didn't abandon you."

"What? No, of course not, don't be silly. Have a cookie." Mabel's mother urged, pouring herself a cup of tea.

"Have you been telling people I've neglected you?" Mabel asked, dropping the damp napkin on the coffee table; she looked with narrowed eyes at her mother.

"Why would I say a thing like that? Really, Mabel."

"Then why does Gemma think I have?"

"I don't think Gemma thinks anything of the kind. You're a good daughter, have a cookie."

"Didn't you hear that crack she made?"

"What crack?"

"The crack about me finally taking an interest in where you live."

"You're being overly sensitive, dear. I think Gemma was paying you a compliment. Don't you, Violet?"

Violet looked from mother to daughter. "It could have been a compliment. Or it might not have been," she evaded, taking a sip of tea.

"It wasn't a compliment; it was an accusation. What have you been saying about me? This little joke of yours. Like, '*who is this*?' And '*Mabel? Mabel who?*' And so on. Does everyone here think you're on your own, with nobody to care about you?"

"No, of course not," Sophie said, shifting in her chair, her eyes not meeting Mabel's.

"You've been doing the helpless little old lady thing, haven't you?"

"I am old."

"But you are far from helpless, and Cyril and I are just a phone call away. I've never abandoned you."

"I never said you did. But you were in Egypt, and that is not a phone call away," defended Sophie. She sat back in her chair and crossed her arms, looking defiantly at Mabel. "My house sold so quickly; I had to make a decision where to move to. So, I picked Gravenhurst Manor. And don't get me wrong, it's a wonderful condo. I made the right decision. But I was so lost when I moved here, I didn't know anyone. And all my furniture was too big and old-fashioned for my suite. Gemma, bless her heart, came to my rescue. She showed me around and helped me shop for new furniture."

Ha thought Mabel Gemma was partly responsible for this garish colour scheme.

"Everyone was new. We were all strangers, and it was Gemma who made us into a community. She started bingo and set up a dance night at the leisure center. She organized music nights, and Gemma can sing and play the piano beautifully. She has a lovely voice. But." Sophie giggled. "Her violin playing could use a little work. Gemma is a gem of a person."

"Okay, I get why you are so enamoured with the woman," Mabel said, feeling guilty. She could see why her mom treated Gemma like a rock star.

"Enamoured?"

"I mean grateful to Gemma."

"Yes, I am, and so are the rest of the residents. Well, most of them are."

Yes, dear Gemma, the gem, had helped her mother, But it didn't give the woman the right to insult her. She bit into her cookie, crumbs sprayed.

Violet brushed the cookie crumbs off her lap. She looked in her teacup, then set it down on the coffee table. "It was nice to see Cyril and the family at Thanksgiving," Violet said, breaking the awkward silence.

Sophie stirred the cream in her tea. "Yes. Too bad about the turkey."

"Cyril told me about the trouble with your savings account," Mabel blurted out.

"Did he now." Sophie's tone turned frosty.

"Yes, he did, why didn't you tell me?"

"What's to tell? The money is back in my account; that's all that matters. Obviously, the bank made an error and fixed it."

"Don't you want to know what happened?"

"No, it's fixed, that's all I care about, have another cookie."

Chapter Thirty-One

"I'm going home," Mabel said, stomping down the hallway; she pressed the call button for the elevator.

"Ah, aren't you forgetting something?" Violet asked.

"Like what? Mom won't let me pursue the strange things going on with her bank account. What else can I do? Maybe she should ask the fabulous Gemma to help her," Mabel said in a petulant tone. She sighed and looked at Violet. "Okay, I know I'm being petty. The woman did help Mom. I should have been here."

Violet put her hands on Mabel's shoulders and turned her to face her. "Stop right there. Get rid of your guilty feelings right now. You had no idea your mom was going to move that fast. When we left for Egypt, she was just talking about moving."

"Yeah, I guess she was," Mabel said slowly.

"And be happy Gemma was here to help her."

"I'll try, no, I will."

"Good, and now, what about Jody? Don't you think we should check out her alibi? We should talk to Mrs. Angus. Jody said she was giving her a bath."

"I wonder what suite Mrs. Angus is in?"

"We could go back and ask your mom," encouraged Violet.

Mabel exhaled and turned around. "Okay, I guess." She plodded back to her mother's door and tapped on it.

Sophie opened the door. "Why hello, long time no see."

Mabel sighed. "You are going to stop this long-lost daughter bit at some point."

"Yes, dear, sorry, my silly little joke has become a bit of a habit," Sophie apologized, beckoning the woman into her suite.

"And stale," Mabel said, stepping through the doorway.

Violet looked over Mabel's shoulder. "We were wondering if you knew where Mrs. Angus lives?"

"She is on the first floor, 110. Why?"

"We want to check out Jody's alibi."

Violet followed Sophie and Mabel into the suite, closing the door behind her. "It all has to do with your friend Mini's death."

"Really? Well, even though I'm not so sure about my worries about Mini's death. I am pleased to hear you're still investigating. You know, just to be sure." Sophie perched on her pink sofa, looking quizzical. "Come sit down." She patted the couch beside her.

Mabel threw off her jacket and sat beside her mother. Sophie squeezed her hand and smiled at her. Mabel smiled back, her anger melting away. So, her mother didn't want to share information about her bank accounts. She'd let that go and get on with the investigation.

"Why are you wavering about the cause of your friend Mini's death? You were so sure it was suspicious, but now you're not. What's changed your mind?" Violet asked.

"I know. One minute, I think I'm being a silly old woman, and Mini died of old age like Randolph said. The next minute, I think maybe I was right, and dear Mini was, well, was murdered." Sophie clasped and unclasped her hands, looking at her daughter. Her bottom lip trembled.

Mabel suddenly thought her mother looked old and frail. "I don't think you are a silly old woman, and neither does Violet."

"Never, you are far from silly," Violet said, laying her jacket on top of Mabel's coat. She gathered up the teacups, setting them on the tray.

"Thank you, dear," Sophie said.

"We think you are right, and Mini's death is suspicious. And so are the so-called accidental deaths of Freda and Hannah. We think their deaths and Mini's are connected," Mabel said. She was sure Freda's death was not accidental. They'd read her diary. Hannah's, well, she wasn't so sure about that death.

"Doesn't anyone in this condo think it's odd those two women fell down the stairs?" Violet asked, picking up Sophie's tea tray; she took it to the kitchen.

"My goodness, everyone thinks the stairs are unsafe. George even wanted to sue the condo board. But Gemma calmed him down."

"You've walked those stairs, Mom. What do you think? Are the stairs mismatched? Or the handrail funky?"

"I've had no trouble with the stairs, mind you. I've only used them on the night Mini died. But there was nothing wrong with the handrail then. And the stairs are well-lit," Sophie said.

"We saw a car parked out front. Maybe the building inspector is here." Violet rinsed out the teapot, setting it in the kitchen sink to drain.

"We'll use the stairs when we go visit Mrs. Angus. Then, we will see for ourselves if there is an issue. Mom, what do you know about Jody?"

"Nothing really; I've seen her around the building. She seems cheerful enough. But I've never had much of a conversation with her. Do you think Jody has something to do with these deaths?"

"So, you do agree Freda and Hannah's deaths are suspicious?"

Sophie looked down at her hands, then back up and said, "I guess I do. If the stairs are safe, then maybe someone did push those women down the stairs. It could be Jody, I guess, although why she would do something like that is beyond me."

"We don't know if Jody did anything. And for goodness' sake, don't utter a word to anyone about any of this." Mabel leaned forward and grasped her mother's hands. It could be dangerous for her mother if the killer suspected she thought there was anything amiss with the deaths. "Mom, I think you should come home with me. You could be in danger."

"Don't be silly. Who would want to murder me?"

"The same person who killed those other women."

"But why me?"

"We don't have a motive. We don't know why someone is killing these women. I'm worried about you. Come home with me."

"Nonsense."

"Have you told anyone else besides us that you suspect Mini died mysteriously?" Violet asked, putting the teacups in the sink and wiping the tea tray.

"Dear me, I haven't breathed a word about my suspicions regarding dear Mini."

"Good, keep it that way," Mabel urged.

Violet rinsed her hands and dried them on a paper towel. "Let's go back to the first suspicious death. You told Mabel you suspected Mini was a gambler?"

"Yes, I did, but I don't know for sure that she was. We mustn't spread rumours about dear Mini. I might be wrong."

"No, of course not," agreed Violet.

"On the night of Mini's death. Did anything seem strange with your friend? Anything odd about her that night?" Mabel asked.

Sophie leaned back on the couch; she picked up a pink cushion, plucking at the tassels. "No, well, she was worried about money. She was very upset about her account at the bank. Unexplained withdrawals is how she put it." Sophie looked sheepishly at Mabel. "I guess I should've twigged then and checked my account. But I thought maybe she lost the money gambling," confessed Sophie.

"Unexplained withdrawals from Mini's bank account and your account?" Mabel's voice rose in frustration. "And you didn't think to tell me?"

"Well, maybe I should have," admitted Sophie. "But I thought Mini lost her money gambling. And the people in the bank are only human. I thought it was probably a clerical error. And I wouldn't have told your brother, but the boy was snooping. He checked my bank statements. Goodness me, just because Cyril is an accountant, he thinks he has the right to muddle in my affairs." Sophie wrinkled her nose.

Mabel grinned. So her mother hadn't confided in Cyril. Her brother was snooping.

"I still think it might have been some kind of a mix-up. Someone new at the bank is my guess."

Mabel threw up her hands. "My God, Mom, you're too darn trusting."

"But dear, it wasn't a lot of money; well, I guess it was a good sum of money. But not as much as Mini. Mini said something like fifty thousand was withdrawn from her account."

"Fifty thousand!" shouted Mabel.

"Well, it might not be fifty. I might have that wrong. Maybe it was five, I'm not sure," Sophie said, twisting the tassels on the cushion.

"Regardless." Mabel leaned back and crossed her arms. "We now have a for sure motive for Mini's murder."

"We do?" Sophie, wrinkling her forehead, tossed the cushion to the side.

"I don't think your friend lost her money gambling. I think someone was stealing from her. We need to find out if Jody had access to Mini's bank accounts."

"Whoa, whoa. You're jumping the gun. Did Mini bank online?" Violet asked.

"You mean on a computer?"

"Yes, did she?"

"No, she didn't hold with computers any more than I do. Neither one of us owns one of those contraptions."

"Like mother like daughter." Violet chuckled, spreading her hands, palms up.

Mabel made a face at Violet.

Violet grinned and continued, "Then Jody couldn't hack their accounts, so it is unlikely she is the culprit. Anyway, Jody said she was giving Mrs. Angus a bath when Hannah fell down the stairs."

"Hannah! Maybe Freda and Hannah were missing money, too," Sophie suggested excitedly.

"Yep, the apple doesn't fall far from the tree; mother and daughter are so much alike."

Mabel pressed her lips and gave Violet a sidelong glance. They knew from Freda's diary that Freda was a blackmailer. But she could have had her bank account fiddled with too. And Hannah, was she missing money? Darn, there were too many possibilities. "Settle down, Mom. We don't know anything yet. And if Jody's alibi holds up, we will have to look elsewhere for the killer."

Violet nodded. "Yes, we are a long way from proving anything."

"But the money, you think that's the motive." Sophie looked up at Violet.

"It could be. If we are right," cautioned Violet.

"Then you can stop worrying about me. I'm not missing any money."

"But you were."

"A coincidence. Remember, my money is back in my bank account."

"But Mini's wasn't. She told you the night of her death she was missing money. So, I think Mini found out who was stealing from her." Mabel jumped up, pacing from the living room to the kitchen. "She confronted them, and they killed her."

"Them? Now, we have more than one killer? Maybe it was just a banking error," Violet said.

Sophie frowned. "But you just said it was a motive."

"No, I didn't; Mabel did; we need to be cautious."

"Speaking of cautious, Mom you should come home with me. I think someone killed those women, and who knows who could be next.?"

"No, I am staying right here. You said the motive is money. I have my money, so no one has any reason to harm me." Sophie folded her arms across her chest and looked defiantly at her daughter.

"We don't know that for sure. Come home with me."

"No, I'm not going anywhere."

Mabel sighed. Her mother was so obstinate. They had to find the killer before something happened to her. She grabbed the jackets, handed Violet hers, and hurried to the door. "Come on, Violet, let's check out Jody's alibi." Sophie followed her to the door. Mabel bit her lip and looked worriedly at her mother. Someone killed Freda because the woman knew too much. She hugged her mother and said, "Please don't say anything about our suspicions about Mini, Freda and Hannah."

Sophie hugged her back. "I won't."

"Not one word, promise."

Sophie's lips turned down. "Oh, for goodness' sake, I promised, stop worrying. I won't say a thing. Good lord, I'm not a gossip."

"And remember, stay the heck away from that stairway," Mabel warned.

Chapter Thirty-Two

Mabel paused at the bottom of the steps. "There's not a thing wrong with these stairs. The steps are wide, and the stairway is well-lit. And the railing is sturdy. There is no reason for anyone to fall. Even if they were feeble."

"Unless they had a dizzy spell or a heart attack." Violet opened the door to the lobby and paused.

"You never agree with me. Why is that?"

"Maybe I'm the voice of reason," Violet replied.

"I'm unreasonable?" Mabel raised an eyebrow.

As they entered the foyer, a tall man with broad shoulders stomped up to them and shouted, "What the hell is the matter with you, women? For God's sake, can't you read? The sign says out of order." The grizzled, grey-haired man rubbed his bulbous nose with the back of his hand.

"Who the heck are you to be ordering us around? Mind your own business." Mabel scowled.

"I'm the building safety inspector, that's who. Obey the damn sign, it was put there for your protection." The inspector looked at the back of his hand, then wiped his hand on his trouser leg.

Violet grimaced and looked away. Farley, the janitor, standing next to the inspector, hitched up the suspenders on his coveralls and smirked.

"How can a stairway be out of order? The sign makes no sense. There is nothing mechanical about a stairway," Mabel said.

"How about dangerous then? Would you understand that?" the large man snarled.

"Then, it should say dangerous. But it didn't, and besides, we don't live here. We are just visiting." Mabel tilted her head back, giving the man a haughty look.

"Yep, they're visitors," echoed Farley, snapping his suspenders.

"The sign is not just for residents. It's for all people." The lanky inspector stuck his laser measuring device in his pocket.

"What did you find?" Mabel asked. "Is there something wrong with the steps? Are they not all the same distance? Or What?"

"I'm writing a report. The public will know soon enough," the inspector said curtly, looking down at Mabel.

Mabel screwed up her face, wrinkling her nose. "It's not like it's a state secret, for goodness' sake. Tell us your findings. Everyone should know, especially the residents."

"You're not a resident," the man shot back, wiping his nose again with the back of his hand.

"Nope, they're just visitors," Farley agreed, grinning.

"I'm sorry we disobeyed the sign. But honestly, we didn't find any difficulty coming down those steps," apologized Violet.

"The name is Monfort," said the big man, smiling at Violet; he offered his hand.

"Nice to meet you. I'm Violet, and this is Mabel," she said, with a smile plastered on her face; she took his hand with her fingertips and looked helplessly at Mabel.

Mabel felt sorry for Violet. Her friend was caught between her fear of germs and her natural good manners. "Violet is right there is nothing wrong with the stairs."

Grimacing, Violet dug into her jacket pockets.

Gemma emerged from the elevator; the tall, imposing woman scanned the lobby as she buttoned her coat.

"So the big question is if the stairs are safe. Why did the women fall?" Mabel asked.

"There is no accounting for stupidity," Farley snorted. "I'm taking that damn sign down." He marched over and pulled the paper sign off the door.

"What a nasty thing to say. Those women fell to their death." Mabel crossed her arms and looked over at the lanky caretaker as he crumpled the paper, sticking it in his pocket.

Gemma stopped buttoning her coat and shouted, "You dreadful uncouth man."

"Gemma, do you happen to have any hand wipes in your purse?" Violet asked.

"Wipes? No, get away from me." Gemma strode over to the janitor. "What a stupid, cruel thing to say. I shall report you to management." Her voice rose to a shrill pitch.

"Yeah, well, we can't see any reason for those women to have fallen down those stairs," Farley snorted again, shoving his hands deep into his coverall pockets.

"Oh, look, I found some," Violet said as she fished out a half-empty packet of hand wipes, happily wiping her hands.

"We? There is no we. Who the hell are you?" Monfort snarled.

"Farley." The janitor looked at the inspector with surprise.

"Try being old and infirm with poor eyesight and arthritic limbs," snapped Gemma. "I am going to inform management of your crude remarks. I don't think they will want to continue to employ a janitor like you." With her phone in her hand, Gemma turned on her heel and marched into the lounge. "I'm calling them right now."

"They won't get anyone else to be at the beck and call of these pampered Nancys. Do you see management here? They didn't even show up for the inspection. It was me who showed this guy around. Not the pansy-ass manager." Farley's wrinkled face reddened. He did an about-face and marched out the door.

The inspector shouted after Gemma. "This guy just showed up and followed me around. Don't lump me in with him. I had no idea who he was." Monfort paused, but Gemma did not respond. "Damn it," muttered the man, following Farley out the door.

As the door closed, Violet said, "Gemma is right. Farley is insensitive, but I kind of feel sorry for the poor man; your buddy Gemma is really upset. I hope he doesn't lose his job over one thoughtless remark." She stuck the near-empty packet of hand wipes in her pocket.

"She is not my buddy," Mabel huffed, starting down the hallway. "Insensitive is Farley's middle name. But you can't really blame him for thinking the women were stupid to fall down those stairs. He doesn't know someone pushed those women." Mabel frowned. "Unless he was the one who pushed them. Maybe their deaths have nothing to do with Mini. Maybe Farley is a nutbar who hates seniors. He's always complaining about them."

"Hey, hey, remember we don't know for sure the women were pushed," reminded Violet.

"Yeah, yeah, the voice of reason again," Mabel grumbled.

"And besides, complaining is one thing. Murder is quite another."

"He does have keys for the building."

"Yes, he does. See, I'm agreeing with you."

"And what does that woman do for fun?"

"What? Who?"

"Gemma, for goodness' sake. That woman is always here. She might as well rent a place in this condo," muttered Mabel as they stopped at suite 110 at the end of the hallway.

"Some people just want to be helpful." Violet rapped on the door.

"There is helpful, and then there's Gemma."

They waited. Violet knocked again, then tried the door. It was unlocked. "Should we?" she asked.

"Yep." Mabel opened the door and stuck her head in. A blast of hot air hit her. "Hello, Mrs. Angus, hello." There was no answer. She motioned for Violet to follow her.

The suite layout was identical to Sophie's. But there was no pink on the walls, only builders' beige. They tiptoed past the kitchen. Cereal bowls with congealed milk set on the counter. On the stove, a greasy frying pan and the remains of a fried egg. The sink had a pile of dirty dishes. Violet wrinkled her nose.

"I don't know why we're tiptoeing," Mabel whispered.

"Or whispering."

The TV blared ominous music from a soap opera. The sound was up, but Mrs. Angus wasn't watching.

"Even if I needed help, I wouldn't ask Jody to clean. This place could do with a good vacuuming and dusting, as well as a good scrub. This smell is overpowering. Maybe she's dead," whispered Violet.

Chapter Thirty-Three

"Well, if she is, she won't hear us." Mabel entered the bedroom. The room was dark, and it was hot. In the bed, with the bedcovers pulled up to her chin, lay Mrs. Angus, snoring.

Violet and Mabel looked at each other and shrugged their shoulders.

"I guess we better let her sleep," Mabel said. As she turned to leave the room, she kicked a chamber pot; the contents sloshed as it banged up against the dresser.

"Yikes," squealed Violet, leaping back, she collided with Mabel.

Mabel jumped out of the way, and her arm bumped into a hairbrush on the dresser, sending it flying into the chamber pot. Mabel looked with dismay from the chamber pot to Violet.

"Don't look at me. I'm not fishing that thing out," Violet said, her lips screwed up into a grimace.

Mrs. Angus elbowed herself up in the bed. "Who's there?"

"Oh, sorry to wake you, it's us. Mabel and Violet, we, ah, we ah. We came to visit you," Mabel sputtered.

"I always take a nap at this time." The thin, pale woman struggled to a sitting position. Her long, stringy grey hair was matted.

"Ah, I see you use a chamber pot," Mabel said lamely, looking into the pot at the floating hairbrush.

"Yes," replied Mrs. Angus in a thin, reedy voice. "The bathroom is too far to go to in the night." Swinging her spindly legs off the bed, she staggered.

Violet put her arm out. Mrs. Angus grasped Violet's offered arm with a white bony hand and shuffled forward.

With her foot, Mabel shoved the pot out of the way.

"I'll leave you to it." Violet grinned, looking from the chamber pot to Mabel. "I'll help Mrs. Angus into the living room."

"Thank you, dear," the old woman said, shuffling to the door, her hand firmly clutching Violet's arm.

Mabel glowered back and picked up the pot, going into the bathroom. "I thought I was through with this when I retired," she grumbled.

When Mabel emerged from the bathroom, Violet had Mrs. Angus sitting on the deep brown velvet couch, and the TV turned down. Mrs. Angus had pulled an afghan over her lap.

Mabel carried the hairbrush in a towel to the kitchen. "Do you mind if I boil your kettle?"

"No, go right ahead; I would love a cup of tea."

"Have you eaten today?" Violet asked.

"Yes, I had an egg, but I wasn't all that hungry."

"I'll make you something."

"No, I get Meals on Wheels today. Someone will deliver my supper around five."

"You sure you don't want something?"

"No, thank you. Tea will be fine."

Mabel backtracked to the kitchen. "How do Meals on Wheels come to your unit? Do they have a key?"

"Oh no, dear, they buzz, and I let them in the building."

"Ah, I'll go make you tea."

Violet sat on a brown upholstered rocking chair, straightening the ivory crochet doilies that decorated the arms and back of the chair. "How do you like your home care worker, Jody? I was thinking of hiring her."

"My dear, I would advise against it. I have had to let Jody go. I phoned the agency this morning. Would you look at my place? Jody was getting worse by the day." Mrs. Angus's reedy voice took on a sharper tone. "Isn't this a shocking state of affairs? I paid that girl good money. And you can see for yourself what kind of cleaner she is." Breathing heavily, the old lady sank back onto her couch.

Mabel filled the sink with hot water and soap and began washing Mrs. Angus's dishes. "It will be just a few minutes for the kettle. I might as well do your dishes while I'm waiting."

"That would be nice, dear," Mrs. Angus said in her thin, reedy voice.

Violet rose from the chair and joined Mabel in the kitchen. Glancing at the hairbrush sitting in a big bowl of hot, soapy water, she grabbed a tea towel.

"I'll rinse the brush with hot water when the kettle boils," Mabel explained as she scrubbed out a cereal bowl.

Violet looked out into the living room. "Mrs. Angus has dozed off." She grinned. "At least I won't be feeling guilty when I tell Jody I don't need her to clean my house."

Mabel wiped her forehead with her forearm. "Look at Mrs. Angus; she's got a lap blanket over her. And I'm sweating buckets here."

MABEL TOSSED THE DISHCLOTH into the sink. The kitchen was clean, and the hairbrush, although wet, was also clean.

Violet carried a mug of tea to the living room.

Mrs. Angus awoke with a start. "Thank you," she said, her hands shaking as she grasped the cup.

Violet stood with her hands on her hips, frowning as she looked around the room.

Picking a doily off the arm of a rocking chair, Mabel sat, fiddling with it. She said, "So, you let Jody go."

"Yes, at first, she was very good. Then, she started to take advantage. I didn't mind at first. She is such a friendly girl." She sipped her tea. "This is just what I needed."

"Where is your vacuum cleaner, Mrs. Angus?"

"My vacuum?"

"Violet, please, we are having a chat with Mrs. Angus. We are not here to clean."

"It wouldn't take long."

Mabel rolled her eyes. "We are here to visit, remember?"

Sighing, Violet perched on the arm of the couch beside Mrs. Angus.

"My vacuum cleaner is in the storage room off the bathroom."

Violet rose.

"Violet," Mabel warned.

Violet compressed her lips and regained her perch.

"Now, what did you mean 'take advantage'?" Mabel asked.

Mrs. Angus frowned. "Take advantage?"

"How did Jody take advantage of you? You said the girl was good at the start. Then she took advantage of you. Did she ask you for money?"

"Oh, no, nothing like that. Although, a few pieces of jewelry went missing. But it was just costume jewelry, nothing valuable. So, I don't really care, and I've got no one to leave it to." She took a sip of tea.

"Did Jody ever shop for you?" Mabel asked.

"Well, she did at first, but then she would forget to get half the items I wanted."

"How did she pay for your groceries? Did you give Jody your credit card? Or your bank card?"

"My debit card." Mrs. Angus set her mug on the coffee table.

Mabel exchanged a knowing look with Violet. "Mrs. Angus, I'm afraid you are too trusting with your bank card. An unscrupulous person could use your card and help themselves to your money. And you gave Jody your bank code."

"Well, yes, dear, I did. But Jody doesn't have my debit card anymore. I got it back. Now I phone the store, and they deliver, and I write them a cheque for my groceries. This works very well," Mrs. Angus said with a satisfied smile.

"That was wise. You can never be too careful," Mabel said.

"I had to let Jody go," repeated Mrs. Angus. "Did I tell you she doesn't clean properly? Well, you can see that for yourself. What a mess. I shall be happy when the agency sends someone else."

Violet ran a finger over the coffee table, leaving a streak behind. "And Jody had your keys to the building and your suite. Did you get the keys back?"

"Oh, I knew I forgot something. I'll phone Jody tomorrow and get my keys back. Nice tea." She took another sip.

Violet went into the kitchen, returning with a wad of paper towels.

"That's not good," Mabel said.

"It will have to do," Violet said, taking magazines off the coffee table and wiping off the dust.

Mabel sighed, "Not the towels, Violet. Jody still has Mrs. Angus's keys."

"What, dear?" Mrs. Angus held out her mug; the cup wavered in the air.

Mabel took the cup from her hand. "Your keys, you said Jody, has your keys?"

"Oh, yes, I must remember to get them back. I should phone Jody." The frail woman's eyes scanned the room. "I wonder where I put her phone number?" Violet moved on to the TV, wiping off the screen.

"Mrs. Angus, do you remember the day when Hannah fell down the stairs? Was Jody here bathing you?"

"She never gave me a bath," snorted Mrs. Angus. "She helps me in and out of the tub."

"On the day Hannah fell, do you remember if Jody was helping you have a bath?"

Mrs. Angus sat silently for a moment. She wrinkled her brow. "I do remember there was bathwater all over the floor. I had to tell her to wipe it up."

"Was this the same day Hannah fell?"

The thin, frail woman bit her lip, and her eyes closed for a moment. "No, sorry, I can't remember if she came that day or not. I wonder where I put Jody's phone number?"

Chapter Thirty-Four

Mabel closed the door to Mrs. Angus's unit. "It looks like we've caught our killer, well, not caught, but we know who the killer is."

"Hold your horses. Mrs. Angus didn't say Jody wasn't helping her with her bath when Hannah fell. She said she couldn't remember."

"But Jody had her debit card and the code. She may have had a card from Mini and Hannah. There were irregularities with Mini's bank account. Money is withdrawn. Most likely, Hannah was missing money too. They confronted Jody and told her they were going to report her. And Jody kills them both."

"Keep your voice down," Violet cautioned. "And from what your mom said, Mini was out a pile of money. That amount could not have come from a checking account."

"I don't know how she did it. But I'm sure Jody is the killer."

Violet stopped in the lobby and turned to Mabel. "I'm not saying it isn't her. We have to be sure, and first things first, we need to get that key back from Jody. If you're right, Mrs. Angus might be the next victim."

"We will, but let's talk to my new friend Homer; he's a wily old devil. I'm sure he knows something. We should visit him. He is always taking the elevator, so he must be on the second floor. I wonder what his suite number is."

"All the units are listed at the entrance. I'll look; let me back in." Violet opened the door and slipped out.

"You know, there is another explanation to how someone can gain entrance," Mabel said as she opened the door for Violet. "Maybe the killer doesn't have a key, and someone lets the murderer in. Maybe the killer has an accomplice, someone living in the building."

"I don't think any of these seniors are cold-blooded killers."

Mabel followed Violet to the elevator. "Just because someone is old, that doesn't make them an angel. Look at Freda. She was a nasty piece of work."

They entered the elevator, and Mabel pressed the button to the second floor. "Anyway, my money is on Jody."

"Yes, but how much does Jody know about banking? As far as we know, she only had access to a debit card," Violet said as the elevator door closed. "And what about your mom? Something was wonky with her account. Jody didn't clean or shop for your mom."

"True, but maybe Jody has a background in banking. We'll know more after we talk to her."

"And what about old Farley, the janitor? He has keys, and he's here most of the time. And as you said, the man sure doesn't like these residents."

Mabel sighed. "Damn, another suspect. Why can't mysteries be easy?"

"Then it wouldn't be a mystery."

The elevator door opened, and standing in front of the doors. Homer and Gemma.

Mabel paused, looked at Homer, and smiled. "Hi, Homer," she said.

"Don't just stand there, gaping woman; get the hell out of the way; we're going down."

Mabel and Violet hurriedly exited the elevator.

"You were up here a few hours ago. Is your mother ill?" Gemma asked, following Homer into the elevator.

Mabel's lips turned down. "And you were up here too. What are you doing? Making the rounds."

Gemma's eyebrows arched, "What do you mean?" Before Gemma could add anything more, Homer pushed the button and the elevator door closed.

Violet grinned. "So much for your new friend."

"Never mind. We take the stairs and head Homer off. I want to talk to that old goat." They hurried to the stairs.

"You'll notice, Violet, even if you take these steps in a hurry, there is no danger of us falling," Mabel panted as they descended the stairs.

Violet grinned as she opened the stairwell door to the lobby. "A little winded?"

"It wasn't a race, you know," Mabel said when she saw her friend's grin.

Gemma watched Mabel and Violet as they entered the lounge. Then, she turned her attention to Abagail and her husband, Ned. The couple were playing cards by the window.

Homer thumped his walker across the carpet to a big armchair. "Do you two just like riding up and down in the elevator?" he snorted, looking at them with his rheumy eyes.

"No, we want to talk to you."

Charlie, sleeping on a long leather couch in front of the muted TV where a curling game was playing, snored. Over by another window, two women were assembling the same puzzle Freda and Hannah had been doing.

"What about?" asked Homer, sitting with a thump on a big, easy chair; his walker fell to the side. Violet picked it up and righted it.

"Well, it is kind of private," whispered Mabel.

"What?"

"I said it's kind of private," Mabel whispered again.

"What? Kind of what?"

"I said it's kind of private," Mabel shouted.

All heads in the room turned to look at her. Charlie set up on the couch, looking blearily around. "What's the score?" He asked.

"Private? What kind of private?" bellowed Homer.

"Good God," Mabel huffed. "How many kinds of private are there?"

"Never mind, Homer, I don't think now is a good time, maybe later," Violet said, poking Mabel.

"When would be a good time to have a chat with you?" Mabel asked.

"I'm a pretty busy man, and I don't know when it would be a good time."

Mabel crossed her arms and glared down at the small man. "You argumentative old—"

"We'll work something out," interrupted Violet. Come on, Mabel. We've got errands to run."

Mabel stared angrily at the old man. Homer, ignoring Mabel, picked up the TV remote and turned up the volume. Violet tugged on her arm, and Mabel reluctantly followed Violet out of the lounge across the lobby and out of the Manor.

Chapter Thirty-Five

"I'd like to take that cantankerous old man and shake him. There is nothing wrong with his hearing. What an old goat." Mabel zipped her jacket up and pulled on her red woollen gloves. It was starting to snow.

"Never mind, old Homer." Violet turned up the collar of her jacket. "And besides, the lounge is the last place to discuss whether Hannah was pushed or if she fell. Not with all those people around."

"I guess you're right," conceded Mabel.

"And we need to get that key back from Jody. Or rather, you have to. I should get home. Neville has been on his own all day."

"It sounds like you're tired of Neville. You should tell him to go home. Hospitality is one thing. But the man is squatting."

"He's not squatting." Violet opened the passenger side door to Mabel's car.

"Pull up your big girl panties, Violet. I think you're being taken advantage of."

"I am not," Violet denied, buckling up her seatbelt.

Mabel turned her car on and waited while the windshield wipers brushed the fluffy snow off the windows. "Whatever, you're a big girl. I'll drop you off and go visit Jody."

"I've changed my mind. If Jody is the killer, I don't think it is wise for you to go alone. Besides, Neville is in a strange mood. He's pouting."

"Really."

"Last night, he borrowed my car. He didn't say where he was going. When he came back, his face and hands were covered with mud and grass stains all over his clothes. And I detected an odour of manure. He didn't say where he'd been, but he had some unkind words to say about you. I told him outright to stop talking that way about you and clean my car. So that's what he is doing now, cleaning my car, or he'd better be." Violet tapped on her phone. "I've got Jody's Address." She recited the address to Mabel.

Grass stains and manure! So, that smug man did go cow-tipping. Mabel's blue eyes twinkled as she thought of what Bugs Bunny used to say, *'What an ultra maroon.'* Grinning, she backed out of the parking lot. The wipers continued to whip the snow off the windshield as they drove down the streets. Snow was beginning to accumulate on the curbs. She turned the car onto a residential avenue.

Jody's bungalow was an old one-story house wedged between two new homes. One had a three-car garage. Who would need three cars? Mabel wondered as she pulled her car into Jody's driveway, parking behind a beat-up old blue hatchback.

Big fluffy flakes of snow blew across the frost-covered lawn into the faces of the women as they walked up the path. Mabel rapped on the bright red door. They waited and knocked again. There was a loud thump at the door, followed by a dog barking and growling.

The door swung open, and a large Rottweiler leapt out. The two women darted back down the step. Jody reached down and grabbed the dog by the collar, dragging the snarling animal back away from the door. The dog resisted, baring its teeth, drool hanging from its jowls.

"Come in, don't worry about Percy; he's really just a pussycat." She jerked on the dog's collar again as it lunged forward.

Mabel and Violet, eyeing the dog, stepped cautiously onto an old, worn doormat that read Welcome. They stomped the snow off their shoes. There was an overpowering smell of cigarettes and stale beer.

"Who is it?" An unshaven young man, holding a can of beer, sauntered out from what appeared to be the kitchen.

"This is Alfie." Jody introduced, yanking the snarling, drooling dog away from the women.

"Hello, I'm Violet Ficher, and this is my friend, Mabel Havelock," Violet said, nervously bending to take off her shoes.

"Leave your shoes on; Jody never washed the floor." Alfie snickered.

Jody punched him on the arm. "Up yours, if you want the floors washed so bad, do it yourself."

The scruffy young man grinned and took a swig from his can of beer.

Jody turned to Violet. "But don't take your shoes off; I got carpets."

Mabel's eyes stayed transfixed on Percy, the Rottweiler. The dog made a low rumbling sound, eyeing Mabel, licking his chops.

Alfie lifted his t-shirt, scratching his potbelly, peering at them with red-rimmed eyes, he asked. "Want a beer?"

"No, thank you," Violet said, edging away from the dog.

"No, they don't want a beer," guffawed Jody. "They came to see me. But you didn't have to come here, Violet, I would have called you. But I haven't had time to look at my schedule." Jody turned to the slovenly dressed man with dirty blond hair slouching in the doorway. "Violet wants me to clean her house."

Alfie burped, then tilted the beer can, taking a gulp. "Good, you could use the work." He turned and wandered back into the kitchen. And much to Mabel's relief, the dog followed him.

Jody giggled. "Alfie is just teasing." She turned and shouted after him. "Alfie is the one out of work. And you got yourself fired, didn't you?"

"Shut the hell up. It wasn't my fault, and you know it." A beer can came sailing through the open kitchen door.

Jody snatched up the beer can and stormed into the kitchen. There was a loud crash; it sounded like furniture was falling over. The dog began barking. And more sounds of falling furniture, followed by a thump as if someone had fallen. The dog continued to bark excitedly.

"Ow, ow. Let me up, let me up, damn it."

"Say you're sorry."

"Okay, okay, I'm sorry I threw the damn can."

"Alright, now clean up this mess and get me a beer."

Violet's eyes widened; she looked uncomfortably at Mabel, who raised her eyebrows and shrugged.

Jody returned to the hallway with a can of beer; she grinned. "You can't take any crap, and that's a fact."

"Oh, no, of course not," Mabel agreed hurriedly.

"Come on in and sit down."

In the middle of the small hallway was a large basket that smelled like a dog. They gingerly stepped over it and entered the living room. Two big-screen TVs and three old sofas filled Jody's living room. Heavy purple drapes covering a window drooped on a sagging curtain rod.

"Sit down, and we can discuss our contract."

Violet sat on the edge of a couch, looking at an overflowing ashtray balanced on the arm of the sagging sofa. "Contract?"

"The terms for me doing your housework. I don't clean windows." She laughed. "Not that windows can be cleaned now. It's snowing out. Did you see the snow? An early winter."

"Yes, we drove through it, but it's not bad. It's just started," replied Mabel politely. She perched on the shabby couch beside Violet.

"And I don't do floors or wash walls." Jody took a swig of beer.

"Well, that's why I'm here. I'm sorry, I've decided not to hire you." Violet looked nervously at Jody.

"You came here to tell me you're not hiring me?"

"I know, I'm sorry, but I ah, I thought I should tell you in person," Violet said lamely.

"This is really sweet of you. I appreciate this. Not many people would go to the trouble of telling me in person."

"Oh, it's no problem; Violet always likes to do the right thing."

"Ha." Came a scoff from the kitchen. "Who's unemployed now?"

"You shut up and mind your own business," Jody shouted. "You want me to come back in there?" she threatened.

"Ha." Then, silence from the kitchen.

"Ah, yes, well, I came because we went to see Mrs. Angus. And well, she asked us to get her keys." Mabel lied; her eyes strayed to the kitchen. The dog stood in the doorway, watching her. Drool fell from his lips.

"She told you then about not wanting me back. Well, I don't care; this home care stuff is pretty heavy going. I think I'll just stick to house cleaning. I'm good at that."

Mabel looked around at the dingy room. "And the keys, dear, could we have her keys?"

"Yeah, sure. I'm glad to get rid of them." Jody set her can of beer on the arm of the couch and walked over to a table piled with remotes. "I bet it's because of nosy Gemma Charbon. She is always checking up on me. I bet that's why Mrs. Angus, let me go." She picked up her bag and dug into it, coming up with a set of keys. She peeled two keys off her key ring and handed them to Mabel.

Percy padded into the living room, emitting a low growl. Mabel slunk behind Jody and stuck the keys in her pocket.

"Thanks, Jody. I'm sure you will soon get lots of work." Violet elbowed Mabel to the door. "If you don't mind me asking, why two TVs? And three sofas?" she asked.

"We don't like the same programs," explained Jody. "And one couch is for Percy. He doesn't like his basket much."

Mabel wondered how each of them heard what was on their TVs. But she didn't ask. The dog was looking at her and licking his chops.

Chapter Thirty-Six

Snow sifted off the roof of Jody's house, blowing across the lawn, and small skiffs of snow started to form. A layer of fluffy snow-covered Mabel's car. She pulled on her red gloves, using her gloved hand to wipe the driver's side window free of snow.

"Have you got winter tires?" Violet asked as she pulled the sleeve of her jacket over her hand, using her arm to clean the accumulated snow off her side of the car.

"No, darn it. I always think I've got lots of time."

"I should have worn gloves," Violet muttered, brushing snow off the rear window with her bare hands. She then hurriedly climbed into Mabel's car. Blowing her warm breath on her hands, rubbing them together.

Mabel shut her car door, and a layer of snow off her car roof settled on her windshield. Shuddering, Mabel started her car and turned on the heater. A blast of cold air came out of the vents.

"If you had a newer car, you could have command-start, and we would have heat by now."

"Never mind, it will warm up in a minute or two."

"My feet are cold," Violet said, stomping her snow-packed runners.

Mabel turned her car lights on; it was getting dark. "You'll be fine. I think it's warming up already."

"Yeah, right." Violet blew on her hands again.

"It is." Mabel switched on her windshield wipers and waited until the wipers cleared a small arc on her windscreen. Then she put her car in reverse, the tires spun, gunning the motor, she backed the car out of Jody's driveway. "What did you think of Jody?"

"She is a lousy housekeeper; I'm glad I don't need her to clean. But I honestly don't think she has the skill to get into any bank accounts." Violet squinted out into the dark, snowy night. "Are you sure you can see? Maybe we should wait until your windshield is completely clear."

"It's fine," Mabel said, peering through the small arc on her windscreen; soft, fluffy snow was Swirling up. She met another car; snowflakes churned, momentarily obstructing her vision; she slowed her car. "Back to Jody, she appears innocent enough, but you never know. She did have a key. And that boyfriend. I don't trust him. But he doesn't appear to be the sharpest tack in the box." Driving slowly to the corner, she applied her brakes; the car skidded and then came to a stop. She looked both ways, then crawled slowly down the street.

"Jody sure put Alfie in his place. I think she's the boss in that house."

Mabel chuckled and turned her car slowly onto the main street. "Jody's right though you can't take crap, and that's a fact," she said. The swirling snow was making the streetlights glow with a halo.

After a long pause, Violet said, "I feel like eating out. Do you want to stop and have supper? We could go to Pam and Ally's. Or do you think it's snowing too hard?"

"No, it's not snowing all that much; it's the wind that is blowing the loose snow around. I'll try to park close to the door."

MABEL SAT IN A BOOTH across from Violet and unzipped her jacket.

"I'm phoning Neville," Violet said, taking her phone out of her pocket.

"Are you asking him to join us?"

"No, I'm telling him to fend for himself."

Mabel tried not to listen to Violet as she gave detailed instructions on how to heat leftovers. She looked around the crowded café. Gemma was sitting at the front of the restaurant by a window. The man sitting with her had his back turned, but Mabel knew who the man was. "Look," she said when Violet finished her call. "It's Randy, the rat. And look who he's having supper with."

Violet shrugged, putting her phone in her pocket. "Oh, your favourite person. Gemma."

The door to the kitchen burst open. Voices were raised, followed by the sounds of pots and pans crashing. Looking over his shoulder, Ally darted out of the kitchen. Pam, a tall, thin Asian woman, followed him. She shouted in a mixture of a Chinese dialect and English. She then turned on her heel and strutted back into the kitchen.

The diners, who had seen this scene played out many times before, turned their attention back to their food.

"Something must be in the air. The women in this town seem to be a tad testy tonight."

"Testy?"

"First, Jody, now Pam and you."

"I'm not testy."

"You didn't invite Neville for supper," Mabel teased.

Violet unrolled her silverware from a white paper napkin and laid the cutlery beside the serviette. "I'm having a night out. Good lord, we are not married."

"I'm just teasing, sorry."

Ally hurried over to their table. "Good evening, ladies. An early snowstorm. But never mind the weather outside. It is nice and cozy in our café, and the special is very good tonight. Deep-fried wontons, mushroom chow mein, honey garlic wings, vegetables with almonds."

"That would be great, and green tea, too, please."

Violet ordered the same.

"Is everything okay with Pam?" Mabel asked, feigning innocence.

"Oh, yes, everything is fine." Ally shrugged. "I suggested we have a menu like the new restaurant on the highway. But Pam says no."

"Your café is nearly full on a snowy weekday evening, so maybe Pam is right," Violet said.

Ally shrugged again as he looked around at the patrons. "I will bring you your tea."

"I wonder what Gemma and Randy have in common?" Mabel mused as she watched Ally hurry away. "They seemed to be in deep conversation. Don't you think they make an odd couple?"

"Why odd?"

"Gemma strikes me as a woman who likes the finer things in life. You've seen the clothes she wears and the car she drives. Old Randy is not fine by any stretch of the imagination. Oh, look, no, don't look. Gemma has just thrown down her napkin, and she is leaning across the table. Randy is shrinking back in his chair." Violet turned to look.

"I told you, don't look."

"Why not?"

"We'll look like nosey parkers. That's why."

"It has never bothered you before."

"Never mind, don't look. I'll give you a play-by-play of the goings-on."

"Goings-on? Now, you have piqued my interest."

Mabel continued to watch the couple. "Gemma is doing all the talking; her elbows are on the table. And now, she is leaning over the table and looks angry. Randy is holding up his hands as if he is fending her off. Oh, and now Randy is nodding. His head is going up and down like a puppet on a string."

"That doesn't sound like any goings-on. Randy and Gemma are having a conversation. Big deal," Violet said, polishing her silverware with her paper napkin.

"No, now Gemma has risen, and she is going around the table to Randy. Now, she is leaning over him, and she is. Oh, oh eww, she is giving Randy a peck on the cheek. Ugh, can you imagine kissing that man? Ugh." Mabel grimaced.

Violet proceeded to unwrap Mabel's cutlery, polishing each item. "You said a peck on the cheek; that's hardly a kiss."

"Whatever," Mabel said, wrinkling her forehead. "There is something not right about that woman."

Violet did an eye roll and lined up Mabel's cutlery.

"Yeah, yeah, I know I might be a tad jealous. But something about her doesn't ring true."

"True or not. Gemma was definitely in the lounge when Hannah fell, and she was driving Homer around when Freda fell."

"I know. And I know it's probably Jody who killed those poor women. But somehow, I'd like it a whole lot better if it was Gemma," Mabel lamented.

"We've been through this. Jody isn't a mastermind. She might have taken some costume jewelry. And Mrs. Angus isn't sure about that. And we know Jody only had Mrs. Angus's debit card. We agree she couldn't steal thousands of dollars with a debit card. And remember the withdrawals from your mom's account? We've already established Jody never cleaned for her. So how would she steal from your mom?"

"I haven't figured that out. Maybe Jody has an accomplice. Follow the money."

"Follow the money? What the heck does that mean?"

"It's the motive, it means follow the money."

"Where did you get that from? It's another mystery on TV. You watch way too much murder and mayhem. You should start watching cooking shows."

"I like murder and mayhem," Mabel said. Alie lifted an eyebrow and shook his head as he delivered their order.

As Mabel ate, she kept glancing over at Randy and Gemma. "When we finish supper, I want to have another go at Homer. Remember, I told you he made a comment about Hannah and those stairs. I think he knows something," Mabel said. "It pains me to say, but I guess I have to try again and talk to that obstinate old fart. But you seem a little testy tonight. After supper, I'll take you home. We can talk to Homer tomorrow."

"Stop saying I'm testy," Violet demanded. "I'm game to go tonight. Although, I don't know how we're going to get him to talk to us. Despite what you told me, you and Homer are still not the best of buddies."

"Mom."

"Pardon me?"

"Mom, he's taken a fancy to my mom. She's our ace in the hole. He'll help us if I play the mom card."

"The mom card?"

"I'm not sure how I'll do it, but I will convince Homer he is helping Mom by helping us." Mabel looked over at the table by the window. "Randy is grinning at something Gemma is saying. Gemma is throwing back her head, and she's laughing. Now Gemma is reaching across the table and pressing Randy's arm," reported Mabel. "That's flirting if I ever saw it," she said, pushing her plate away and picking up her teacup.

Violet swallowed and said, "I don't know how you managed to eat so fast. You were spying on those two by the window the whole time."

Mabel shrugged and sipped her tea, her eyes still on Randy and Gemma. Randy rose from the table, helped Gemma with her coat, and then went to the long counter. A petite girl of eleven or twelve sat on a high stool behind the cash register. She handed Randy a credit card reader. Randy paid the young girl and turned, spotting Mabel and Violet; he sauntered to their table.

Mabel set her cup down and peered up at him. "Hi, Randy. Are you and Gemma out on the town?"

"It's Randolph, and we're just friends," blurted Randy, his faded blue eyes darting to look at Gemma.

Mabel grinned. "Well, I would think so; one rarely eats with an enemy."

Randy's face turned red, his long white lashes blinking rapidly, he sputtered. "Oh, ah, no, not an enemy."

Standing beside Randy, Gemma buttoned her coat. "Never mind, her. Mabel always thinks she's funny." The tall, imposing woman pulled on a pair of black leather gloves, pursed her lips, and asked. "Where is dear Sophie? Didn't you invite your mom out for supper?"

"Ah, well, no, I hadn't thought..." Mabel's voice trailed off.

"I see, poor dear Sophie." Gemma looked down at Mabel with a superior smile. She tugged on Randy's arm. "We'd better be going Randolph. We don't want to interrupt Mabel's fun night out on the town."

Randy tugged a blue and white toque on his head, his long white-blond hair stuck out in a fringe around his face.

As the couple left, the door swung open, and a blast of cold wind chilled the room.

Mabel bit her lip and sighed. She should have invited her mom out for supper. Gemma was right. She was a thoughtless daughter.

THEY DARTED TO MABEL'S car. The snow had stopped falling, but the wind was whipping up the new-fallen snow, driving it into their faces.

Mabel started her car. The windshield wipers flipped back and forth, brushing off the snow, but she still couldn't see out. The windows were frosted. "To heck with old Homer. I'm for going home. The night is too nasty to go sleuthing." Mabel turned her car heater on full blast, watching as the frost gradually melted on the windshield.

"I agree. Neville will wonder if I'm okay. I doubt if he's seen this much snow back in England."

A small arc of frost cleared on the driver-side windshield. "I think it's interesting; Gemma was having supper with Randy, the rat."

"You have to let your childhood prejudice go. Get over it; we all change when we grow up."

Mabel looked out the car window, the snow was blowing, piling up on the sidewalk. "You weren't there when Mom and I went to his office. Randy hasn't changed; he's still a rat." She put the car in gear and backed up. The tires spun, then got traction. As she drove cautiously down the street, another car's lights flashed in her eyes. "Idiot, put your lights on dim," she shouted.

"He's not going to hear you." Chuckled Violet. "It would probably help if you got your cataracts taken care of."

"Yes, Doctor Violet, I will." Mabel drove slowly down the snow-covered street and parked at the curb in front of Violet's house.

Neville, wearing a light sweater and covered in snow, bounded up to the car. He opened the car door for Violet and exclaimed excitedly, "Isn't this wonderful? Look at all this snow; we should build a snowman."

"It's the wrong kind of snow," Mabel said.

"Wrong kind of snow?"

"The snow is too fluffy; it won't pack. Oh, never mind, Violet will tell you, shut the door; you're freezing me out."

"You're Canadian. Don't you like the cold?" he snarled.

Mabel grinned. She so wanted to ask how the cow tipping went. But she decided not to. Instead, she said, "Canadians don't stand around in a snowstorm in their shirtsleeves like you. If you stay here long enough, the thrill of the first snowfall will soon diminish."

Chapter Thirty-Seven

Sipping her coffee, Mabel looked out her kitchen window at the new-fallen snow. The morning was bright and sunny; the snow glistened, and the temperature had risen. Neville would be happy; the snow would be perfect for making a snowman. But it was Remembrance Day, time for that later. Mabel checked her watch. She'd better find her winter boots and jacket before setting off to the ceremony. Setting her empty cup in the sink, Mabel went off in search of her winter coat.

There was a sharp rap at her door, and when the door opened, Violet entered, dressed in a red down-filled jacket. Followed by Neville, he had on a white and green ski jacket that had seen better days, big black earmuffs over his ears, and a green scarf wrapped around his neck. They stomped the snow off their boots on the black mat that lay in front of the door,

Mabel smiled. "I see you got some winter clothes."

"I went around to my neighbour, Miles, and he outfitted Neville," Violet answered, adjusting the poppy pinned to her jacket.

"I was afraid the snow would be melted by now, and I'm very pleased to see it hasn't. What a nice brisk walk we've had to your house." Neville took off his mitts and grinned.

"This will melt. Hopefully, by March, if we're lucky."

"Seriously?"

"Yes, and soon it will get cold."

"Get cold? It's quite chilly now." He looked expectantly at Violet.

Violet shrugged indifferently and pulled off her gloves.

"The word is chilly, not cold. If you want a warmer winter, you have to go to the west coast. Out here on the prairies, this is it until the spring. Anyway, I'll dig out my winter jacket; we need to get a move on it. We have to be at the cenotaph before eleven o'clock." Time to have a chat with Neville, Mabel thought as she opened her closet door. Violet was just too soft-hearted; she was sure Violet was tired of his freeloading.

MABEL, VIOLET, AND Neville joined the large group of townspeople who were wearing red poppies and gathered around the tall cenotaph. Everyone was chatting and commenting on the early snowfall. The Sound of bagpipes brought all the conversations to a stop. They stood silent as a young Air Cadet piped the small legion of veterans with medals pinned to their chests to the war memorial. Two RCMP officers followed in their full-dress uniform. More Air Cadets and local dignitaries brought up the rear. They lined up in neat military rows in front of the cenotaph. On top of the monument was a statue of a soldier from the First World War. The soldier's hands rested on the butt of a rifle. His head bowed down as if he were looking at the long list of soldiers from Glenhaven who died fighting for peace and freedom.

A tall young cadet with curly red hair sang the national anthem, *Oh Canada*. The crowd joined in, faltering when the boy sang the second verse in French. A young blonde girl straightened her cadet jacket and marched to stand in front of the dignitaries. She paused, took a deep breath, and then recited the poem, In Flanders Fields, in a crystal-clear voice. When the young girl concluded the poem, a cadet played *The Last Post* on his trumpet as the Canadian and Legion flags were lowered. All heads bowed in the two minutes of silence. No one stamped their feet, even in the icy chill. The trumpet sounded again with the reveille, and flags rose. Then, wreaths were placed at the foot of the monument.

A tall, gaunt, grey-haired minister wearing a long black robe with a brown padded parka zipped over it strode to stand in front of the cenotaph. As he opened his bible, the bottom of his robe flared out. He began with a scripture reading from the bible. He then proceeded to give a lengthy explanation of the passage and why he chose it, launching into a sermon. The adults in the crowd began to shift their feet. And as the minister droned on, children tugged on their parent's arms, grumbling and whining.

Mathew Hamilton, the mayor of Glenhaven, walked up to the minister. The big barrel-chested man pulled up a sleeve of his red and black ski jacket and tapped on his watch. The minister looked at the mayor, stopped mid-sermon and finished with a short prayer.

"Thank you, Reverend Windgate. And now, ladies and gentlemen, please join us at the community center for more speeches." He chuckled, "I promise not to talk too long. And our wonderful ladies' auxiliary will serve lunch."

The crowd followed the veterans and the RCMP down the snowy streets. The cadets ran ahead, as did the school children, shrieking and yelling, tossing snowballs.

"Snowballs," shouted Neville, excitably scooping up a handful of snow.

Mabel was quicker and was an old hand at snowball fights. She packed the snow in her hands and fired a snowball at Neville, but her aim was off, and it only grazed his shoulder. He turned and hurled his snowball at Mabel, who ducked; the snowball slammed into Violet. Violet let out a hoot, returning fire. The children howled with joy as their parents joined in the snowball fight. Soon, the children and the adults were hurling snowballs at each other.

"Really, on a day like today, you people should show some decorum," shouted the mayor's wife, Gloria Hamilton. A snowball sailed over Mabel's head and smashed into a snow-laden tree. The branches vibrated, and snow fell, showering the tall blonde woman. "Stop this right now," Gloria shrieked angrily, brushing and shaking her head; snow cascaded off her hair and coat.

"Never mind, Gloria," called a wizened little veteran with a chest full of medals. He was hobbling down the street, leaning heavily on a wooden cane. "I don't think any of us think good, clean fun is disrespectful."

"And don't forget lunch is waiting for us at the hall," voiced Constable Shamanski. The big man slowed his steps to walk slowly alongside the old veteran.

"Food," yelled the redheaded cadet. And a mad dash to the community hall ensued. The adults laughed, brushed off their snow-covered mitts and gloves, and followed the children.

Neville grinned, shaking snow off his mitts. "That was fun."

Mabel and Violet smiled in agreement, dropping their snowballs.

IT WAS HOT IN THE COMMUNITY hall. Coats were hung over the backs of the chairs or piled on top. The chairs that were once set in straight, uniform lines were now pushed into untidy rows. The speeches were finally over, and as usual, Mayor Hamilton's remarks were long-winded. The mayor had been no better than the Reverend Windgate. People were milling around, waiting for the luncheon to begin. As Mabel removed her coat, she spotted Gemma and her brother Paul conversing with the reverend. Gemma was holding onto Reverend Windgate's arm. He appeared to be lapping up every word she said. The reverend threw back his head, laughing at some witticism Gemma shared. Her brother Paul joined in.

"She is quite the social butterfly," muttered Mabel.

"Yes, Violet sure is," agreed Neville, his thumb and index flattening his mustache.

Across the hall, Violet was visiting with Helen and Mary.

"No, not Violet, I meant Gemma," corrected Mabel. Then she smiled and draped her jacket on the back of a chair. Now was her chance. If she could get this man alone, she'd read the riot act to him. Taking Neville by the arm, she said, "There is a plaque at the back of the hall; I think you would be interested to see."

"I'm not going anywhere with you. What prank do you have in mind at this time?"

"No, prank, and I'm sorry I played that little joke on you," Mabel said, hoping he would believe her.

"Fool me once and shame on you, fool me twice, shame on me." Neville turned to go.

"No, really, no prank, no joke, it's something I think as an English man you will be interested in. You'll see how the Canadians joined in the war to help Britain."

Neville eyed Mabel suspiciously but followed her through the throng of people to the back of the room.

Mabel stopped under a large brass plate with the names of the veterans who had served in the First World War. "What are you up to?"

"What do you mean up to?" Neville looked at Mabel. "You're the one up to something, sending me on that wild goose chase. Cow Tipping!"

"This isn't about my little joke. And I wouldn't have played it, if you weren't such a jerk."

"A jerk!"

Mabel waited until two old Vets with medals on their chests moved away. "Yes, a jerk. And you've been freeloading off Violet since, well, for months."

"You are the rudest person I have ever had the misfortune to meet. Violet invited me to visit."

Mabel crossed her arms. "I don't care what you consider rude. You are taking advantage of Violet's good nature. You've been here way too long for any house guest."

"Has Violet complained to you?"

"No, she hasn't."

"Well, there you are then."

A couple with two small children came to look at the plaque. "Your great grandad's name is on here. Let's see if we can find it?" The kids gathered around as the woman ran her finger down the list of names.

Mabel took Neville's arm and maneuvered him to a quieter corner of the hall. "No one comes for a visit and stays as long as you have. I don't care that Violet invited you. Three months is too long."

"It's none of your business how long I stay, and Violet isn't complaining. In fact, we're having a delightful time. I'm getting to know a part of Canada I've never seen. And I'm enjoying it."

"Are you planning to immigrate?"

Neville, turning to leave, said, "You're jealous, that's what you are."

Mabel grabbed his arm. "Jealous? Of what? Of You? You have a very inflated ego. I have no interest in you other than thinking you're up to something. I don't know what your game is. But I'm watching you. If you are up to no good, I will be your worst nightmare."

Neville yanked his arm from Mabel's grasp. "Up to no good? I am insulted you think so little of me."

Mabel eyed the outraged man. Had she gone too far? She did have a suspicious nature. "Why are you still here?"

"Not that it's any of your business, but." Neville paused and looked across the hall at Violet. "I've been enamoured with Violet since I first saw her in Egypt. She's everything a man like me could want. But after a few days, Violet kind of lost interest in me. I think if I stay longer, she will get to know me better. And well, maybe she will feel the way I do." His voice trailed off, and he turned and walked away.

Mabel's face reddened, and her mouth hung open. She'd really put her foot in it. Neville was in love with Violet. She watched as Neville maneuvered through the crowd on his way to Violet. Darn it, why did she say anything? She hoped Neville didn't tell Violet she had accused him of freeloading. Violet would be furious. She frowned. Did Neville say a part of Canada? That could mean he'd been to Canada before, but it didn't mean anything, did it? She'd worry about that later; her stomach rumbled; lunch was being served.

Long lines of adults and children lined up at the booths where the ladies' auxiliary served coffee, bunwiches and dainties. The people dropped money in a basket, donations for the Legion Auxiliary that provided the lunch.

Mabel spied Homer on the far side of the hall. She would corner the old goat and see what he knew about Hannah. Maybe he even knew or suspected something about Mini's death.

She balanced a small paper plate with a bunwich and a selection of dainties and made her way through the crowd to where Homer sat.

"I brought you some lunch," Mabel said, offering him the plate.

"What do you want?" Homer looked at her with his rheumy eyes.

"I'm just being nice. Why can't you accept that?"

Homer snorted. "I doubt that." He took the plate. "Where is my coffee? You didn't bring coffee?"

Mabel's eyes narrowed; she had half a mind to take the plate back. But she guessed he was right. It was a bribe. "Coming right up," she said with forced cheerfulness. She returned with two coffees and a plate of food for herself and sat beside Homer. She offered him the Styrofoam cup of coffee.

Homer looked at the cup. "I can't eat and hold that coffee." He took a bite out of the bunwich.

Mabel pressed her lips together, fighting back a retort. She smiled and placed the coffee cups on the floor beside her chair.

"Hi, Homer, wasn't that a nice service? But then it always is," Violet said, joining them. She pulled a chair beside Mabel, balancing the plate and her coffee cup.

"Yup." Homer's mouth muffled as he munched on his bunwich.

"Where's Neville?" Mabel asked, wondering if he snitched on her.

"Visiting with Alfred." Violet selected her bunwich, giving it the once over.

Mabel relaxed. So far, so good; Neville hadn't squealed on her. At least not yet.

"Coffee, I'd like a drink of my coffee. Did you put cream in it?"

Mabel, fed up with catering, snapped, "I don't know what you take in your coffee. You're lucky I even brought you any."

Homer grinned. "Well, it's a good thing you didn't. I take my coffee black."

Mabel bit her tongue and gave Homer his coffee. She brushed a crumb off her lap, took a deep breath, and said, "You're a very perceptive man, Homer. I bet you know something about Hannah's fall down the stairs."

"Your lame attempts to flatter me won't work. But bribery will. Get me another piece of that peanut butter marshmallow cake thingy."

"You mean confetti squares?"

"I don't know what it's called, but it has peanut butter and marshmallows in it."

Mabel gave Violet a surprised look. Was this all it took? "Sure, Homer, I'll get you a piece of cake."

"Two, I want two."

Mabel made her way through the crowd to the counter. The peanut butter marshmallow cake pan was empty. She spotted her friend Mary, who had a piece of the cake on her plate. Mabel grabbed a paper napkin and darted over to Mary.

"May I have your slice of confetti square?"

Mary gave her a questioning look. "You want my cake?"

"It's not for me. The cake is for Homer. It's vital that I give him that piece of peanut butter marshmallow cake."

Mary raised her eyebrows. "Okay, sure, if you think he needs it."

"Thanks, Mary, you're a pal." Mabel took the slice of the cake and looked around for another. She spotted Alice, and Alice had a slice of the cake. No, not Alice. Detecting was all well and good, but she drew the line at asking Alice.

She prowled through the crowd, searching for the cake. She spied Mayor Hamilton; the man had a slice of the confetti square. He was talking to Constable Robert Shamanski, who Mabel thought looked very smart in his red serge. She snuck around behind the mayor's back and waited. The man was extolling the benefits of living in Glenhaven. When the mayor gestured with his hands, the paper plate with the slice of cake was near at hand. Quickly, Mabel plucked the cake off his plate and slunk away. Out of the corner of her eye, she saw Robert watching her; he had a grin on his face.

"Here you go, Homer, and you better enjoy it. And what you have to tell us had better be good. I could be arrested for stealing cake."

She waited while Homer happily consumed the two slices of confetti squares, then asked. "Okay, shoot, what do you know?"

"Know about what?"

"What do you know about these unfortunate deaths at the condo?"

"Which one?"

"What do you mean which one?"

"Do you mean Freda or Hannah?" Violet asked. She and Mabel pulled their chairs closer to Homer's.

"Why should I give you fodder for gossip?"

"We are not interested in gossip. Violet and I are trying to figure out what is going on at the condo. Three deaths in as many months."

"Why should I tell you?"

"I brought you cake," Mabel fumed. What an obstinate old goat.

"We're worried someone else could be in danger. Like Mabel's mom."

Homer crushed the corners of his Styrofoam cup, looking thoughtful.

"Do you have any information that would help us? You said something the day Hannah fell. You said Hannah falling down those stairs was no accident. What did you mean?" Mabel asked.

"All I know is no one in the building takes the stairs except for Farley. And Hannah certainly didn't. She was all hunched over. She would never go down those stairs, never. Besides, her condo was on the first floor. Of course, she might have been visiting someone. Still, she would never take the stairs. No one does."

"Is that all? I stole a piece of cake from the mayor for this?" Mabel folded her arms and glared at Homer.

"You stole a slice of cake from the mayor?" Violet looked askance.

"There is more." Homer grinned, licking the peanut butter off his fingers.

"What?" Mabel's eyes narrowed with suspicion. "This better be good."

"Remember when you left your purse in the lounge?"

"I remember."

"I brought you your purse. For all the thanks I got," Homer grumbled.

"You might get a thank you if you were a little more—"

"How nice of you, Homer. I'm sure Mabel means thank you, don't you?" interrupted Violet.

"Whatever. I'm sure I thanked you."

Violet eyed Mabel and shook her head.

Mabel sighed and said, "Thank you, Homer, for retrieving my purse."

"I made sure you got it back. Because Hannah was a kleptomaniac," Homer said triumphantly.

"Again, this is not news to us. We already know Hannah was light-fingered." Mabel gave Homer a dismissive look.

"Yeah, well, that loony woman stole stuff from everyone." Homer curled his lip. "She'd sneak into our apartments and lift stuff. Hannah was nuts. I know for a fact the woman even snuck into Freda's suite right after Freda fell down the stairs. Some friend she was. Mind you, old Freda knew where all the bodies were buried, if you get my drift."

"As in, Freda knew secrets," Violet said.

"Yep, that old bitch tried it on with me once. She said she knew stuff about me."

"Language, Homer, watch your language," rebuked Violet.

"And please lower your voice. It's not nice to speak ill of the dead," Mabel said.

"What's she gonna do? Come back and haunt me, although I wouldn't put it past the old bitch, and she was an old—"

"Homer," Violet warned.

"Anyway, I told the old bat to get lost. I don't give a damn who knows what about me. I'm not ashamed of anything I've done."

Mabel grinned. "I bet you're not."

Violet shook her head at Mabel, then said, "Homer, you said Hannah snuck into Freda's suite right after she fell down the stairs. How do you know she did?"

"Yeah. Are you perhaps gossiping?" Mabel asked.

"I'm not gossiping, you fool, woman. Hannah showed me Freda's phone."

"Hannah bragged she took Freda's phone?" Violet exchanged a jubilant look with Mabel.

"No, Hannah didn't brag. But when she asked why, the phone didn't work. I asked her where she got it from. That's when Hannah let it slip; she'd stolen it from Freda's suite. So, I told the stupid woman she had to have the password. Everyone knows you have to have a password." Homer held up his phone and grinned a superior smile.

"Did you tell anyone Hannah stole Freda's phone?" Mabel asked.

Homer shrugged. "Why would I do that? I mind my own business. Besides, the phone was of no use to Freda. She was dead. Hannah might as well get some use out of it. If she could figure out how to get into it."

Mabel gave Violet a sidelong look. The killer didn't take Freda's phone. Hannah did. "So, what did Hannah do with the phone?"

"She said she'd ask Gemma how to unlock the phone. Like a dim bulb like Gemma would be able to get into Freda's phone," snorted Homer.

Chapter Thirty-Eight

"Where's Neville?" Mabel asked anxiously. "I didn't see him after the Remembrance Day Service." She filled her kettle with water and put it on the stove, turning on the burner.

"Yes, you did; I saw you showing him the veteran's plaque at the back of the hall. What were you talking about?" Violet sat on a kitchen chair, fidgeting with her scarf.

"Oh, yeah, right." Mabel bit her bottom lip and looked nervously at Violet.

"So, what did you two talk about?" Violet gave Mabel a searching look, folding her scarf into squares on her knee.

"Oh, this and that." Mabel didn't meet Violet's eyes. She rinsed her teapot, added two tea bags, and stalled for time. Did that rat tattle on her?

Violet unfolded and re-folded her scarf; she bit her lip and then asked, "Did Neville mention a trip?"

Mabel took out two cups from her cupboard and asked. "A trip? Is he going home?"

"Eventually. I was going to tell you about it, so don't get all huffy," Violet said hurriedly.

"Tell me about what?" Mabel set the cups on the table.

"A trip, a tour to the Nordic countries ending in Russia."

"So, Neville is going to Russia, that's nice."

"I planned on taking the tour too." Violet tugged on her scarf. "Of course, I wanted you to come as well."

"I'm not sure I can. Mom was miffed that I went to Egypt."

"It doesn't matter, anyway."

"Why not? If you want to go with Neville, you should go." Mabel pasted a smile on her face. Darn it, she'd love to go, but just because she couldn't, there was no reason Violet should stay home.

"I'm not going, and I suspect neither will Neville."

"You're not going to Russia because of me?"

"No." Violet rolled her scarf into a ball. "But you were right."

"I was right?"

"Neville is a moocher."

"Am I hearing you right? You're saying Neville is a moocher?"

"Yes, I am. Last night, he tried to convince me to pay for the tour, for me and for him. He said he would pay me back, but he's short of funds at the moment."

"He wants you to pay for the trip?"

"I was taken aback." Violet tied her scarf in a knot. "I said no, and then we had a loud discussion."

"I bet you did," Mabel said grimly. She pulled out a chair from the table and sat across from Violet.

"Yes, we did. I told him to pack his bag and leave." Violet sighed. "That was when Neville told me he had no money for a return ticket back to England."

That slimy dog fumed Mabel silently. Neville had convinced her that he was in love with her friend. She'd been right all along. The man was a con artist. "If I were a better person, I wouldn't say I told you so. But I'm not. I told you so; he is a con artist."

Violet threw down her scarf. "That's exactly why I didn't want to tell you. I knew you would lord it over me."

"I'm not lording it over you, but I was right. I knew something was fishy about that man. You're not going to loan him money, are you?"

Violet glowered. "Did I say I was lending Neville money?"

Mabel leaned across the table. "Are you?"

"No, I'm not. Neville is waiting for the money from his brother."

Mabel rolled her eyes. "I hope the money isn't coming by packhorse over the mountains. When is the man leaving?"

"I don't know. But I can tell you, as soon as his brother sends him the money, he is leaving. Get your kettle; it's boiling."

Mabel rose, went to the stove, and poured hot water into her teapot. "So, in the meantime, what are you going to do?"

"I'm not giving him any money. But I can't just kick him out; he has nowhere to go. But I did give him a deadline. He's got until the end of the week to get his finances sorted out."

Mabel brought the teapot to the table. "Your problem is you're too nice."

"I know now he was just taking advantage of me. And Neville would have continued to do so if I had let him."

"If it's any consolation, I think Neville was or is infatuated with you."

"Yeah, right, I've been a fool. I never learn. You'd think I would after three marriages."

"You're a romantic soul at heart. That's why you have a hard-hearted old friend like me."

Violet sighed and gave Mabel a half-smile.

"I'm sorry I was right," Mabel apologized.

"No, you're not. You like being right," Violet said with a lopsided grin.

"So, you are going to put up with him until the end of the week?"

"Yes, he's harmless. He's just a very bad con man. I promise you, one way or another, he will leave."

Mabel returned to her counter and opened her cutlery drawer, retrieving two teaspoons. Violet was never good with confrontation. She slammed the drawer shut; she'd make sure that creep left. Placing the spoons on the table, she asked. "Are you sure you're okay? We don't have to continue our investigations if you'd rather not."

"No, I want to. I was flattered by his attention. And I confess my ego is bruised. I feel like a chump. I'd rather take my mind off that annoying man."

"Good, he's not worth your time," Mabel said, pouring the tea, relieved Violet was taking Neville's betrayal well. They were back to sleuthing.

"Homer had quite the revelation about Freda's stolen cell phone. We should begin there," Violet said, accepting the mug of tea. "If Hannah asked Gemma for help with Freda's phone, we are back to her."

"I know. I thought we could rule her out. Gemma was driving old Homer around the day Freda died, and she was calling bingo when Hannah fell." Mabel stirred the sugar in her tea.

"If Hannah went to Gemma and asked her to unlock the phone, it probably didn't take her long to find out Hannah stole the phone from Freda's suite. Gemma must have told someone." Violet took a sip of tea.

"But maybe Gemma didn't tell anyone. Maybe she has an accomplice," speculated Mabel.

"Like who?"

"How about old Randy, the rat? Remember the natural cause he wrote in his report? Maybe he isn't the incompetent boob I thought he was. Maybe he is in cahoots with Gemma and did a cover-up. They looked pretty cozy at the café." Mabel said.

"You think Randy pushed those women down the stairs?"

"I don't know. For all I know, he killed Mini, too."

"Randy murdered three women?"

"He could have. Who would suspect the corner?"

"Medical Examiner."

Mabel made a face. "Whatever, there is a motive, and the motive is money. Someone was stealing from Mini. She confronted them and was killed. The other two died in an attempt to cover up the first," Mabel said thoughtfully.

"And you think Randy and Gemma are in it together."

"It's possible."

"If Gemma is in on it. How did she steal so much money from Mini?" asked Violet. "Not with a bank card. She had to have access to her account."

"Right."

They sat in silence, drinking their tea.

"I think I've figured it out."

"What's your theory?" Mabel crossed her arms, leaning back in her chair.

"Randy is probably involved. And, of course, Gemma."

"We've already considered them."

"Yes, but I've figured out the how." Violet held up her hand, ticking the reasons off on her fingers. "One, Gemma is always hanging around the condo. She would know which senior seemed to be alone with no family near at hand. Two, as you have pointed out many times, that woman is always doing things for the seniors living in Gravenhurst Manor, running errands, and taking them to their appointments, building up trust. At some point, she probably took them to the bank. And somehow, she or Randy got access to their bank accounts. Third, this scenario would fit Mini, as she had no family nearby. Four, well, there is no four, but I bet Mini and your mom are not the only ones who had money stolen from their accounts."

"But your scenario doesn't fit, Mom. I live here in town."

"Ah, but you weren't when she moved into the condo. You were in Egypt with me. And then you went to Edmonton to be with Melina when she gave birth to your granddaughter Rene. And don't forget how your mom always acts like she never sees you."

"Yeah, her big dumb joke."

"But what if the bank scammer didn't think it was a joke? The people who live in the condo are always surprised to see you. Gemma, we will say, Gemma, for now. She thought you had abandoned your mom. Your mom appeared to be easy pickings, so she steals the money out of your mom's bank account."

Mabel nodded.

"Then, when you do turn up, Gemma gets scared you'll find out about the fiddling with your mom's account, so she redeposits the money."

Mabel stared at Violet, her mouth open in a silent oh. "Good lord, you've hit the nail on the head. Get your coat. We're going to interrogate my mother."

MABEL REVERSED HER car, and the tires spun. "Darn it," she muttered, taking her car out of gear. She got out, letting the motor idle, and walked to the back of the car. Snow had been falling all day. A small drift had blown up behind Mabel's car: "Darn it," she said again.

"Snow tires, you need winter tires. You have no traction," Violet said, joining her at the rear of the car.

"Snow tires? This is a snowbank. It's not ice." Mabel tramped through the snow into her garage and grabbed a snow shovel. "The streets didn't look all that bad when we walked to the cenotaph. I just need to scoop out this bank."

Violet stood by while Mabel shoved her shovel into the snow piled up behind the back wheels of the car. "Let me help. I feel useless watching you do all the work."

"No, it's okay, this won't take long."

Violet shrugged and retreated to the warmth of the car.

"Hey, Mabel, let me do this; you get in the car with Violet." Fred Granger trotted up with his little Scottie dog Pokey on a leash. The small sandy-haired man in a red ski jacket took the shovel from Mabel and handed her the white terrier's leash.

"Fred, you are a friend indeed. Do you think the streets are clear? I want to visit my mom at the condo." The little dog dashed toward the back tire of Mabel's car. Mabel yanked on the leash.

Fred dug the shovel into the snowbank, taking big clumps of snow out from behind Mabel's car and tossing the snow onto her lawn. "Nah, the town snow plow has been out. The main streets are clear."

"What about the rest of this street?" The leash slipped from Mabel's hand, and the dog bounded onto her lawn.

"You should be fine." Fred paid no attention to his dog as he shovelled another scoop of snow. "I came from the main street. Just a bit of snow is piled up at the curb by the stop sign before you turn onto the main."

Mabel dashed after the dog, her boots sinking into the newly fallen snow. She caught Pokey as he lifted his leg. "No, you don't; that's my rosebush," Mabel scolded the furry little dog. Picking him up, she carried him back to her driveway.

Fred paused, leaning on the shovel. "But I don't know about the condo parking lot." He sniffed and ran a mittened hand under his nose, then resumed his shovelling.

"I guess I'll take my chances." The little white terrier squirmed in her arms, barking his disapproval. "Is Helen Graham a dog lover, do you know?"

"Helen? A dog lover? Why do you ask?"

"No reason, I'm just wondering." Mabel petted the little dog, and Pokey stretched out his neck and gave Mabel a lick on the cheek.

Fred paused. "The poor woman is a nervous wreck; she is even afraid of little Pokey. He barks, and she jumps." Fred snickered; going back to his task, he made quick work removing the snowdrift. Grinning, he stuck the shovel into the snow on the lawn. "You should have no trouble now. I'll watch until you're safely on your way."

Mabel smiled. "Thanks, Fred, I'll make you some cinnamon buns."

Fred brushed the frost off his bushy mustache and picked up Pokey. "Great, I love cinnamon buns."

Mabel waved and reversed out of her driveway and down the street.

Fred was right; the streets were relatively clear of snow. She slowed the car down as they drove past the Gravenhurst sign. A flock of ravens had perched on the sign, cawing loudly.

Farley, wearing an oversized blue parka and a Winnipeg Jet's hockey toque, was shovelling the snow off the steps of the condo.

"A never-ending job in the winter," Mabel said by way of a greeting. She was glad that Gemma's threats of having the man fired because of his crude remarks had fallen on deaf ears.

"Yep. We wouldn't want some frail old bugger to land on their keister," Farley said, scraping the snow into a pile by the sidewalk.

"Stay warm," Violet said over her shoulder as she opened the front door.

"Hump," Farley grunted, ignoring her greeting, flinging more snow up onto a pile.

"Charming as always." Mabel grinned as the outside door swung shut behind them.

"Since we still have Mrs. Angus's key, we might as well let ourselves in." They opened the inside door and entered the foyer. "

"I'll return Mrs. Angus's keys to her," volunteered Violet. "Are you waiting down here or going up to see your mom?" Violet asked as she turned to go down the hallway leading to Mrs. Angus's suite.

"No, I'll wait here." Mabel wandered into the lounge and out again. No one was about.

"Mrs. Angus didn't even remember that she gave her key to Jody," Violet said, striding up to the elevator and pushing the call button.

"That is not good. The woman really should be panelled for the home."

"When you ask your mom about the money. Don't be too hard on her. She is probably embarrassed she let someone have access to her bank account," Violet cautioned as they rode up in the elevator.

"I'm getting to the bottom of this. Mom may look like a delicate flower, but she is tougher than old boots."

Violet grinned. "Something like her daughter. You must have learnt that at your mother's knee."

"Maybe," Mabel acknowledged, rapping on her mother's door. "It's me, your long-lost daughter," she called.

"Come on in, I've got the kettle on," greeted Sophie.

"Will you please sit down for a minute? There are some things we have to talk about," Mabel said as she shed her coat.

"Is it about my will?" Sophie grinned. "Don't be so much in a hurry, dear, I feel quite fine." She bustled back into her kitchen.

"Good lord, no, not your will." Mabel stood by the kitchen counter and folded her arms.

"Go sit down. I'll get you some peanut butter cookies fresh from the oven."

Mabel's tummy won out, and she followed Violet to the small round table in the kitchen. She waited until her mother had prepared the tea and set the cookie plate on the table.

"There," Sophie said, adding cream to her tea, stirring it with a teaspoon.

"Great cookies," complemented Violet.

"Thank you, dear. And you, Mabel, do you like my cookies? It's a new recipe."

"You sure make a lot of cookies, Sophie," Violet said. "What do you do with them? You can't possibly eat them all."

Sophie laughed. "I give them away to my neighbours. Homer is always happy to receive a plate of cookies."

Mabel munched on her cookie and took a sip of tea; she swallowed and said, "Great cookies, Mom. But now for some serious talk. I want you to come clean. No more evasions. Tell me about your bank account, the mysterious withdrawals and deposits."

"Oh, for goodness' sake, you're still on about that. The money is back in my account. You sure are curious about my money. You're as bad as your brother. I find this curiosity of yours very unattractive." Sophie sniffed.

"I don't care about your money."

"You could have fooled me. You're the one always asking about it."

Mabel bit her lip and looked helplessly at Violet.

"The problem is Sophie," Violet said, "We think someone is messing with seniors' bank accounts. The people who live alone in this condo, the Seniors who have no family. We think someone is taking advantage of them. Don't get me wrong, but people your age tend to be too trusting."

"Poppycock," rebuked Sophie. "I'm not that trusting."

"I think maybe you are, and you're just a little embarrassed to admit it." Violet smiled kindly at the little white-haired lady.

Sophie set her teaspoon on her saucer, then picked it back up again, stirring her tea rapidly. "Besides, I'm not alone, am I?"

"No, but you've been playing that silly little game that I never come around to see you," reminded Mabel. "And because of your silly joke, someone thought you were alone and a good target for this scam. That is, until I turned up.

I bet if we look back into the transactions, the deposit into your savings coincides with me returning to Glenhaven."

Sophie pressed her lips, shifting in her chair. "Well," she said finally. "When I moved here from Kipling, I decided to move all my accounts to Glenhaven Saving and Loans. And I needed a little help it was all very confusing."

"And?" prompted Mabel.

"Gemma took me down to the bank to help me."

"Aha, I knew it," Mabel said triumphantly.

"You knew what?" Sophie asked.

"I knew that woman was too good to be true."

"No, no, you're wrong. Gemma would never steal from me or anyone else. What a ridiculous idea."

"I know you don't want to think Saint Gemma has done anything underhanded. But there's the motive. You told us Mini was upset, fifty thousand withdrawn from her bank account."

"I told you I might have been mistaken; maybe it was five thousand," Sophie said worriedly.

"The same amount is withdrawn from yours. Remember when you said you heard Mini asking Gemma for money? I don't think she was asking for money. I think she was demanding money. I think she was going to report Gemma."

"But, but I thought you were looking at Jody for these, ah... terrible events." Sophie shivered.

"We were, but now Gemma is our prime suspect."

"Gemma couldn't have anything to do with Mini's death. I must be mistaken. Mini must have died of natural causes." Sophie's eyes darted to Violet, then Mabel. "And you said all these dreadful deaths are related. Gemma was calling bingo in the lounge the day Hannah fell down the stairs. And I remember the day Freda fell. We had just come home from Kegsworthy. Gemma and Homer had just driven up too."

"True, but we don't know how long Freda lay at the bottom of those stairs. She could have been there for a long time until Jody found her. The residents here tell us they don't use the stairs. Gemma could have killed her and still taken Homer on his errands." Mabel leaned forward, pressing her point.

"But Sophie is right; Gemma was in the lounge when Hannah fell down the stairs." Violet tapped her fingers on the table with each word.

Mabel sat back in her chair.

"And how did Gemma withdraw that much money from Mini's accounts? Mini wouldn't have kept that much in her checking. She'd have to have an accomplice in the bank." Violet crossed her arms.

Sophie looked uncomfortable; she twisted her teacup one way and then the other. "She might," she said softly.

"She might what, Mom?"

"Gemma might have an accomplice."

"Who?"

"Well, it was Gemma who suggested I move my banking to Glenhaven Saving and Loan—"

"Ah-ha," Mabel said, she slapped her hand on the table. The teacups rattled.

Violet shook her head at Mabel. "Continue, please, Sophie."

"Gemma took me to the bank and the one who helped me transfer my accounts. The financial advisor she took me to see was Paul, her brother."

Mabel and Violet sat silently, staring wide-eyed at Mabel's mother.

Chapter Thirty-Nine

The women sat hunched in Mabel's car, waiting for the fan from the heater to defrost the windshield. The howling wind whipped the newly fallen snow across the condo parking lot. A flock of ravens circled over the manor and lit on the roof.

"Don't those ravens ever fly south?" asked Violet.

"Ravens?"

"The ones on the roof."

Mabel tilted her head, peering through a small melted spot on the windshield into the darkening night. "Oh yeah, tough birds." A small animal darted across the parking lot. She marvelled briefly at how tiny animals and birds much smaller than ravens survived the cold winters on the prairies. "But back to Mom's revelation. We now know Gemma and her brother are the culprits, but unfortunately, we have no proof."

"We should phone Robert. After the golf course fiasco, I'm sure he knows we're not crazy old ladies. If we tell him what we know, I'm sure he'll look into it," Violet suggested.

"Look into the banking maybe, but not the murders. When old people die, no one looks very hard at the cause.

Freda and Hannah fell down perfectly good stairs, and no one is looking into it. You heard Farley, you can't fix stupid, he said, and even though the building inspector didn't say it, I think he agreed with Farley. There will be no investigation into those women's deaths. Those two villains won't spend a day in jail for those murders," Mabel said, drumming her fingers on her steering wheel.

"But remember, Gemma came out in defence of the women."

"Very smart on her part."

"What are we going to do? Sitting out here in the dark is just silly."

"I want to do something." Mabel's stomach rumbled; she hadn't eaten a proper meal all day.

"I wonder how many residents have had their money stolen?"

"And my mom. Don't forget, my mom was a victim of their money scheme too. If I hadn't come home, God knows what else they had in mind for her."

"I agree, but what do we do?"

"I don't know, but I want that conniving woman and her no-good brother to pay for what they did. Those three women did not deserve to end their lives like that," Mabel said, trying to ignore her empty tummy's complaint.

"I wish we could lay a trap."

"Me too." Mabel paused, then brightened, "You know, a trap might just work."

"I hope it's not a just might work. What's your plan? You're not going to use your mother as a decoy?"

"Good lord, no, but I bet she would if I asked her. Anyway, they wouldn't believe Mom if she tried the plan I have in mind." Mabel shut off her car and opened the door. "Come with me. If Homer cooperates, I think there is a way."

Violet and Mabel ran across the snow-covered parking lot and into the condo entrance. Farley and his snow shovel were gone. The snow was piled up against the wall. Mabel looked for Homer's name on the wall plaque and buzzed his unit.

"What?" Homer snarled. His voice sounded tinny over the intercom.

"It's me, Mabel, and Violet. We want to talk to you."

"At this time of night?" Homer snorted. The door did not open.

Mabel pushed the buzzer again. She waited, but there was no answer. So, she pressed it a third time.

"What the heck is wrong with you? It's night; let a man get some sleep."

"It's only nine o'clock. You can't possibly be going to bed."

"Well, I am."

"No, you are not, and I'm going to keep pressing this buzzer until you let us in."

"If you want in, call your mother."

"It's you we want to talk to, so give up and let us in."

"Dang, fool woman," he snarled. The door opened.

"At least you've caught him in a good frame of mind," Violet said, rolling her eyes.

Mabel and Violet stamped their feet on the carpet, knocking the snow off their boots, and strode briskly across the lobby. Mabel pressed the call button for the elevator; the door opened immediately. "He's putting on a good front. But he's curious."

"What if he's going to bed? I hope we don't catch him in his PJs." Violet worried as they rode the elevator to his floor.

They tiptoed down the hallway past her mother's suite and lightly tapped on Homer's door. Mabel could hear the TV blaring from the other side of the door. "In bed," she scoffed, knocking harder.

"Since you're here, you might as well come in," Homer grumbled, opening the door. He wasn't in his pyjamas. He was dressed but wearing bedroom slippers. As the women entered, he swung his walker around and stomped to the living room to drop down on a couch. The layout of Homer's suite was a carbon copy of Sophie's but sparsely furnished with builders' white walls. White vertical blinds covered his windows. In front of the old, worn brown leather couch set a coffee table that had seen better days. In the tiny kitchen, set a small, round wooden table and four chairs. The main feature of the living room was a large plasma-screen TV.

"Homer, turn down the TV. We have to talk."

"I'm watching the hockey game. Sit down and wait for a commercial."

Mabel strutted over to the TV and turned it off. "Homer, I have a plan, and we need your help."

"I don't care what your blame plan is." He grabbed his remote and turned the TV back on.

Mabel took it from his hand, shut off the TV and tucked the remote in her pocket. "This is more important than some stupid hockey game."

"Stupid hockey game, that is very un-Canadian. Give me the damn remote."

Mabel, with her hands on her hips, stood in front of the TV and said, "No, I will not. You have to listen to me."

Violet took her coat off and neatly placed it on a stool by an old rocker across from the couch. She sat in the rocker, rocking back and forth, and said, "Homer, please, this is important; Mabel has a plan to catch the killers."

"Killers," scoffed Homer. "What killers? Have you women been drinking?"

Violet held up her hand, motioning for Mabel to be quiet. "No, Homer, we haven't, and yes, there are killers."

Homer sat back on his couch; his head swivelled from woman to woman. "I think you're both nuts."

Mabel took off her coat, tossing it to the floor; she sat beside him and sank into the cushions of the couch. "Freda and Hannah. Falling down the stairs. They didn't fall. Those women were pushed."

"Ha," snorted Homer, shifting away from her.

"You know you don't believe those falls were accidents. You said so yourself, no one uses the stairs. Everyone takes the elevator." Violet's rocker swung back and forth as she stood up, moving to perch on the coffee table in front of Homer.

"I didn't push them. Is that what you're after?"

"No, we know you didn't." Violet reached out to pat his hand.

Homer jerked his hand back. "So, why are you here bothering me? I'm missing the hockey game. Give me my damn remote."

"Never mind your darn remote. Someone pushed those women down the stairs. This is serious."

"You got it all figured out, have you? Then tell me why someone pushed those old gals down the stairs?"

"Because they both knew something dangerous."

"Dangerous to who?"

Mabel rolled her eyes and blew out a long breath. "To the killers, pay attention."

"What Mabel means is that Freda and Hannah were both in possession of incriminating evidence."

"Incriminating evidence of what?"

"Incriminating evidence of Mini's murder." Mabel sat back and gave Homer a superior look.

"Mini's murder?"

"You do remember when Mini died?"

"Of course I do; I'm not senile."

"By the way, where were you the night Mini died?" Mabel asked.

"Don't go pinning her death on me. I was at a movie with Pete, my nephew, he took me to this stupid movie. It was crap, some stupid science fiction thing. Totally ridiculous, unbelievable."

"Of course, we don't think you killed Mini. But haven't you ever suspected something was odd about her death?" Violet folded her hands, looking intently into Homer's face.

Homer blinked and rubbed his rheumy eyes. "I can't say as I do," he denied.

"You will if you listen to us." Mabel rose, pacing back and forth in front of Homer, explaining the motive for Mini's murder, ending with her mother's story of the events on the night of her death.

"I like your mother, but how do you know for certain someone blocked the elevator and the door to the stairway? She might have been confused. It happens to the best of us."

"We found proof."

"What proof?"

"We found proof in Freda's diary. We read her diary."

"You snoopy old broads."

Mabel twisted her lips. She'd let that crack pass. They did need Homer's help. "It was a good thing we did. If we hadn't, we wouldn't know what we know now, would we? Freda's diary backed up everything my mom said. She had a video or pictures on her phone of the murderer blocking the elevator and the door. And of the killer going into Mini's unit. Freda wrote she was going to blackmail the killer. We think Freda told the killer she had evidence. Then, the killer pushed Freda down the stairs, but unfortunately for the killer, Freda didn't have the phone on her. And before they could search her condo, light-fingered Hannah had been there and pinched the phone."

"Yeah, right, she did take Freda's phone," Homer said slowly.

"And you told us Hannah wanted to use the phone and needed help to unlock it."

"Yeah."

"And who did she say she was going to get help with it?"

"Gemma, she was going to see if she could unlock it."

"Right," Mabel said triumphantly.

"So, Gemma had to kill Hannah to get the phone," Violet added.

"Ha," snorted Homer. "I can blow a hole right through your cockamamie theory. Gemma was calling bingo when old Hannah fell down the stairs. You were there."

"Yes, you're right, she was. But she has an accomplice. The accomplice gave her the alibi." Mabel lifted her chin and smiled smugly.

"Who?"

"Gemma's brother Paul."

"Paul?"

"Yes, Paul, he's the financial adviser at Glenhaven Savings and Loans. That's how they scammed the money off Mini. And God knows how many other seniors."

"Paul killed Hannah?"

"I think he did. I remember the sound of Hannah falling; there was a pause, and then she screamed. I think he pushed her down the stairs, but she wasn't quite dead, so he finished the job. Then, he ran back up the stairs, out on the fire escape and around the building. He waited until the ambulance came and pretended to have just arrived. I remember him having a disagreement with one of the firemen about not being called. Thus creating alibis for both him and his sister."

Homer sat silent; his head hung down. Finally, he looked up at Mabel with his red, rheumy eyes. "Okay, saying all this is true. Why should I get involved?"

"They have killed three helpless women. And who knows? My Mom might be next."

Homer was silent; he bent his head, looked up, sighed and asked, "What the hell do you want me to do?"

"We have a plan," Mabel said eagerly.

"A plan?"

"It's Mabel's plan," Violet said. "I'm in the dark as much as you are."

"It's the best plan I've ever had."

"She always says that." Violet rolled her eyes and sat beside the small old man, watching her friend pace.

"This time it really is," Mabel said confidently; her stomach was growling. "By the way, do you have anything to eat? I'm starving."

"I thought you had some half-baked plan to catch these so-called killers. Not come up here and scam food off me."

"I brought you lunch at the hall, and I even stole cake for you. What kind of host are you?"

"I didn't invite you. You barged in."

"Homer, Homer. We have a serious situation here. Someone is offing your friends. For God's sake, give Mabel a cracker or something."

"Who said they were my friends?"

Violet sighed. "But you want to protect Sophie and stop whoever it is that killed these women."

"If! Someone killed them," snorted Homer, casting a skeptical look at Mabel.

"Don't be such a skinflint," Mabel scolded. "A crummy cracker. Is that too much to ask for? You're hungry too, aren't you, Violet?" Violet shrugged.

"Okay, fine, eat me out of my house and home. Top left-hand cupboard by the fridge."

Mabel wrinkled her nose and trotted to his kitchen. She took out a box of soda crackers. "Seriously, when I said crummy crackers, I didn't think that was what you were going to give me."

"You're lucky I'm feeding you at all. I didn't ask you here. You came here uninvited with some cockamamie idea."

"Crackers are fine, aren't they, Mabel?" Violet interceded. "We do want Homer's help, right?"

Mabel nodded; opening the box, she removed a cracker sleeve and ripped the top off. "Yes, thank you so much, Homer. For your dry old crackers."

"Mabel," warned Violet.

Homer glared up at Mabel as she leaned against the kitchen counter, munching on the crackers, crumbs spilling down onto her shirt.

Violet waited until Mabel had devoured half the sleeve of crackers. "You said you had a plan? And for goodness' sake, brush your shirt off. You got cracker crumbs all over."

Mabel brushed her shirt off as she opened a cupboard door, closed it, and opened another. She took out a glass, went to the kitchen sink and turned the water tap on, filling the glass. She chugged the water down, wiping her lips off with the back of her hand. She said, "I have a plan, and Homer, I need your cooperation."

Homer looked at Mabel, suspicion in his eyes. "Yeah, you said that before. Just what do you have in mind."

Mabel set her empty glass on the counter and gave Homer a wide smile. "I want you to phone Paul and then Gemma. I want you to tell them you know what they did."

"That sounds like that movie," Violet said.

"Movie?" Mabel asked.

"That movie, '*I Know What You Did Last Summer.*' Don't you remember it?"

"No, I don't recall it."

"It came out in the 90s. Teenagers or someone phoned people and pretended they knew what they did."

"What the hell are you two women talking about? Is this part of your cockamamie plan?" growled Homer.

"I hope not that was a slasher movie; I don't think it ended well," Violet said.

"Oh great. Some plan this is."

"No, no, Homer, this is completely different."

"Yes, that was a slasher movie," assured Violet.

Homer gave them a wary look.

"Would you stop saying slasher," Mabel demanded.

"I was just saying—"

"Well, don't," interrupted Mabel. "Anyway, Homer isn't a teenager."

"What the hell does that mean?" Homer folded his arms and snorted. "You two are nuts. I'm not having anything to do with your cockamamie plan. You don't even make sense."

"Forget about the dumb movie. This is my plan. I want you to phone Paul and then Gemma. I want you to tell them you got proof of their wrongdoing."

"Wrongdoing?"

"Right, let's call it what it is. Tell them you know they are responsible for the deaths of Mini, Freda, and Hannah. And that you have proof. Tell them you want money, or you will give your evidence to the RCMP."

"But, I don't got proof of anything."

"I know that, but they won't. Gemma and Paul can't afford to take a chance. I'm positive they will come here to confront you."

"So, I'm the bait, is that it?"

"No harm will come to you, I promise."

"Yeah, right, people are dropping like flies around these two maniacs, and you're going to protect me. Ha."

"You haven't heard my whole plan. The police will be here."

"How? How do you figure that?"

"No worries. I have a plan to get the RCMP here."

"No worries," Homer gave a harsh laugh. "Anyway, what if you're wrong, and Gemma and her brother didn't do a thing?"

"Oh, they did something. Those two swindled seniors out of their hard-earned money. I believe Mini confronted them, and they killed her to cover it up."

"Yeah, but what if you're wrong?"

"If we're wrong, nothing happens. And you can go back to watching your hockey game."

"Except, I'll look like a fool."

Mabel rolled her eyes and said nothing.

"Why not just phone the cops?"

"Because we've no proof."

"Why me? I'm an old man with a walker. Why should I be the sacrificial lamb?"

"Because I think they will believe you would want money in exchange for proof. You're not exactly Mr. Friendly. You always act like you have a chip on your shoulder."

"Thanks a bunch."

"Don't be modest; you know it's true."

"How much money should he ask for?" Violet asked.

"Oh, right, I wonder what a good blackmail amount would be? How about a thousand?" suggested Mabel.

"If I'm going to ask for money, I want a lot of money, not a paltry thousand," complained Homer.

"Oh, for God's sake, it's not like you're going to get the money."

"Hump," snorted Homer.

"Anyway, phone our suspects and tell them you know what they did and have proof. Demand any amount you want. I'll hide in your closet."

"Sure, you hide in the closet. Oh, that's a good plan."

"I'll be your witness to back you up."

"And you can record everything they say on your phone," Violet suggested. "Give me your phone, Homer, and I'll show you how."

"I know how to record, damn it. Just because I'm old doesn't mean I'm stupid," grumbled Homer. Pulling his phone from his pocket, he hobbled to the table.

"Am I the only one who doesn't know how?" Mabel asked.

"Yes," they said in unison.

Mabel wrinkled her nose. "Anyway, I'll still hide in the closet, and you can record the conversations, the confessions."

"It's still not getting any better for me," Homer said, looking doubtful.

"Violet, you wait downstairs. As soon as Gemma and Paul enter the condo, you text Homer." Mabel gave them both a superior smile. "I know what texting is."

Violet and Homer exchanged an amused smile.

"Violet, you text Homer as soon as they get into the elevator, and we'll get prepared. And I'll hide."

"Oh, yeah, great, you hide. Leaving me to face the killers," Homer grumbled unhappily.

"Stop worrying, you'll be fine. As soon as Violet texts you, she will phone the RCMP. Simple, right?"

"Simple? How the hell long do I have to keep them talking? What if the cops are busy elsewhere?" Homer's eyes darted between the two women.

Mabel looked uncertain.

Violet picked up her coat and put it on. "I know; as soon as I go downstairs, I'll report a burglary at my house. That way, the RCMP will be in town. Then, when I see Gemma and Paul come into the building and they're in the elevator, I'll phone again. And tell the police they have to come here to the condo, that there is an emergency."

"Yes, and scream like you're being attacked. That way, they will drop everything and rush over."

"Should I go that far?"

"Yes, it's a matter of life or death."

"Great, that makes me feel a whole lot better," muttered Homer.

Chapter Forty

Violet got out of the elevator and dialled 911. "There is someone in my house," she whispered, thinking a whisper would ring truer if she heard a burglar. "Please hurry, this is Violet Ficher. I live at 325 Manitoba Avenue, Glenhaven. Hurry, I think he's coming." Shutting off her phone, she entered the lounge, pacing back and forth by the window, waiting for the car lights of the killers.

"THIS IS A WASTE OF time; Gemma sounded like I was some demented old lunatic." Homer stuck his phone in his pocket and hobbled to the kitchen table.

"Well, she's hardly going to admit she killed people over the phone." Mabel opened Homer's curtains, peering out into the dark. Homer's condo didn't face the parking lot. All she could see was the snow swirling under the streetlights.

"And now her brother Paul just hung up on me." Homer pushed his walker to one side and slowly settled back on a kitchen chair.

"Do you have your phone ready?" Mabel dropped the curtain and returned to the kitchen table.

"Yeah, yeah." Homer spun his phone around on the table.

"Cover it with something, for goodness' sake."

Homer threw an IGA advertising flier that was lying on the table over the phone. "Satisfied?"

"Are the batteries charged? Oh my gosh, are they?"

"A fine time to think of that." Homer lifted the ad flier and checked his phone. "Yeah, the batteries are good. Can I watch the game now?"

"No, if they come and the TV is on, we won't be able to record their confessions."

"Yeah, their confessions. How the hell do I get them to confess?"

"I can't think of everything. You'll come up with something." Mabel opened the hall closet. "Good lord, your closet smells."

"I didn't ask you to hide in my closet," snarled Homer, then frowned, "What does it smell like?"

"It smells like old men."

"What did you expect? I'm an old man." Homer snickered.

VIOLET, PEERING OUT the large window, saw car lights flash against the glass. A car came to a stop in the parking lot. She ran, ducking down behind a large armchair, where she had a clear view of the front door. Her heart pounded wildly as she waited.

She held her breath as the door opened. Mabel was right; the killer had a key.

It was Paul, Gemma's brother. The tall, freckled-faced man strode to the elevator and pushed the button.

The door opened, and Abagail and her husband, Ned, stepped out.

"Good evening," greeted Ned.

"We are off to play cards with the Hanovers," volunteered Abagail.

"Really," muttered Paul.

"They just moved in a few days ago; they are in suite 103, a nice couple there from..."

Paul stepped into the elevator before Ned could complete his explanation.

"He sure is in a hurry," Abagail said as the elevator door closed.

Hunched behind the chair, Violet took her phone from her pocket and texted, '*Killer number one was on his way.*' She peeked out at Ned and Abagail. Should she phone the police? Or wait for Gemma?

"You forgot the bottle of wine," accused Abagail.

"I thought you were going to bring it," her husband retorted.

"No, I told you to bring it."

Violet wished the pair would quit bickering and leave.

HOMER'S PHONE BEEPED.

"What's that sound?"

"A text."

"Who texted you? Is it Violet?"

"Who the hell do you think it was? The suspect is on his way up."

"Only one?"

"She texted; killer number one is on his way. So, what does that tell you?"

"And it's Paul," Mabel said excitedly.

"That doesn't take a genius to figure out that it's Paul. She texted he was on his way. I must be out of my mind to let you persuade me to do this." Homer covered the phone with the ad flier. "Get the hell in the closet."

"There's lots of time." Mabel gave him a sour look and walked to the closet.

"Get in the closet, get in the closet," Homer yelled at her.

"I am, I am, hold your horses." Mabel positioned herself in the closet.

"You fool woman, you forgot your coat; get your damn coat," Homer called.

Mabel darted out and grabbed her coat, putting it on as she dashed back into the closet. She peeked out, opening and closing the door.

"What the hell are you doing? Get in the closet."

"I am. You just make sure you have your phone on."

There was a sharp rap on the condo door. Mabel peeked out the closet door she'd left partially open.

"Who is it?" squeaked Homer.

Mabel bit her lip. Homer was scared; the man was going to be useless.

The door opened, and Paul stepped in, closing the door. The big, handsome man with auburn hair stepped closer to Homer and said, "So, old fellow, what's this about proof? Proof about what?"

"Don't old fellow me. I've got a name," Homer snapped.

Ah, this is more like Homer, Mabel thought gleefully, shifting so she could see the table where Homer sat.

"Okay, Homer, what do you have to say for yourself? You say you have proof? Proof of what?" Paul crossed his arms and leaned against the kitchen counter.

"I've got it, and I want money. If you want my proof, come up with the cash," snarled Homer.

"First, the proof, if it's worth anything, I might be prepared to pay you. What is it you've got?"

"How much? How much is it worth to you? I'm not taking chicken feed."

Mabel grinned; Homer was getting into character. She shifted to get a good look at Paul's face. The remote in her parka pocket turned on the TV. *'He shoots, he scores,'* the announcer shouted excitedly. "Shit," Mabel said, pressing the remote.

"What the hell?" Paul looked first at the TV, then over at the closet.

Chapter Forty-One

The front door opened. Ah, Violet thought, this will be Gemma. She peeked over the chair.

Jody Harris, with her big bag slung over her shoulder, entered.

"Hello, Jody, this is a late-night visit," greeted Ned.

"I got a call from Mrs. Bevin. She needs my help; she has twisted her knee or something and needs help to get into bed." Jody pressed the call button for the elevator.

Violet, squatting behind the chair, silently fretted. Ned and Abagail chatting with Jody could ruin everything. Paul might already be at Homer's.

"It is very nice of you to come out at this time of night."

Jody stepped into the elevator. "It's money; I have to do what I do; it is all about money." The door closed.

Good, thought Violet; now that Jody has gone, Abagail and Ned will leave. Her legs were cramping from crouching behind the chair.

The door to the condo opened again, and Farley entered, stomping the snow off his boots. He looked at Ned and Abagail. He grunted, his keys jingling on his belt as he ambled to the elevator.

"Hello, Farley, late-night call. I didn't know you worked evenings," commented Ned.

Violet's heart sank. Good lord, she thought, this place is like Grand Central Station. Everybody and his dog has a key.

"I don't; that damn fool Sweeny is complaining they have no hot water. The clown probably doesn't know hot from cold," Farley grumbled, pushing the call button for the elevator.

"Jody just went up in the elevator," volunteered Abagail.

"I'll take the stairs then. It's a damn sight quicker than this thing," grumbled Farley opening the stairway door.

"Don't fall," shouted Ned as the door closed.

"I do wish you'd brought the wine; maybe you should go back up and get it," mulled Abagail. "We'll have a bit of an edge if we get them a little snockered."

"Forget about the darn wine. Just pay attention to the game."

Violet listened to their voices fade as they turned down the hallway. Should she wait for Gemma or phone the police?

PAUL GRABBED MABEL by the arm and dragged her out of the closet. "What the hell are you doing in there?" He turned, glaring at Homer. "What do you two think you're going to do? Shake me down for more money?"

Mabel scurried over to Homer's side; her heart was beating wildly. "We, we know what you did. You stole money from Mini and, and you killed her. Then you killed poor Freda and Hannah."

"You don't know anything," sneered Paul. The freckles on his face appeared redder.

"I notice you don't deny it," Mabel said, her voice raspy; her mouth was dry; she licked her lips.

"I didn't kill anyone," he said as the door opened.

Jody stomped in, slamming the door shut behind her.

Mabel's hopes soared; she didn't know why Jody had barged in and she didn't care. Whatever the reason, it was bad news for Paul. He wouldn't dare hurt Homer or her. Not with a witness present.

"No, Pauly didn't do it."

"What?"

Jody threw her bag on the floor. "You heard me. Pauly didn't kill anyone." She wrapped her arms around Paul, hugging him.

"You!" Mabel exclaimed, flabbergasted. "You're in on it?"

"Me and my boyfriend," Jody said proudly. She nestled her head on his shoulder and smiled up at him.

"Your boyfriend? I thought Alfie was your boyfriend."

"Alfie." Jody giggled. "He's my baby brother. Pauly is my boyfriend." She pulled his head down and kissed him on the lips.

Mabel noticed Paul didn't put his arm around Jody. He looked uncomfortable.

Homer snorted. "Ha."

"What are you snickering at, old man?" The big girl turned to eye Homer suspiciously.

"The brain and the brawn," smirked Homer.

"What do you mean by that?" Jody glowered, stepping toward him.

"He doesn't mean anything," Mabel assured her, plopping down on a chair beside Homer.

"Was that a dig at me?" Jody put both hands on the table, leaning over it; she eyeballed Homer.

"Jody, we have more important things than a little name-calling." Paul put his hand on her arm, pulling her back to the kitchen.

"If that was a slur, you better watch it, old man, I don't put up with crap."

"It will take more than you, girly," snarled Homer.

"For God's sake," snapped Mabel. "Shut up."

"Who the hell are you to tell me to shut up?" railed Homer.

"Both of you shut up. I can't think with your bickering," stormed Paul.

Mabel and Homer exchanged glares but remained quiet.

Paul ran a hand through his wavy auburn hair, pacing in the small kitchen. He stopped in front of Jody. "We have to figure out what the hell we're going to do with these two?"

"Ever since you phoned me, Pauly, I've been going over a plan. And I have a good plan. Of course, I can't use the stairs again. It wouldn't fly." She giggled, laying her head on Paul's shoulder." Fly. Like, fly down the stairs."

Paul recoiled, took a breath, and then put his arm around Jody.

"You killed both of those women, Freda and Hannah?" Mabel's eyes widened in surprise. She was glad she was sitting down. This woman was a psychopath. When would the police get here? Did Violet even phone them? Was she still waiting for Gemma? Good lord, they had gotten it wrong. Gemma was innocent. She'd let her jealousy cloud her judgment. Violet was waiting for Gemma. She wouldn't phone the RCMP. Mabel felt sick to her stomach.

"I only helped those old biddies along to their final destination," defended Jody. "They were going to die soon enough anyway. They were old. And besides, Freda was a blackmailer; she tried to get money out of me. She deserved it."

"What did Freda have on you?" Mabel asked, knowing Homer's phone was recording.

Jody ignored Mabel and grabbed Paul's arm, draping it over her shoulder and snuggling up to him. "And I did it all for you, Pauly and I'd do it all over again." Jody offered up her lips to him.

Paul gave her a peck on the lips. "We have to concentrate, Jody," he said, gently disentangling himself from her embrace. "The plan. You have a plan."

Jody tugged on his arm, draping it back around her shoulders; she cuddled up to him. "Pauly, don't be embarrassed in front of these two old birds," she purred, caressing his cheek. "They know love when they see it. Or maybe they can't remember that far back." She giggled as she looked over at Homer and Mabel.

Panic mounted as Mabel looked around the room for something she could use as a weapon. Homer was tough, but he was incapable of putting up a fight. Should she try for the door? But Jody and Paul were between her and the door.

VIOLET PACED BACK AND forth by the windows, peeking through the curtains and debating whether she should phone. To her relief, she saw another set of car lights. She watched as the car stopped in front of the manor and parked. Violet skittered back behind the big chair.

Moments later, Gemma stocked through the lobby and went to the elevator.

Violet's phone blared out *Gangnam Style*. She had forgotten to mute the phone.

"Who's there?" Gemma strode into the lounge.

Violet's redhead stuck up from behind the chair. She shut off her phone and jammed it in her pocket.

"What the heck are you doing here at this time of night? Were you hiding?"

"I, I didn't know who was coming in. I, I got nervous," stammered Violet.

"Really?" Gemma raised her eyebrows. "Sweetie, turn on the lights. Where is your friend Mabel? Is her mother ill?"

"Ah, ah, yeah, she took a turn for the worse," Violet sputtered, edging away from Gemma.

"A turn for the worse? I didn't know she was ill." Gemma followed Violet into the lounge.

"It came on suddenly."

"What? What came on suddenly?"

"Her, her illness," Violet said lamely.

"Her illness?"

"Yes, I, it's the flu, the flu came on suddenly. Sophie, she is ...and yeah, that's why she's ill." Violet's voice was getting shrill with each answer. "I don't want to catch the flu. That's why I'm waiting for Mabel here."

"Some friend you are. I have an errand to run, and then I'll go check on Sophie." Gemma turned on her heel and walked rapidly to the elevator.

Violet waited until the elevator door closed, then dialled 911. "Help, help, I'm at the Gravenhurst Manor in Glenhaven." She gasped. "I'm in danger. Someone is trying to kill me, oh, no, he, they, her, him, is coming to kill me." She let out a blood-curdling scream, then hung up. Forgetting to text Homer, she hurried to the front door and waited.

PAUL ATTEMPTED TO SHRUG off Jody's grasp, running his fingers through his hair again. "Jody, please. What the hell are we going to do? You said you had a plan."

Pouting, Jody released his arm. "Well, I did when it was just old Homer here. I thought we could take the old guy outside and leave him to die of the cold. I think it's called hypothermia. But now that we have two to get rid of, I'll have to think of something else."

"You think I'm that easy to get rid of, do you? Well, think again," snarled Homer. With a determined look on his face, he rose from his chair, grabbed his walker, and thumped toward Jody. "No tattooed green-haired idiot is going to get rid of me."

Jody, with a malicious grin, sprang toward him. "I told you I don't take crap."

Paul grabbed her arm. "Don't Jody, we don't want any marks on him."

Jody curled her lips in a sneer. "You're going to die, old man. The easy way or the hard way depends on how I feel."

Paul put his arm around Jody. "Settle down, dear, he's harmless. We've got to think about what to do." Jody looked up at Paul, smiled, and snuggled into his embrace.

Mabel placed a hand on Homer's shoulder, pushing the reluctant man back on his chair. Her thoughts raced; oh, *Violet, please, please phone the police*. Forcing herself to calm down, she turned to Jody. "Did Hannah ask you to unlock Freda's phone?" Mabel asked, aware that Homer's phone was still recording.

"Yep, I couldn't believe my luck. And actually, Hannah did fall down the stairs accidentally. We struggled over the phone. She wouldn't let go of it, and when I ripped it out of her hands, she fell. Unfortunately, she wasn't quite dead." Jody shrugged. "So, I had to finish her off."

Paul gave Jody a sidelong look and shuttered. She looked up at Paul. "Don't worry, Pauly, that phone is long gone. No one will find it now."

"Who killed Mini? Was it Gemma?" Mabel asked, stalling for time, edging her way toward the door.

Jody giggled. "Gemma? You mean Goody Two Shoes. She wouldn't want anything to happen to her precious seniors."

The door swung open, and Gemma strode in.

Chapter Forty-Two

"What is going on here? I thought you were looking after your mother."

"You're talking to me?" Mabel asked, her eyes widened.

"My dear, do you see anyone else here with a sick mother?"

"My mother is sick?"

"Sophie isn't sick?"

"No."

"If she isn't sick. What are you doing here?" Gemma dropped her oversized purse on the kitchen counter.

"Your cohorts have just confessed how Freda and Hannah died," Homer snarled.

Mabel glanced down at the newspaper and saw the edge of the phone. She moved toward Gemma, diverting her gaze from the table. "Are you going to confess how you murdered Mini?"

Jody stomped up to Mabel and planted a hand on her chest, shoving her backward. Mabel stumbled against Homer's walker. She straightened the walker, glancing toward the door. Was the cavalry coming?

"Me murder Mini? What nonsense are you spinning? First, I get this weird call from Homer." Gemma turned to face Homer. "Your absurd allegations that Freda and Hannah's deaths were not accidents. And that somehow, I'm to blame is crazy. And now this disgusting accusation that I killed Mini? Where are you getting these ridiculous ideas from?"

"Give it up, Gemma. Jody has spilt her guts," sneered Homer.

"Spilled her guts? What the heck is this old man railing about?"

"I killed old Mini. No use hiding it," Jody said proudly.

"What? Impossible?" gasped Gemma.

"Oh no, you think I'm too stupid? I know you think I'm not good enough for Pauly. You think I'm a dumb old house cleaner, only good enough to scrub floors. You have always underestimated me," Jody shouted, marching up to face Gemma. Gemma's eyebrows shot up; she put her hand over her mouth and backed away.

Paul grabbed Jody's arm, dragging her back to the kitchen. "Settle down," he cautioned, putting an arm around her shoulder.

"Your sister has always treated me like I'm a moron. Well, I'm not." Her lips curled in a pout as she looked across the room at Gemma. She lifted her chin and said, "I was the one who planned the murder of Mini. Mrs. Angus is a diabetic. I'd watched her use her insulin pen. I saw how easy the pen was to use." Jody smiled gleefully at Paul. "When I told Pauly about the insulin, he said it would be the perfect way to get rid of that troublemaker, Mini."

A sly, sinister smile crept over Paul's face. "And it was perfect. We had to get rid of that old lady."

Mabel shivered; Paul's smile was even more frightening than Jody's.

"It was easy. I stole an insulin pen from Mrs. Angus. Then, I waited until it was dance night at the leisure center, and all the seniors were out of the building. But to be on the safe side, I blocked the stairway door and the elevator. Then I went to Mini's unit and let myself in. The old lady was in her bedroom, changing clothes. It was easy to overpower the old gal and give her an injection in the bum. It wasn't all that hard to do. Just stick in the pen and push. When she became unconscious, I put her in her nightgown and stuck her into bed." Jody finished with a triumphant grin. "You see, Mrs. High and mighty. I'm not the dummy you thought I was, am I?"

"Good God, you pair of lunatics." Gemma put her hand to her mouth in shock.

Jody sighed and turned to Paul. "Now we have to get rid of these two. And Miss High and Mighty. I'm out of ideas."

"We are not going to kill my sister."

"Kill me? Paul, for God's sake."

Mabel looked wide-eyed at Gemma. She'd been wrong about her. Gemma was innocent. Gemma was their saviour.

"Whoa, whoa, hold it right there, Jody, you are not going to harm my sister."

"Paul, you better talk some sense into this woman." Gemma gave Jody a scathing look.

Mabel smiled hopefully at Gemma, feeling guilty for thinking the worst of her. Gemma wasn't afraid of Jody. And

Paul wasn't going to let Jody hurt his sister. If the cops didn't come, Gemma was their ticket out of here.

"Pauly, Gemma should pay for the mess we're in. This is all her fault. She picked the suckers for us, she picked Mini." Jody's voice was rising to a high pitch. Her breathing accelerated, her eyes narrowing as she looked at Gemma.

Paul placed his hands on Jody's shoulders, turning her to face him. With his face inches from hers, he smiled into her eyes. "Relax, dear heart, and think about all the good things," he said softly, stroking her cheek. "Remember all the lucrative senior accounts my sister pointed our way? Gemma has been a great help to us. It's not her fault Mini found out." Paul gave the big girl a chase kiss on her lips. "We'll think of something. But we are not going to harm Gemma. Is that clear?"

Jody relaxed in his arms and smiled up at him. "Okay, Pauly, I promise."

Mabel's fear turned into anger and disgust. "You pretended to be everyone's friend, and all the time, you were systematically stealing from them. I knew you were too good to be true," Mabel stormed. Gemma wasn't their saviour. Now what? What happened to Violet? Where was the RCMP?

"I'm good to all these old people. I do a lot for these seniors. And most don't even thank me. So, we help ourselves to their money. Big deal; we deserve it. What are they going to do with it? They're not going to spend it. They're only going to leave it to their ungrateful children. Children never come to see them. I do more for these old people than their children ever do."

"You picked on my mother because you thought I wasn't around."

"You weren't, were you?"

"Then, when I turned up, you put the money back in her account."

"So, you have nothing to complain about. Your mom got her money back. And we would have done the same with Mini. But the poor woman died."

"Mini didn't just die. She was murdered," snarled Homer.

"Whatever," Gemma said, then turning to Jody, she raged, "And Mini needn't have been murdered. That was a stupid mistake. The other night at the café, Randolph tried to persuade me there should be an inquest into Mini's death. But I pooh-poohed it. You're lucky I did."

"I don't care about this, Randolph guy." Jody's eyes flashed. "I saved us. You didn't."

"No, you didn't, you idiot. You've put us in a bind." Gemma's face was flushed with anger. "You didn't have to kill Mini. We never had a problem before. I could have explained things to her. I'm good with old ladies. Paul, you know I could."

"You're fooling yourself," Paul accused his sister. "We had to get rid of the old girl. She was going to report us. Mini had to go. What else could we do? Anyway, I didn't kill Mini. Jody did."

"Pauly, you better back me up here. What I did, I did for you." Jody grabbed his arm. Paul shook her off.

Gemma rounded on Jody. "This is all your fault. The one we should get rid of is you."

"Bitch," screamed Jody.

The door burst open, and three RCMP officers entered. They stood in the doorway, surveying the room.

"About time," Homer greeted them.

"Never mind, they are here." Mabel beamed at the officers as they crowded into the suite. "And you can arrest the lot of them."

"Pay no attention to these two old people, officers," Gemma said, "They are a little confused and are raving and muttering all kinds of gibberish."

"Old," blustered Mabel.

"Confused," growled Homer.

"Yes, the poor old dears are making outlandish accusations. I don't know who called you. Probably that silly woman from downstairs. But everything is in hand." Gemma flashed them a big, broad smile.

"Hi, Robert," greeted Mabel.

"Ah, Mabel, why am I not surprised?" Constable Robert Shamanski grinned, taking up a stance by the kitchen cupboards.

"We have heard some disturbing accusations," said a small blonde police officer standing beside the constable.

Mabel recognized the sergeant. "Hi, Sergeant Russell."

Sergeant Russell ignored Mabel and issued an order. "All of you come with us. And this is not a suggestion."

"You can't be serious?" objected Gemma.

"I'm perfectly serious. Please come with us, and we will sort this out."

Mabel smiled smugly and said, "I think handcuffs all around, except for Homer and me."

"Mrs. Havelock," cautioned Constable Shamanski.

"Handcuffs, really. That won't be necessary," screeched Gemma, looking wildly around her. "My brother and I haven't done anything." Her voice rose another octave. "This woman here is the one you need to arrest. Jody is a killer. And she is crazy," Gemma screamed. Grabbing her big purse from the counter, she swung the bag like a windmill.

Paul looked at his sister, then sprang into action, dragging Homer off his chair. Taking his car keys from his pocket, he jammed the keys into Homer's neck. "Stay back, or this old man dies," he shouted.

Homer lifted his walker and drove it down into Paul's foot. Paul screamed and staggered on one foot.

Constable Shamanski seized Paul by the arm and pushed him into the kitchen. Paul stood with his face pressed up against the fridge as the constable snapped handcuffs on his wrists.

Jody shoved her elbow into Sergeant Russell, making a break for the door. The officer grunted and spun on her heel. She grabbed Jody by the arm, throwing her to the floor. She put her knee on her back and fastened handcuffs on Jody's wrists.

"Gemma is right. Jody, Jody is the killer. We just found out tonight," Paul yelled.

Gemma continued to flail her handbag in a circle. A young officer's hat went flying. He ducked and grabbed the bag. Looking sheepishly, he seized Gemma and fixed a set of handcuffs on her wrists.

"Liar, it was all your idea. Bastard, you said you loved me. I did it all for you. You're going down with me, both of you," snarled Jody from the floor.

"And we have a little gift for you too." Mabel smiled proudly, folding her arms across her chest as she watched the culprits being handcuffed.

Homer held up his phone. "I've recorded everything on this phone. You thought you could outsmart an old senior like me. Underestimating a senior, see where that attitude gets you?" he sneered at the brother and sister.

"Thank you, sir. I'll take charge of it." Constable Shamanski bagged the phone. "We'll need to take your statements. Mabel, you know the drill." Mabel grinned and nodded.

Two officers ushered Jody, Gemma, and her brother Paul out the door.

Violet stuck her head around the corner. "Can I come in now?"

"Yes, all clear," the constable said. "But you will have to come to the station as well. We apprehended the burglar at your house. We had to leave him in the car while we dealt with this emergency."

"You apprehended a burglar?" Violet asked worriedly.

"The man said he was a house guest," Constable Shamanski said.

"More like a freeloader," Mabel said.

Violet shook her head. "Mabel, please."

"I have to tell you, Violet, this guy started spilling out all sorts of information the moment we put cuffs on him."

Violet bit her lip. "You put cuffs on Neville!"

Mabel grinned.

"This guy you call Neville confessed his name is Jake Hanson. He is a con artist from Vancouver."

"He's not English?" asked Violet.

"Nope, he's a homegrown con man. His accent disappeared as soon as we arrested him. And he's not a very good con man. He babbled all the way from your house to here. We ran his name through the computer. He's wanted back in Vancouver on fraud charges. The man scammed some woman out of her travel ticket for a trip to Egypt."

The End

Don't miss out!

Visit the website below and you can sign up to receive emails whenever Joan Havelange publishes a new book. There's no charge and no obligation.

https://books2read.com/r/B-A-CCKUC-XJRMF

BOOKS 2 READ

Connecting independent readers to independent writers.

Did you love *The Trouble with Funerals*? Then you should read *Wayward Shot*[1] by Joan Havelange!

2

When Mabel slices her golf ball into the town cemetery, she and her best friend Violet, think the worst that could happen would be a lost ball. Until they discover a dead body, and it isn't six feet under.

Mabel's ball lies in the middle of his forehead. It can't be murder, can it? The ladies take it upon themselves to solve the mystery of the dead body in the graveyard.

Using the information gleaned from Coffee Row, a collection of eccentric townspeople leads them to investigate

---

1. https://books2read.com/u/3JqeqK

2. https://books2read.com/u/3JqeqK

golfers and relatives of the deceased. Their investigation frustrates a newly appointed RCMP officer, who does his best to put a stop to their interference. But nothing stops the intrepid detectives. Not the RCMP, a stampede of cattle or even shots fired at them in the dark. They have an uncanny ability to find trouble and dead bodies.

Also by Joan Havelange

Mabel and Violet Mysteries
Wayward Shot
Death and Denial
The Trouble with Funerals